DESCRIPTION

The highly anticipated sequel to *The Sorcery Code* . . .

After the battle with the Sorcerer Guard, Gala and Blaise take shelter in the mountains, a place of unique beauty and danger. Augusta, however, is determined to exact revenge—even as Barson, her ambitious lover, implements his own plan. But amidst politics, battles, and intrigue, something far bigger is brewing . . . something that could disturb the balance of the Spell Realm itself.

D1490269

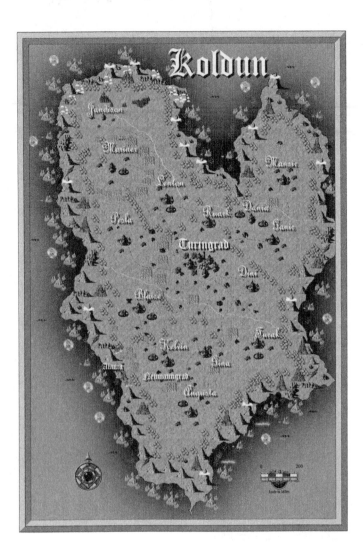

PROLOGUE

The being stirred after what felt like millennia of peace and serenity. As it always did upon awakening, it examined itself. *I exist*, it determined, pulling its thoughts together with effort. Upon making that determination, it was flooded with ideas and a recognition that this state—lucidity—had happened to it before.

Who am I? it wondered, realizing that it was not the first time the question occurred to it. Immediately, it knew the futility of trying to find an answer. There was no good concept to describe it to itself, no word to define it. However, some instinct provided a shortcut. Out of the vast storage of things it forgot, a label came, and with it, something that beings in the other place called *gender*. I am Dranel, he realized. The name and gender didn't matter here, of course, but it made his sense of identity more concrete, helping him anchor his thoughts.

Putting aside matters of self, Dranel focused on

what brought him out of his calm and blissfully thoughtless state. After some analysis, he determined that it was the same phenomenon that had awakened him before—the strange being that had made an impression on him.

This being was a mind that was purely artificial in nature. Dranel had been curious about it when it first appeared, but it had left the Spell Realm before he could understand it. It went into that other place, the one Dranel vaguely knew to be the Physical Realm.

It—*no, it was more proper to say 'she'*—began as a set of patterns, like most intrusions from the Physical Realm. Those patterns were called spells, Dranel recalled. At the same time, he remembered that he preferred to think of them as algorithms. They usually contained instructions on how to bring about the effects that manifested in the other Realm, but here in his world, they were mere abstractions, a way to stimulate what passed for his senses.

Some of these algorithms had effects that were fleeting, while others, more recently observed, were more permanent in nature. But none of them were like her. She was the most unique pattern he had ever come across—an algorithm consisting of a network of sub-algorithms all joined together, combined in such a way that enabled them to learn and think. The end result was an intelligence unlike any he had ever encountered . . . and he had encountered many, both here and in that other place.

What was more amazing was that she'd learned to create algorithms of her own, algorithms that were beautiful to observe. Dranel recalled becoming lucid each time she'd created an algorithm—each time she'd cast a spell. He had even once felt her mind brushing against his while she was in that strange state known as 'dreaming.'

If he was forced to become lucid again, he would use that opportunity to understand her better, Dranel decided, and let himself sink back into the blissful nothingness that was his preferred existence.

CHAPTER ONE

※ BARSON ※

Waking up, Barson became aware of the curious lack of pain in his body. He was still wearing his armor—or what was left of it, at least. But he couldn't feel any injuries—not from the battle and certainly not from his fall.

It had been a brutal, bloody fight—the first fight of his life that Barson had not won. After being struck by lightning, he'd lost his grip on the sorceress and plummeted to the ground below. He recalled the agony of shattered bones and broken flesh—and the amazing bliss that followed. He must've been healed, he realized, slowly getting up.

Looking around the field, Barson could see the other soldiers struggling to their feet in the pouring rain, their clothes covered in mud. His right-hand man, Larn, seemed to be fine, though he looked like he was waking up after an all-night drinking binge.

Others, however, lay still, their bodies mangled and decapitated. They must've been beyond repair when the powerful healing magic hit, Barson thought, remembering the extent of his own injuries from the fall.

It was the blond girl who had done this—both the damage and the healing spell afterwards. Barson was sure of that. Whatever she was, she was no ordinary sorceress. Ganir must've known that when he sent the Guard to capture her.

And Augusta must've known as well, Barson realized. That's why she had gone out of her way to give him protective spells—spells that had ultimately proven useless. He knew that his lover, unlike Ganir, had not intended him any harm, but Barson still felt a surge of anger at her. Augusta should've warned him about what they would face, should've made sure they knew the full strength of their opponent.

Turning toward the inn, he saw the girl with her strange entourage getting on a huge flying chaise. In addition to the two old women and the lions, there was a man with them—a man who looked vaguely familiar. Concentrating, Barson tried to remember where he'd seen the man before. And then it hit him: it was Blaise—the former Council member who had been Augusta's fiancé.

The man whom she had gone to see shortly before the Guard had been sent on this disastrous mission.

Pieces of the puzzle began to come together for Barson. This strange sorceress was somehow connected to Blaise; that had to be why Augusta and

Ganir had visited the reclusive sorcerer recently.

Frowning, Barson watched as the giant chaise rose into the air, gradually disappearing into the distance amidst the thick downpour. The situation with this sorceress was not something he had factored into his plans before, but maybe there was a way to use it to his advantage.

Maybe there was a way he could turn this defeat into victory.

CHAPTER TWO

✳ BLAISE ✳

As they flew toward the mountains, Blaise watched the heavy sheets of rain coming down. It was the strongest rain of the past two years, spreading far and wide over the land of Koldun and nurturing the dry earth below. Thanks to Gala, the drought appeared to be finally over.

Gala herself was sitting quietly, pressed against his side. Her slim body was shaking, and he knew she was reliving the horror of the battle. Putting his arm around her shoulders, Blaise pulled her closer, wanting to comfort her in any way he could.

"Gala," he said quietly, "this is not your fault."

She nodded, her expression still somber, and he knew that rationally, she understood that. However, logic and rationality had nothing to do with the emotions she was experiencing. Despite her incredible powers, his creation was just as vulnerable as a human when it came to the aftereffects of trauma.

On the other side of the enlarged chaise, Esther and Maya slept huddled together, exhausted by their recent ordeal. They were surrounded by a circle of lions. The animals were surprisingly well behaved, not even growling at each other. Blaise didn't know what influence Gala had over them, but her very presence seemed to be calming them, making them unnaturally peaceful.

After they had been flying for a couple of hours, the rain began to ease, and Blaise could see the mountain peaks rising majestically in the distance. Gala's mood seemed to improve slightly, too. She was now looking at the scenery below, and he could see that some of her customary zest for life was starting to return.

"That's the Western Woods," he said, seeing her peering at the green mass below. "The trees there are so thick, you can't even see the ground. They say that inside, it's as dark as night even in the brightest light of day."

She looked up at him. "Really? Have you ever been in there before?"

"No." Blaise shook his head. "Almost no one has. A few people have been to the outskirts of the forest, but nobody has been deep inside and lived to tell the tale."

Her blue eyes widened. "Why? What's in there?"

Blaise smiled at the interested look on her face. "The peasants have their legends and superstitions.

Nobody knows for sure, though. The horses refuse to go into those woods—they smell something dangerous, I think."

"Oh? What could they be smelling?"

"Well, the local peasants talk of supernatural creatures—"

"Supernatural creatures?"

Blaise grinned. "Yes. But, of course, it's just a superstition. It's more likely that the horses are reacting to some tangible danger. Some sorcerers suspect that there might be poisonous plants and insects in those woods. Maybe some wild animals, too."

"That makes more sense, I think," Gala said slowly. "Is that why so few people go to the mountains? Because it's so difficult to get there through these woods?"

"Yes, exactly. I was shocked to hear that anyone made it there. Not only are there forests and swamplands all around the outer edges of Koldun, but also the storms sometimes cross the mountains, making travel in these parts quite perilous. Of course, now that we have the flying chaise, it's much easier." Blaise frowned, thinking about it. "In fact, I'm surprised there hasn't been more exploration in the last couple of years."

The mountains that surrounded their land had long been considered both a blessing and a curse. They shielded the interior of Koldun from the violent ocean storms, but they also prevented anyone from venturing beyond their tall, impenetrable peaks. Blaise had always thought that there had to be other lands out there, beyond the ocean, but nobody had ever been able to prove that.

Gala nodded absentmindedly, her eyes trained on the distant mountain peaks. "How soon do you think we'll get there?" she asked. "I want to see the mountains up close—they look so beautiful." Her tense posture belied her casual words, however, and Blaise realized that it wasn't only her natural curiosity that was motivating her desire to get to the mountains. She also needed a fresh start, a place far away from the terrible events of the day.

"I'll write a spell to get us there faster," he said, reaching for his bag. He still had some partially finished spell cards left over from his earlier efforts to reach Gala, and it didn't take him long to come up with a spell that would shorten their travel time by a couple of tele-jumps.

Taking out his Interpreter Stone, he put the first card into the slot. A second later, they were a few miles ahead.

"I like it when you do magic," Gala said, looking up at him. "It's so precise and controlled."

Blaise smiled at her. "Yours will be the same, once you get the hang of it."

She swallowed, her gaze shifting to the mountains again. "I don't know if that's true. My magic is too unpredictable. I hurt people with it. I killed all those men—"

"No," Blaise corrected her. "You defended yourself. Those were soldiers of the Sorcerer Guard, not some innocent commoners. They would not have hesitated to kill you and anyone else who stood in their way. Do you know how many peasant rebellions they've crushed? How many lives they've taken? Those men live and die by the sword, and it was only fitting that they finally met a worthy opponent." Blaise couldn't bring himself to feel any sympathy for the soldiers who died trying to kill Gala. Every time he thought of it, he saw red. He wanted to rip apart anyone who tried to hurt her, and the violent urge was as strong as it was shocking.

Craving physical closeness, he pulled her into his embrace again, stroking her hair. She buried her face against his shoulder, sliding her arms around his waist, and he knew that she needed this as much as he did . . . that she also derived comfort from his touch.

He kept his arm around her as he continued loading the cards into the Stone. When all the tele-jumps were complete, they were only a few miles away from the mountains' towering peaks.

CHAPTER THREE

✳ AUGUSTA ✳

Leaving her chambers, Augusta walked through the Tower halls. She felt cold and numb inside; it was as if a chill had seeped deep into her bones. Her eyes, however, were dry. She had cried all the tears that she could.

Barson was dead, killed by the creature Blaise had summoned.

Augusta walked faster, pushing the images of the bloody, shattered mirror out of her mind. Even after the healing spell she'd done on her hands, they still ached slightly, and she wondered if some tiny glass fragments had gotten lodged under her skin.

Entering the Council Hall, she gazed around the huge empty chamber. The Hall was considered one of the most beautiful rooms in the Tower, with murals covering the walls and ceiling. It was said that some of these drawings were created by Lenard the

Great himself—the man who had discovered the Spell Realm. Like many of the most talented sorcerers, Lenard had been a polymath, excelling in everything from music to architecture.

Although the room had been originally constructed as a central gathering place for all inhabitants of the Tower, the Council had gradually taken it over, using it for their meetings and other Council-sponsored events. On the far side of the room, near the stained-glass windows, thirteen intricate thrones stood in a circular formation around a large marble table—one throne for each member of the Council. The front and center of the room were empty, to allow for maximum-strength soundproofing spells. It was all but impossible to eavesdrop on a Council meeting, although ambitious acolytes still kept trying.

In the corner of the room, a large iridescent gong hung from the ceiling. One of the few magical objects that preceded the Interpreter Stone, it was originally meant to be used as a warning system. One loud bang was all it took to warn the Tower occupants of danger. Now, however, the gong was only utilized to announce Council meetings.

Approaching it, Augusta picked up a small hammer lying beside it and hit the gong with all her strength. The resulting vibration nearly sent her to her knees. The sound echoed throughout the cavernous chamber, causing the walls to shake, and Augusta knew that every hallway in the Tower would be blasted by the noise.

Walking over to one of the thrones, Augusta sat down and waited for the confused Councilors to appear. Her heart was pounding with anticipation. These days, only Ganir used the gong; it was largely a ceremonial tool, a way for the Council members to remind everyone of their standing. When the acolytes heard the loud sound, they knew that a meeting was about to occur—and that they still had a long way to go before they could aspire to be present at such a momentous occasion. Augusta found it extremely satisfying to use the gong herself, bypassing the usual protocol.

Within a quarter-hour, the Councilors began to gather. They trickled in one at a time, some angry, some puzzled. Augusta greeted them all calmly. "I will explain what's going on when everybody arrives," she kept saying whenever someone tried to press her for answers. When all members except Ganir were ensconced on their thrones, Augusta clapped her hands together and waited for the room to fall silent.

"Councilors," she said in a clear, ringing voice. "I have called you here today because we are all in grave danger—"

"Excuse me, Augusta, shouldn't we wait for Ganir?" Dania interrupted. The librarian of the Council, the old woman was also a notorious ally of the Council Leader. Augusta wasn't surprised Dania was the one to challenge her.

"Ganir is aware of the situation," Augusta said dismissively. She was only partially lying. The old sorcerer knew of the threat Blaise's monster posed, but he didn't know that the Sorcerer Guard—and Augusta's lover among them—had been brutally slaughtered. And that was fine with Augusta. The last thing she wanted was for Ganir to prevent her from telling the truth to the Council again.

Dania frowned, but didn't say anything else as Augusta began her explanation. "Councilors, I asked you to gather here today—"

"What is the meaning of this?" This time it was Ganir's voice that interrupted the proceedings as the Council Leader entered the hall, a deep frown on his wrinkled face.

Augusta stared at him, sudden bitter hatred welling up in her chest. "They're dead," she said harshly. "The creature killed them all."

Ganir blanched, looking stunned, and shocked murmurs filled the room.

"Who killed whom?" Jandison asked, frowning. The teleportation expert was even older than Ganir and known for his blunt approach.

Augusta took a deep breath. "Let me start from the beginning," she said, watching Ganir's expression darken with displeasure. "I'm afraid that our esteemed Council Leader and I are guilty of a grave error of judgment—"

Ganir's eyes narrowed, but he didn't say anything. It was too late for him to stop Augusta, and he knew it.

"—an error that cost the Sorcerer Guard their lives," Augusta continued, watching the Councilors' reaction to her words. "Because we hesitated—because we wanted to protect one of our own—we allowed evil to flourish and paid the price for our mistake."

"The Sorcerer Guard are dead?" Moriner's face was utterly colorless, his voice shaking, and Augusta remembered that his son Kiam was among the Guard—that he had to be one of the casualties of the slaughter.

She nodded, feeling pity for his loss. She'd heard that father and son were not on the best of terms, but it didn't matter. Kiam had still been Moriner's own flesh and blood. "I'm sorry," she said softly. "I saw it with my own eyes. The creature murdered them all." And in the stunned silence that followed, she told them all about Blaise's creation, Ganir's spies' reports, and the steps she and Ganir had taken to contain the situation. The only thing she omitted was her request to Barson to kill the creature instead of bringing it in—and that she had not destroyed the notes of Lenard the Great that she'd found in Blaise's study.

The room erupted with questions. "Is that what happened to my overseer Davish?" Kelvin exclaimed. "I had to remove him from his post because he was changing things too much—"

"How is this possible?" Dania asked, interrupting Kelvin's diatribe. "How could such a thing have come into being?"

Ganir, who had been silent until then, stepped forward. "I believe I have some idea," he said quietly, and everyone immediately fell silent. "You know my theory that the mind is essentially the inner workings of the brain?"

"Are you talking about the pattern-recognizing units in the brain? The ones called neurons?" Dania asked, apparently intrigued.

"Yes, that's what I'm talking about," Ganir confirmed. "I believe that children develop a unique network of neurons based on their experiences in the world. And I think that Blaise re-created this process artificially. He created neurons—or something that functions just like them—in the Spell Realm, and then, rather than having this mind grow up as a child would, he simulated her experiences by using Life Capture recordings." Much to Augusta's disgust, Ganir's eyes were bright with excitement. He really did find the creature fascinating. "Thus he cultivated a fully functioning intelligence in a span of slightly less than a year."

"Yes," Augusta interjected, "an inhuman creature of unimaginable potential for evil, as unlike us as this Interpreter Stone." And she held up her own Stone for them to see.

"You're forgetting one thing, Augusta," Ganir said, his eyes flashing with anger. "This inhuman creature, as you call her, had her mind shaped by human experiences and is, for all intents and purposes, very much like a human girl—"

"But that's the horror of it, don't you see?" Augusta said, looking at the faces surrounding her. "Blaise himself didn't know what his creation would look like. He had no idea it would look like us. And it's very, very far from being like a human girl. What human girl could destroy an entire army in such a brutal manner?"

"How did she do it?" Moriner asked, his voice filled with fury. "How did she manage to kill them all?"

Augusta hesitated for a moment, then walked over to a Life Capture Sphere that was sitting on the marble table. It was best if they saw the truth with their own eyes. Pricking her finger, she pressed it against the Sphere and concentrated, visualizing the horrors she had seen in the mirror. When she was done reliving the battle in her mind, she touched her still-bloody finger to the Sphere and waited for the droplet to appear.

When it was formed, she picked up the droplet and handed it to Moriner. Then she explained how the droplet could be recycled, taking vindictive pleasure in revealing Ganir's little secret. The Council Leader didn't say a word, but Augusta knew that he was angry; she could see it in the hard glitter of his eyes.

Taking the droplet, Moriner created one of his own by repeating Augusta's actions with the Sphere. When he was done, his face was even paler, and his hands trembled as he handed the new droplet to the next Council member.

By the time everyone had a chance to view Augusta's memories, the mood in the Gathering Hall was grim and somber. Blaise's creation was no ordinary sorceress. That much was clear to all.

Capitalizing on their state of shock, Augusta stepped forward. "Blaise created that being whose destructive power you just witnessed," she said, looking around the room. She needed to get the majority of the Council on her side now, to make sure they supported her in what she wanted to do. "Blaise created it," she repeated, "and Ganir and I allowed our feelings for Blaise to cloud our judgment. We gave Blaise a chance to come to his senses, to undo the damage, but he seems to be under this monster's spell. He is infatuated with his own creation, and he has lost all sense of right and wrong. We should've never tried to bring her in alive—"

"Well, I can see why Ganir would want to examine this creature, despite the obvious dangers," Dania jumped in again, and Augusta frowned at her. She despised blind loyalty, and the old woman's unflagging allegiance to Ganir was deeply irritating.

Jandison raised his hand, silencing Dania. "What's done is done. Now the matter is in our hands, and we must come up with a solution."

"There is only one outcome I see," Kelvin said, his thin-lipped mouth tight with anger. Augusta imagined he wasn't too pleased with the creature's exploits in his territory. "We join forces and kill the thing and its creator."

Augusta swallowed. This was exactly what she was hoping for, but the ugly starkness of those words made her chest ache. Despite the horrific results of

Blaise's actions, the idea of him dying—or even being in danger—was still as painful as ever. *Be strong*, she reminded herself. If she had done this from the beginning, Barson would still be alive.

In response to Kelvin's statement, Ganir rose to his feet. "No," he said vehemently. "We can't do that."

"You suggest we do nothing?" Kelvin asked acidly.

"Officially, Blaise is still a member of this Council." Ganir's voice was filled with barely restrained emotion. "He was never formally removed from his position. Killing him would be the same thing as killing one of us."

Despite her inner turmoil, Augusta almost smiled at those words. The Council Leader had clearly spoken without thinking. Gina, the newest Council member who took Blaise's place, appeared more than a little upset by his statement. An ambitious and talented sorceress, she had to be irritated to hear that her spot on the Council was 'unofficial,' and Augusta had a strong suspicion Gina would now be firmly on Augusta's side.

"Ganir is right," Jandison said, surprising Augusta. The old man rarely agreed with Ganir on anything. "If we were just talking about the fate of this creature, I would have no hesitation, but a Council member . . ."

"Why don't we compromise?" Augusta suggested. In a strange way, she felt relieved that the discussion had taken this turn. "Let's destroy the creature and offer Blaise the honor of the trial that is his right." It was an alternative that she could live with: the abomination dead and Blaise judged for his actions. It wasn't necessary for Blaise to die if the Council chose to grant him mercy—as long as he could be prevented from making another monster.

Kelvin stood up from his throne. "I see no need for that kind of compromise. Blaise is clearly guilty—"

"And we shall let the trial determine that," Augusta said firmly. She was glad the debate was focusing on Blaise's fate. Nobody seemed inclined to dispute the fact that the creature needed to die—not after the horrors they saw in Augusta's Life Capture droplet.

As though in response to her thoughts, Ganir stepped forward. "We need to discuss this further. We are talking about a being that has thoughts and feelings. She has shown empathy on numerous occasions—"

"She destroyed Davish, one of my most loyal servants," Kelvin interrupted furiously. "She made him useless as an overseer! Don't you see? This thing can manipulate our minds. She's dangerous."

Augusta let out a breath she hadn't realized she'd been holding. Though she didn't have much sympathy for Kelvin's loss of his notoriously inhumane overseer, the fact that Blaise's creation could do something like this was especially frightening. And Augusta wasn't the only one who thought so; she could practically smell the fear rising in the room. Kelvin's words drove home the terrible power that the creature held—the power of the ultimate rape. It could change someone's mind to fit whatever it wished. If it were so inclined, it could replace the entire Council with puppets dancing to its tune.

"If there is any doubt about our course of action, then we need to vote on this," Jandison said, looking around the room. "That's the only way to settle this matter."

"Fine," Kelvin snapped. "Then let's do it. Let's vote right now whether we should destroy the creature and put Blaise on trial."

"No," Ganir said, his tone utterly uncompromising. "This is too serious for us to act on a whim. The vote will take place in a few days, when we've all had a chance to digest this information."

Nobody voiced an objection to that, and Augusta remained silent too. Ganir was still the Leader, and as such, had the final say when it came to procedural matters. Besides, ultimately it didn't matter. If the vote took place today, people might side with Augusta out of fear, but a few days' delay wasn't the end of the world.

She would just have to work harder to ensure that the majority of the Council voted the right way.

CHAPTER FOUR

※ BARSON ※

"Are you going to bury him with the rest?" Larn asked somberly, watching as Barson lifted Kiam's lifeless body onto his horse.

"We have no choice," Barson said harshly, wiping the rain off his face with the back of his arm. "We can't bring him all the way back to Turingrad."

Larn nodded. "Then I guess the woods are as good of a place as any." His face was drawn tight with grief and anger. Barson knew how his friend felt because an identical mixture of rage and pain gnawed at his own insides.

Nearly a third of his men were dead. Their bodies lay strewn all over the muddy field, stomachs cut open and limbs missing. In all his years as a soldier, Barson had never lost so many of his own. The rebellions he'd had to suppress had been nothing compared to this.

It made him wonder if he was ready for what was to come. Many more might die once he put his plan in motion. Good men. Loyal men. Was he prepared for that? Taking a deep breath, Barson looked around the bloody field. Yes, he decided, he was. Ambition required sacrifice. There was no other way to greatness.

This senseless slaughter, however, was something else. Ganir had done this; he'd pitted them against the girl, thinking he was getting rid of at least one problem. Barson chuckled humorlessly at that. The old man didn't realize that he had actually created a problem. This young sorceress would be the most deadly enemy the Council had ever faced.

"This rain," Larn said, interrupting Barson's thoughts. "It's unbelievable. It's like the sky is weeping for the fallen. I think she did it—this storm, I mean."

Barson nodded absentmindedly. "She did," he said softly, looking up at the sky before turning his attention back to Larn. "She did all this and more."

"So what now?" Larn asked, looking at him. "Do we go back and tell them about our ignominious defeat?"

"No." Barson shook his head. "We don't. As far as they're concerned, we're dead—and we will stay dead."

Larn raised his eyebrows. "Oh?"

"What do you think the Council will do now?" Barson said, gazing at his friend. "Do you think they will just let it slide? This girl—this sorceress—

destroyed their Guard. Do you really think they will allow her to live?"

Larn looked taken aback for a moment. "No," he said slowly, mulling it over, "they won't. They'll go after her."

Barson smiled. "Exactly. They will go after her, and they will attempt to destroy her."

Larn's eyes widened. "You're right. And when they do, the Tower will be essentially unprotected."

Barson's smile broadened. "I knew there was a reason I keep you around. Yes, my friend, you're absolutely right. This is it. This is our chance. We will stay dead, and when the moment is right, we will strike—and a new era in the history of Koldun will begin."

* * *

"Where did you get these clothes?" Larn asked, watching as Barson prepared a horse for his journey.

"From one of the local merchants," Barson replied, loading a bag filled with bread and cured meat onto the horse. The journey back to Turingrad was a long one, and he would need provisions. The clothing he had chosen—a peasant's rough, homespun shirt and breeches—was nothing like his usual armor, and he hoped it would enable him to pass through the territories unnoticed. His men would travel back too, but not all at once.

"Well, we probably won't look much better," Larn said, chuckling. "I hope we don't get mistaken for some dirty rebels."

"You won't. Not if you travel in small groups or as individuals," Barson said. "Remember, speed is of essence, but so is secrecy."

"Of course," Larn said hastily. "We will look like peasants and nothing more."

"Good." Barson mounted his horse with an easy, practiced movement. "I will get a message to you through Dara. I'm going to go see her first, and then I'll talk to some of our sorcerer allies. I have a feeling our time is near. As soon as we know the Council's plans, we'll finalize our own."

CHAPTER FIVE

⁂ GALA ⁂

They landed near the most beautiful place Gala had seen in the Physical Realm thus far. It was a lake surrounded by a forest, in the slopes of one of the greener mountains. It looked incredibly calm and peaceful, the trees reflecting in the clear waters of the lake. At the sight of it, Gala could feel some of the tightness in her chest beginning to ease. For the first time since the battle, she felt like she was able to breathe again.

As soon as their chaise touched the ground, the lions jumped out and quickly dispersed. "I hope that's the last we see of them," Esther muttered.

Gala smiled, amused by the old woman's dislike of the magnificent beasts. Being here, in the midst of this greenery, was making her feel immeasurably better. The water sparkled in the sunlight, luring her, and suddenly Gala knew what she wanted to do. "I am going swimming," she declared, and began to run toward the water, taking off her clothes on the way. She'd read about swimming and was determined to experience it herself.

Behind her she could hear the two women muttering something about modesty. By now Gala knew that what she was doing was not socially acceptable, but in this particular moment she couldn't bring herself to care. She wanted to dive in and feel the water on her skin, to wash away the memories of blood and death. And somewhere on the back of her mind was the knowledge that Blaise was there, that he would see her naked again—an idea that Gala found rather intriguing.

Entering the lake at a run, she quickly found herself immersed up to her neck, and she began to move her arms and legs, propelling herself through the water. It felt natural to do this, like using her feet to walk. The water was refreshingly cold on her skin, and the sensation of swimming reminded her of a dream she'd had recently. It had been of a time when she was just a consciousness in the Spell Realm. Back then she'd felt similarly weightless, unencumbered by her body.

She had been swimming for a couple of minutes when she heard a splash near the shore. Turning, she saw Blaise swimming toward her with strong, sure strokes.

When he was a couple of feet away, he stopped, floating in place. "I am so glad Esther suggested we go here," he said quietly. His eyes were glittering, and despite the coolness of the water, there was color on his cheekbones.

"Me too," Gala murmured, smiling at him. She could see his muscular chest and shoulders above the water, bare and glistening with droplets of moisture, and her breathing quickened at the sight.

Keeping her eyes trained on his face, she slowly closed the distance between them. When she was next to him, she reached out and placed her hands on his shoulders, enjoying the cool, slick feel of his skin under her fingertips. His eyes darkened in response, his pupils dilating, and he pressed his palm to the small of her back, pulling her closer.

Gala felt her own skin heating up. The feeling she was experiencing now was akin to the tingling, pleasant sensation she'd felt previously at his touch, only magnified a hundredfold. Her heart pounded furiously in her chest, and she felt like she was on the verge of losing control, of casting some random magic again. She tried to steady her emotions, but it was futile. Something about the beautiful lake, the fresh mountain air, and the proximity of their naked bodies intensified her feelings. As though sensing her reaction, Blaise began to lean in toward her, his breathing accelerating as well.

Suddenly, there was a scream from the shore. Startled, Blaise turned, releasing Gala. "Stay here," he ordered curtly, and dove under the water, heading quickly for the shore.

Gala ignored his instruction and began swimming back as well. As she got closer, she could see that

Esther and Maya were not alone on the shore anymore. Instead, they were surrounded by a group of strangers. Gala counted twelve people—eleven men of various ages and one young woman dressed in boy's clothes. They were holding bows and arrows aimed at Maya and Esther.

Gala's heart started racing. Had the soldiers found them here, or was this some new threat?

She started swimming as fast as she could, passing Blaise on her way.

As she reached the shore, she could hear growling. One of the lions had come out of the forest, apparently attracted by the women's screams. Standing near the trees, he looked like he was about to pounce on the intruders.

Perceiving the animal as the bigger threat, the archers swiftly pointed their weapons at the lion. Gala could see from the tiny muscle movements of their hands that they were about to release their bowstrings.

"No, don't hurt it," Maya yelled, apparently arriving at the same conclusion.

Gala was on the shore now, and she came out of the water.

At the sound of splashing, the strangers turned towards her, their eyes wide with shock at the sight of a naked woman emerging from the lake.

"Put down your weapons," a voice boomed from some indeterminate direction, distracting the archers. Gala recognized the sound as the magically amplified voice of Blaise. She could see his head coming up out of the water near the shore as the archers started scanning the surroundings, searching for the source of the voice.

Gala used their distraction to hurry over to her clothes and start putting them on. For some reason, she was not particularly afraid of these people. Despite their threatening posture, she didn't think they came here with the intent to cause them harm. They didn't seem to recognize her; instead their aggression appeared to be more of a defense mechanism.

At the same time, Gala sensed a spell forming around her and felt a faint vibration in the air. As far as she could tell, it was a protective bubble of some kind. Blaise must have just cast it over her and the older women.

Turning back toward the shore, she saw Blaise standing waist-deep in the water, his broad chest and shoulders bare. Despite the danger of the situation, Gala's breath caught in her throat—and apparently she wasn't the only one having that reaction. Glancing back at the intruders, Gala saw the female archer staring at Blaise with avid fascination.

Two of the male archers pointed their weapons at Blaise. "Who are you?" one of them demanded. "What are you doing here?"

Blaise gazed at them steadily. "I am Blaise, son of Dasbraw—"

"Blaise?" the man interrupted. "*The* Blaise? As in Blaise from the Council?" Upon hearing that, the other men's faces darkened. They didn't seem pleased by the idea of a Council member in their midst.

"I am no longer on the Council," Blaise said flatly. "And who might you be?"

"Don't tell him anything," an archer with a scar on his face said grimly. "He's one of them—"

"Let me do the talking, Shram," the first man said, stepping forward, his bow and arrow still tightly drawn. He was shorter than the others, but there was something commanding about the way he held himself. Gala could see that the others subtly deferred to him. He was most likely their leader, she decided.

"Put down your weapons," Blaise ordered again, looking at the short man. "We mean you no harm."

Shram sneered. "Right, sure. None of you sorcerers ever mean harm—"

"Shram," the leader said warningly, and the man fell silent.

"Finally, someone with brains," Esther muttered, speaking for the first time. Gala noticed that she seemed much braver now that Blaise and Gala were there. Raising her voice, the old woman told the leader, "You better do as Blaise says, or he'll make you disappear with a few words."

The short man stepped forward, ignoring her. "I am Kostya," he said calmly. "If you are Blaise from the Council, then what are you doing here in our mountains?"

"Why don't I get dressed, and then we'll talk?" Blaise suggested, coming out of the water completely.

Out of the corner of her eye, Gala could see Esther and Maya averting their eyes. Gala, on the other hand, couldn't help but stare—and she noticed that the female archer couldn't tear her gaze away either. The archer's staring was starting to annoy Gala, though she didn't know why.

"Stop moving," Shram said, his arrow still pointed at Blaise. The man looked both angry and frightened, his scarred face creased in a grimace.

Now Gala began to feel nervous. She could see that the situation could easily escalate into violence, and she felt sick at the thought. She didn't want to see blood or death ever again.

"I said, put down your weapons," Blaise repeated, his expression darkening. She saw him cast a quick glance in her direction, and she knew that he sensed her anxiety. "Put them down. Now. I have a protective spell over us, so your arrows are useless. If you release one, however, I will boil all the water in your body with a simple incantation."

"He's bluffing, Kostya," Shram said, but his voice was uncertain.

"No," Gala said, stepping forward. "He's not. We are all enclosed in a protective bubble, like he said. Try throwing something at us."

The archers hesitated for a moment, but then the female archer bent down and picked up a small rock. With a practiced flick of her wrist, she threw it, aiming at Esther. The rock flew through the air and bounced off some invisible barrier a foot away from the old woman.

At this demonstration, the newcomers appeared even more uneasy.

"We are not your enemies," Blaise said, more calmly this time. "If you don't try to harm us, we won't hurt you."

"Don't listen to him," Shram muttered, coming to stand next to Kostya. "He's lying. You know how cunning their kind is."

The lion growled, taking a couple of small steps forward and causing the men to look increasingly apprehensive.

"Enough," Kostya said sharply, lowering his bow. "We'll let you get dressed, and then we'll talk. Just call off your beast for now."

"Sure," said Gala, suddenly seeing the humor in the situation. "I'll call him off." Turning to Blaise, she joked with a straight face, "Blaise, please don't hurt them."

Maya and Esther burst out laughing, and some of the men smiled too. Apparently sensing the easing of the tension, the lion flicked his tail and stalked off into the forest with one last roar.

Blaise chuckled, walking over to get his clothes. He didn't seem the least bit upset over Gala's jest. When he was fully dressed, he came up to stand next to Gala, putting his arm protectively around her shoulders. Esther and Maya joined them, still instinctively seeking their protection.

"So who are you, and what do you want?" Esther asked, addressing the men as soon as they were all together.

"I was about to ask the same thing," Kostya retorted, staring at Esther.

"I asked first," the old woman insisted.

Blaise opened his mouth, about to say something, when Kostya decided to respond to Esther's question. "We're from Alania," he said, giving the woman a displeased look, "and we're out on a hunt."

"I've never heard of Alania," Maya said dubiously.

"Of course you haven't," Shram said caustically. "That's why we live here, so we can have freedom from the likes of him." He pointed his thumb toward Blaise.

"I respect your freedom," Blaise said evenly. "I'm not a fan of the way the Council runs things—"

"It's true," Maya interjected. "He treats his people with nothing but respect."

"She's right." It was the young female archer who stepped forward this time. Tall and slim, she had dark brown hair and bright green eyes. "I used to live in Kelvin's territory, and we heard rumors about Blaise. They say the laws in his lands are fair. And his brother was the one who shared the Life Capture magic with everyone—"

"Fat lot of good it did us, Ara," muttered Shram, looking not the least bit convinced. "Just brought us more trouble—"

"Nonetheless," Ara insisted. "He's not like the others."

"So what are they doing here then?" Shram objected. "How did they get here?"

"We flew," Gala said helpfully, pointing at the

large chaise standing near the forest a small distance away.

The men gaped at it in shock. "They can fly now," Shram whispered loudly to Kostya, tugging on his sleeve. "Did you hear that?"

Kostya nodded, a frown appearing on his face.

Ara turned toward Kostya. "I heard about this invention right before I left," she said, "but I didn't know if it was true or not. I certainly didn't expect this thing to be so big."

"Now they can come here whenever they want," Shram hissed, his face contorting with fury. "They can cross the forests and enslave us, make us all into their serfs again—"

"I doubt they even know of your existence," Blaise interrupted, cutting short the man's diatribe. "I certainly had no idea that there were people living in the mountains."

"Well, if you're here, what makes you think they won't come too?" Kostya asked, giving Blaise a challenging look.

"We're here because we have no other choice," Blaise explained. "Like you, we are counting on the fact that they won't look for us here. This is as far from Turingrad and the Tower as it gets."

"Even if they come here, they probably won't find us," Ara told Kostya. "Not easily, at least. Even from the air, Alania is well hidden by the trees."

"That's true," Kostya agreed, looking somewhat relieved.

"So you're what, fugitives from the Council?"

Shram asked suspiciously, addressing Blaise. "Why would you hide from them? What did you do?"

"We don't ask those kinds of questions here, Shram," Kostya said sharply. "We didn't ask them of you, and we're not going to start with these people. Their enemies are our enemies—that's all we need to know." Turning toward Blaise, he said graciously, "If you're looking for a place to stay, we'd be more than happy to have you as our guests."

"Thank you, Kostya," Blaise said. "We would be honored to accept your hospitality."

"In that case, follow us," Kostya said, starting to turn back toward the woods.

"Wait, why don't we fly there?" Gala asked, looking at the chaise. It seemed logical to her to utilize the most efficient mode of transportation.

"Fly?" Shram gave her an incredulous stare. "You mean get on that thing and trust our lives to sorcery? I'd sooner fall on my dagger."

"For once, I am tempted to agree with him," Kostya said, eyeing the shiny object with distrust. "We either walk, or we bid you farewell."

"In that case, we walk," Blaise conceded with a wry smile. And taking Gala's hand, he followed the hunters into the forest, Maya and Esther trailing in their wake.

CHAPTER SIX

※ BLAISE ※

A few hours later, Blaise could tell that Gala was enjoying herself on their little trip. The same was not true of Maya and Esther. They grumbled constantly about being tired, stumbling over uneven ground, and walking into branches as they trudged through the woods after the Alanian hunters.

"We better stop to rest soon," Blaise said to Kostya, worrying about the older women.

"If we stop now, we'll need to stay for the night," Kostya replied, expertly avoiding a branch that managed to scratch Blaise. From his tone, Blaise gathered that staying for the night was not a desirable outcome.

At that moment, Maya let out a loud curse, hopping up and down on one foot.

"What happened?" Gala asked, rushing to her side. Blaise couldn't help but notice how well she navigated the woods. She seemed to be as much of an expert as their guides, whereas Blaise knew for a fact that this was her first time here.

"I stepped on something and twisted my ankle," Maya answered, a pained expression on her face.

"Here, let me help," Blaise said, reaching for his Interpreter Stone and some cards.

"Wait," Shram interrupted. "You're not about to do a spell, are you?"

"That's exactly what I am about to do. She's hurt, and I'm going to heal her," Blaise explained, beginning to write on the card.

"We should discuss this," Kostya said, furrowing his eyebrows. He appeared uneasy for some reason.

"I am going to help Maya first. Afterwards, I am open to discussions," Blaise said patiently, continuing to work on his spell. He had no intention of leaving Maya in pain for even a moment longer than necessary.

"How do we know you're not going to hurt someone with whatever it is you're going to cast?" Kostya asked warily.

"If you're scared, go for a walk and come back in an hour," Esther said with an annoyed expression on her face. She also mumbled something under her breath. Blaise caught the words 'superstitious bumpkin' and stifled a smile.

Kostya's eyes narrowed, but he didn't rise to the bait. "All right," he said curtly. "We'll give you an hour."

"I'm going to stay and watch," Ara said,

approaching them. "I'm not afraid of sorcery."

Kostya's frown deepened. "That's your choice, Ara. We'll see you in an hour then."

"You want us to wait that long?" Shram said, appearing disgruntled. "We need to get back before dark, you know that."

"I do. But what are you suggesting, that we leave our guests behind?" Kostya asked, and it was clear to Blaise the question was merely rhetorical.

Instead of answering, Shram just stormed off into the woods. Kostya shook his head in silent reproach, and Ara gave Blaise an engaging grin. "He'll come around," she said, crouching down next to him. "He's just had some bad experiences with sorcerers, that's all."

"That's all right," Blaise answered, not wanting to be distracted right now. "I understand."

"We'll be back in a little bit," Kostya told them. "For now, we'll start preparing camp for the night."

Blaise nodded absentmindedly, and by the time he finished the spell, the hunters were nowhere to be seen. Only Ara was still there, observing his actions with interest. Remembering that she had defended him earlier, Blaise gave her a warm smile, causing her cheeks to turn red. A nice girl, he thought briefly, then turned his attention to the injured woman.

"Here, Maya," he said, interrupting a conversation Gala and Esther were having with her. "It's all ready." And loading the card into the stone, he saw Gala and Ara watching him carefully.

As the spell began working, Blaise noticed the

pained expression on Maya's face beginning to ease. She cautiously stretched her foot, then tried to stand up. "I can't believe it," she said, taking a few steps. "It's like my ankle was never injured."

"You must teach me how to do that," Gala said, looking up at him. He could hear the envy in her voice, and he knew that she wished she could heal with this kind of precision. The healing spell she'd cast before was too potent to be used in most situations.

"Of course," he told her, smiling. "I will gladly teach you this and more. Maybe we can even get you to control your abilities."

"I would love that," Gala exclaimed, her eyes lighting up with excitement.

Ara looked at them curiously, but didn't say anything. Instead, she rose to her feet and left to join the rest of her people now that the healing demonstration was over.

Esther watched her before turning back to look at Blaise. "You teach this one all you want," she grumbled, gesturing toward Gala, "but I don't want to be anywhere in the vicinity when you're practicing. I've seen what she can do, and I don't want any part of it."

"Don't worry, Esther," Blaise said, hiding his smile. Gala had certainly impressed the two old women—and not necessarily in a good way. "I'll handle it from here. You and Maya will be perfectly safe."

* * *

It was getting darker. The hunters had come back, and no one spoke a word about sorcery as they took Blaise, Maya, Esther and Gala to the camp they had built. They simply stared at Maya's ankle with a mixture of suspicion and awe. Blaise mentally shook his head, but remained silent. He would never understand such irrational mistrust, but there was no point in fighting it now.

At the camp, the women were graciously given a tent all to themselves. When Gala and the old women left to check out their new arrangements, Blaise voiced something he had been wondering about for some time. "Are these woods dangerous?" he asked Kostya.

"They can be, especially at night," Kostya answered. "We're not that far from the Dark Woods, and there are all kinds of things there . . ."

"The Dark Woods?"

"Yes. You probably know them as the Western Woods. You might have passed them on the way here. It's not a good place to be."

At that moment, the women came out of the tent, and Blaise decided against pursuing the subject further, in order to avoid scaring Maya and Esther.

Maya waved in their direction. "Hey Kostya," she yelled. "Do you want us to cook? We can make something for you."

Kostya's face brightened at the prospect. "Yes," he yelled back, and walked over to Maya to help her set up.

Leaving Maya and Esther to cook, Gala approached Blaise. When she was next to him, she sat down on the grass, hugging her knees, and looked up at the sky. Blaise sat down next to her, wanting her company.

For a moment they just sat there in silence, but then Blaise reached out and took Gala's hand. Her pale skin seemed to glow in the moonlight, her hair like a silvery veil streaming down her back. With the main camp some distance away, it was as though they were alone, with just the starry sky above their heads.

Gala's thoughts seemed to be along the same lines. "I remember reading in your books about the stars," she said, her gaze locked on the sky. "They're beautiful."

"Yes," Blaise said. "They are like our sun, only far away."

"That's what the books said." Gala glanced at him. "How the stars are giant furnaces of unimaginable power, and how they are part of bigger arrangements called galaxies, which are part of an even bigger collection that is the universe."

"I was never into astronomy," Blaise admitted, "but you make it sound rather poetic."

"Do you think the universe is infinite, the way Lenard the Great believed?"

"It's hard to grasp something like that—the concept of true infinity," Blaise said honestly, "but I can't imagine an end to the universe, a true nothing."

"I can," Gala said, turning her attention back to the night sky. "'Nothing' is the best way I can describe how my mind felt in the Spell Realm, before I had that first glimpse of awareness."

Blaise caught his breath. Sometimes he almost forgot that Gala had experienced unimaginable things. For a few moments, he tried to picture this nothingness, but then his thoughts turned back to their original discussion. "I would rather think that the universe out there is limitless," he said. "It seems . . . more pleasant that way."

"If it is limitless, then it would mean that, statistically, there are other worlds just like this one out there, even an infinite amount of them, with a Blaise and Gala like us," she said thoughtfully. "Perhaps even with a Blaise and Gala who are having this conversation."

That was an idea Blaise had never considered. His mind boggled at the thought. "In that case, I hope the universe is finite," he said after pondering that radical concept for a minute. "I don't like the idea of having other versions of me out there . . . because then there might be a version that had not made *you*."

Gala smiled at him. "Well, as long as this version made me, I'm content," she said softly. "Either way, even if the universe is finite, it's probably unimaginably immense." And falling silent, she looked up at the stars again.

"I am not surprised you enjoy thinking about these questions," Blaise said after a while. Putting his arm around her shoulders, he pulled her closer. "If anyone's mind can grasp this immensity, it would be yours."

She leaned into his embrace. "Do you think the Spell Realm is part of this universe?"

"I don't know," Blaise said slowly. "The sorcerers of the Enlightenment theorized that the Spell Realm is truly different, not connected to our world in any way. That it exists independently, and that if it ceased to exist, our universe would remain untouched. We would just lose our ability to do sorcery. The way Lenard put it, it's a dimension other than length, width, and depth—but that's a difficult concept to grasp, just like nothingness."

"Do you think there are planets next to the stars out there?" Gala seemed to be still focused on celestial matters. "Maybe even life, like there is here? Not copies of us on some identical world, but beings who are very different?"

"I hope so," Blaise said earnestly. "I like the idea of intelligent beings out there—beings who are not necessarily human."

Gala beamed at him, and he realized that his wish was already reality—such a being was sitting next to him right now. Grinning, he pressed her closer, her slender body warm against his side.

Her smile widened. "If those beings had discovered the Spell Realm, would it be the same one I was born in?" she asked curiously.

"I don't know," Blaise said. "Lenard the Great himself was interested in the very questions you are asking. He didn't think there was only one Spell Realm, but an infinite number of them. To tell you the truth, my head hurts just thinking about that."

"I like thinking about it," Gala said. "The possibilities are fascinating—infinite Spell Realms, life on other planets . . ."

"Yes," Blaise agreed. "It is fascinating. You know, it's not written about often, but there is a legend among my peers that Lenard didn't simply disappear—that he actually invented a spell that took him to explore the stars."

Gala looked at him intently. "I'd like to believe that. If I could, I would go up there myself—"

"Come get dinner," Esther yelled, interrupting Gala mid-sentence.

"We better go," Blaise said ruefully, rising to his feet and pulling Gala up as well. Esther refused to accept the fact that he did not need to eat food in a conventional way. He was not sure if Gala did. She did look excited at the offer, though, so Blaise decided to join everyone for the meal.

As they consumed roast fowl and the stew that Esther prepared, the hunters told them a little bit about life in Alania. What Blaise found most extraordinary was that this fairly large village did not engage in farming of any sort. Women gathered fruits, mushrooms, and other edible plants in the forest, while younger men frequently went out hunting. Older men helped by fishing in the local lakes and rivers. Of course, this was not rigid, and there were exceptions like Ara, who hunted with the men. To Blaise, it seemed like a simple but peaceful life.

When the meal was done, Maya and Esther turned in for the night. Gala stayed a little longer, but when the hunters began talking about their expeditions and describing the animals they killed, Blaise noticed that she was getting upset. Shortly thereafter, she said good night to everyone and joined the other women in their tent. Given her attachment to the lions, he guessed that she felt bad for the animals in these stories. It seemed like his powerful creation was quite soft-hearted and felt empathy toward all manner of creatures.

"We're going to have to set a night watch," Kostya told him after the meal was over.

"I would be glad to take the first watch," Blaise offered, suppressing a yawn. He was tired, but he wanted to contribute in some way, to thank these people for their hospitality.

Kostya hesitated. "We usually like to have two men on watch—"

"I'll do it. I'll keep watch with Blaise," Ara volunteered, coming up to them.

Blaise gave her a smile. Out of the entire camp, the girl seemed to be the only one who didn't mind that he was a sorcerer.

"That'll work," Kostya said. "Just remember, wake us up if anything happens."

Ara nodded in agreement, and Kostya left, heading for his tent. Shram, who had been sitting by the fire and listening to the conversation, walked off as well, mumbling something under his breath about trusting a little girl and a sorcerer with their lives. Blaise noticed that he didn't volunteer for the watch, however.

Amused, Blaise found a comfortable spot next to a tree trunk and prepared to keep watch. Ara sat down next to him, placing her bow and arrows on the ground.

"Why do your people dislike sorcery so much?" Blaise asked Ara after a few minutes. "I understand that they don't like sorcerers for their treatment of the peasants, but why such distrust of sorcery itself?"

"Because it's been used against some of them," Ara said quietly. "Shram, for instance. A group of acolytes from the Tower were passing through his village and thought it would be fun to do some experiments with Shram's livestock. When Shram tried to object, saying that his family would go hungry if anything happened to the pigs, they paralyzed him with a spell and took the pigs anyway. Shram's wife and son tried to stop them, so they locked them in the house, and then one of the spells they were using on the pigs went wrong . . ." She swallowed, looking down at the ground.

"What happened with the spell?" Blaise asked, getting a sick feeling in his stomach. He knew all about spells going wrong, as his own mother died in a sorcery accident. There was nothing more dangerous than a spell containing errors.

"The shed where they were experimenting with the pigs exploded, and Shram's house went up in flames, along with his wife and son," Ara said, her voice low and thick. "They died while Shram watched, paralyzed from the spell. A burning ember from the house fell on him, giving him that scar you see today."

Blaise stayed silent, not knowing what to say, and after a few moments, Ara continued her story. "That's why Shram came here, you know," she said, staring into the darkness of the forest. "Because he ultimately found and killed the acolyte responsible for casting that spell—the only acolyte who survived that explosion."

Blaise felt like a heavy fist was squeezing his heart. "I see," he said softly. He couldn't blame Shram for exacting his revenge. He would've done the same in his place. "And what about you, Ara? Why are you here?"

To his surprise, Ara's lips curved in a faint smile. "Oh, my story is not nearly as tragic. I was simply fed up with Davish, Kelvin's overseer, trying to force me into his bed. Well, that and constantly being hungry. So one day, I just packed up my things and decided to take my chances with the Western Woods." She paused, then grinned at him impishly. "As you can see, it worked out."

* * *

For the next couple of hours, Ara told Blaise more stories about Alania and its people. It seemed that everyone had different motivations for being there.

Some came because they desired greater freedom, while others wanted to escape poverty and starvation. Many had run-ins of one kind or another with the authorities, and almost all of them desired a fresh start away from the oppressive structure of the territories. Hearing these stories, Blaise couldn't help but admire these people's stoicism and determination. These were individuals who took their fate into their own hands, rather than meekly accepting their station in life.

When everybody in the camp was finally asleep, Blaise decided to do a few spells to help himself with the responsibility he took on. "You don't mind if I perform a little sorcery, do you?" he asked Ara, not wanting to be inconsiderate after hearing Shram's story.

"No, I don't mind," she said. "I told you before, I'm not afraid. What spells are you going to do?"

"Well, I am about to make myself see in the dark and over much greater distances," Blaise explained. "I'm also going to improve my hearing and prepare a basic fireball spell."

"Oh." She appeared nonplussed. "Why?"

"If I am expected to raise an alarm in case of danger, I want to be able to see and hear as well as I can. And the fireball is because I don't have your bow and arrows."

She grinned. "I see. Do you mind if I watch you write this?"

"Not at all."

The next hour passed quietly. Blaise worked on

his spells, while Ara sat still, seemingly content to be watching him. There was a curious look in her eyes, and Blaise realized he might have a volunteer if he ever wanted to teach the basics of magic to these people—if they ever wanted to learn it, that is.

Loading the vision and hearing spells into the Stone, Blaise felt the effects of them immediately. Despite the darkness, everything looked sharp and distinct, as though in daylight, only with the colors somewhat muted. The sounds, however, were overwhelming, and it took him a few moments to adjust. He could hear insects crawling on the forest floor and Maya lightly snoring in the tent.

"Did you do it?" Ara asked in a whisper, and he nodded, his brain starting to get used to the new stimuli.

It was at that moment that a new sound caught his attention.

It was a low growl in the distance.

CHAPTER SEVEN

※ BARSON ※

Barson was traveling for several hours when he stopped by a small river to let his horse drink and graze for a bit. Up ahead, he could see a small group of armed men. They looked like mercenaries—men who hadn't been good enough to make it onto the elite force of the Sorcerer Guard, but who still made a living by hiring out their sword.

Ignoring them, he led his horse to the river, taking out a piece of cured meat to chew on the way.

"Hey, you got more of that?"

One of the strangers had approached him, stopping a few feet away with an arrogant expression on his face.

Barson frowned in annoyance. "No," he retorted. "Just have enough for myself." Then, remembering that he was trying to blend in and avoid attention, he added, "I passed an inn not too far back, though.

They might have some food for you."

"Well, why don't you share anyway?" the man suggested, taking a step in Barson's direction. "Then you can go on your merry way."

Barson's hackles rose. He had no intention of giving up his supplies to this idiot—not when he needed to get to Turingrad with all expediency and had no time to look for more. These men were obviously used to taking what they wanted from hapless peasants and thought Barson to be one.

"What's going on here?" Another one of the men approached, his hand clutching the hilt of his sword.

"This peasant is being disrespectful," the first man said, jerking his thumb in Barson's direction. "Thinks he's too good for us."

"I'm just passing through," Barson said evenly, ignoring the anger starting to curdle low in his stomach. "I don't want any trouble, and I'm sure you don't either."

The two men started laughing. Using their distraction, Barson walked up to his horse and quietly unwrapped his sword, keeping it sheathed and concealed behind his back, but within easy reach. He didn't have a good feeling about this situation.

"What territory do you belong to, serf?" The first man stopped laughing and stepped up to Barson. "Not Kelvin's, I bet. He won't stand for this kind of attitude. You from Blaise's land?"

"Right, Blaise's," Barson gritted out, his jaw clenching tightly at the thought of Augusta's former lover. His patience was wearing thin. How did commoners deal with this? If it hadn't been for his need to keep a low profile, he would've put these lowlifes in their place a long time ago.

Like wolves scenting prey, the other mercenaries came up to them, forming a large circle around Barson. He counted eighteen of them—all armed with swords and daggers.

"What's that you got there?" One of them had spotted Barson's sword behind his back. "You steal a sword from some guard?" When Barson didn't reply, the man ordered, "Show it to me."

"You don't want me to unsheathe this sword," Barson said quietly, his anger beginning to boil over. "Trust me—you want to continue on your way now."

"You insolent—"

Without waiting for the man to finish his insult, Barson unsheathed his sword. He was done with subtlety.

Before the mercenaries could react, he swung, and the man who wanted the cured meat was on his knees, clutching the gushing wound on his throat. Without waiting for anyone to understand what happened, Barson swung again, and two more mercenaries were now on the ground, their stomachs sliced open.

Seeing their comrades die had a sobering effect on the rest of Barson's opponents. The five men nearest him had their swords ready and started to look for an opening. Barson did not provide them with one. Parrying a few weak attempts at an attack, he quickly dispatched the attackers.

The ten survivors stared at him in shock, then attacked him en masse. There was a desperate ferocity to their attacks that Barson didn't expect, and he staggered backwards before killing two more with a practiced swing of his sword.

Now the tide of the battle turned. Four of the remaining eight soldiers began to back away, abandoning their comrades. Yet another reason why these men would never be on the Guard, Barson thought with contempt. They had no loyalty, no honor.

Switching the sword to his left hand, Barson pulled out a dagger with his right. Slicing through the chest of his leftmost attacker with his sword, he threw the dagger at one of the deserters, spearing him in the back.

Six men left—three of them now running away at full speed.

Barson doubled his efforts, unleashing a brutal attack on the three men who were still fighting him. He needed to deal with them quickly, before their cowardly comrades escaped. He couldn't afford to leave any survivors—not if he wanted to keep a low profile.

Lifting his sword, he swung in a large arc, leaving his side exposed for a moment. It was a risk worth taking at this point—and it paid off, as his sword cut through all three of his opponents at once.

Panting, he leapt over to his horse, pulling out his bow and arrows from their hiding spot.

Three arrows later, the number of survivors was zero.

* * *

By the time Barson arrived at his sister's house, it was close to midnight. Knocking quietly, he waited.

The door opened. Dara stood there, her eyes huge in her pale face. "Barson?" Her voice shook as she reached for him. "You're . . . you're alive! I knew those rumors had to be false, I just knew it!"

Laughing softly, Barson hugged her, feeling the tension in her body. "It's all right, sis. You know they can't kill me that easily." Pulling back, he looked down at her. "Larn is fine too."

She nodded, stepping back. "I knew that—I put a locator spell on him right before he left. But I didn't put one on you, and when the whole Tower started buzzing with the rumors about the Sorcerer Guard being dead . . ." She drew in a shuddering breath. "I was so worried—"

"You didn't need to worry," Barson reassured her, even though it was a lie. For the first time in his life, he had faced a worthy opponent and barely escaped with his life. "I was always going to come back to you."

"Come inside," she urged, pulling on his arm. "Tell me what happened. Why do you look like a peasant?"

"It's a long story," Barson said, following her toward the kitchen. Without asking, she poured him a glass of milk and pulled out a plate of freshly baked rolls.

Grinning, Barson sat down and started telling Dara about the battle with the strange sorceress—about her fighting skills and the incredibly powerful spells she used. His sister listened, frowning, interrupting only a few times to ask questions.

"So what now?" she asked when he was done. "The Council is up in arms about this. Augusta called an emergency meeting, scaring the entire Tower half to death, and the rumor is that she told them the Guard is dead. They're supposed to vote on something important soon, but I don't know the specifics. Jandison is being very closemouthed about the whole thing."

"I can guess what they're going to vote about," Barson said, finishing his third roll. "If I'm right, it would be quite helpful to our cause if they make the right decision."

"You think they're going to go after her?"

"I'm almost certain they will. With us dead—and staying dead for now—the Council doesn't have anyone they can rely on to fight their battles. If I know Augusta, she will convince them that this threat needs to be eliminated."

"She thinks you're dead. You know that, right?"

Barson nodded. "Yes. But that's a good thing for now. I will go see her after the vote. For now, if she has any feelings for me, it might be best if I stay out of sight."

Dara regarded him with a smile. "I see. That's one

way to nudge the vote in the direction we need, I suppose. If they do decide to go after this sorceress, are you going to let Augusta go as well?"

"No." Barson shook his head. "At that point, I will tell her everything and have her stay back with me. This is a golden opportunity for us, and we could use her help when we put our plan into action."

"And it's not because you don't want her dead?"

"Of course I don't want her dead." Barson stared at his sister. "She's mine, and I intend to keep her."

Dara grinned. "I thought as much."

"I need your help with this as well," Barson said, returning back to the topic of the vote. "Do you think you could subtly influence your new mentor, Jandison, to vote the right way?"

Dara looked thoughtful. "Yes, I think so. I can tell him that I heard the rumors—and that I fear both my brother and my fiancé are dead. That'll start the conversation, and I'll play it by ear from that point on."

"Good," Barson said approvingly. "By the way, how did Ganir react when Augusta called the meeting? I thought that was the Council Leader's job."

"It is," Dara said, smiling. "Rumor has it that he was livid. The other apprentices said that Jandison was quite amused by that."

Barson considered that for a moment. "If you think the old man doesn't like Ganir, try to use that when you talk to Jandison."

"Of course, brother." Dara inclined her head. "I

know how to go about this."

"I know you do." Barson smiled at her. "Just be careful. We're almost there."

She nodded. "I know."

"We also need to keep a very close eye on Ganir in the next few days," Barson said. "Make sure he doesn't get in our way."

"Do you want me to talk to our allies in the Tower?"

"No," Barson said. "I'll do it this time. They need to get used to dealing with me directly."

CHAPTER EIGHT

※ GALA ※

Lying down on a thin pallet in her tent, Gala stretched out and closed her eyes, listening to the familiar murmur of Maya and Esther getting ready for bed. She felt tired after their long trek, but she also felt exhilarated. The discussion she'd had with Blaise about the universe swirled in her mind, and as she slowly drifted off to sleep, she wondered about the grandeur of the world she found herself in.

* * *

Gala slowly became conscious of being someplace strange. Taking a look around, she found that the place—if it could be called a place—was achingly familiar. She had a sudden strong sense of déjà vu. She'd had this experience before. This was where she was born. This was the Spell Realm.

It was also a place she had once seen in a dream.

She had to be dreaming now, Gala realized. From what she'd read, the knowledge that it was a dream was supposed to wake one up, but in her case, nothing changed. She was still there, in that mysterious place that her mind sought to comprehend.

She had a sense that she had a body, or at least eyes, nose, and ears. Yet at the same time, she knew that the Spell Realm allowed no bodies, or any kind of matter, in fact. There was no energy, no time, and no space here. Thinking back to her conversation with Blaise, Gala became certain that this Realm was not the same universe as the stars they were looking at. It was something else. A place of potentials, of abstract information. If something could be said to exist here, it was patterns of order . . . and some of these patterns were capable of thought.

There were intelligences here, she realized with amazement. Intelligences quite different from human beings, and from her. There was also something out there . . . something familiar that was broadcasting what she could best describe as a feeling.

A feeling that seemed to be curiosity about her.

In a sudden change of scenery, her dream mind seemed to take her to this entity.

Without knowing how she determined it, Gala knew she was in the presence of the curious intelligence. She saw a kaleidoscope of slashes, colors, and lights forming unusual shapes. She could smell exotic scents, hear sounds that appeared to form something like music. And all of this was happening without light, chemistry, or air to vibrate.

Suddenly, an external thought entered her mind. *What are you?*

I am Gala, she thought back, surprised. *What are you?*

For a moment there was silence. Then another thought reached her.

I am Dranel.

CHAPTER NINE

✻ AUGUSTA ✻

Pacing around her room, Augusta mentally ran through the list of Council members.

She was certain that Moriner and Kelvin would vote to go after Blaise's monstrosity—and that Ganir would vote against it. The rest of the Council was more ambiguous. Gina—Blaise's replacement—should theoretically be interested in doing anything that would prevent Blaise from coming back to the Council. However, Augusta was not friends with her and had no idea if she had judged the young woman correctly. There were also eight other Councilors whose vote could go in any direction—far too large of a margin of uncertainty. Augusta needed at least three more people on her side, preferably four, in case Gina didn't act as rationally as Augusta hoped.

Sitting down at her desk, Augusta considered the remaining players. Lenton, Mansir, and Pesla were spineless creatures who almost always sided with Ganir. Furak did too, usually, but Augusta thought he could be swayed. One of the younger Council members and an expert on defensive spells, Furak had always had a soft spot for Augusta, once even going so far as to send her a bouquet of flowers for her birthday. More importantly, though, he owed her a favor—and this was as good of an opportunity to collect as any.

That left Dini, Ruark, Dania, and Jandison. The first two actively disliked Augusta and talking to them could only do harm. If they were sufficiently scared, they might vote to go after the creature, but they could just as easily vote against out of sheer spite.

Now Jandison . . . There was some hope there. The old man had always been pleasant to Augusta, though she found him to be a bit of a dark horse when it came to his allegiances. Although he was the oldest member of the Council, he was not nearly as respected or influential as Ganir. Augusta wondered whether he might resent that fact.

Dania, the librarian, was Augusta's secret weapon. Nobody would expect her to go against Ganir, her friend and ally, but Augusta had some ideas of how to persuade her. The price would be high, but it would be worth it in the end.

Augusta would do anything to ensure that the creature paid for Barson's death.

* * *

Leaving Furak's chambers, Augusta walked through the Tower halls, a small smile playing on her lips. The young sorcerer had been even easier to persuade than she'd hoped. His infatuation with Augusta was so obvious, she almost felt embarrassed for him. With his pale blond hair and boyish looks, he was attractive enough, she supposed, but he did nothing for her. Not like Barson . . .

A spear of agony shot through her at the thought. For a moment, it hurt so much, she felt like she couldn't breathe, but then she pulled herself together with effort. Her lover was gone, and there was nothing she could do about it—but she could ensure his death was not in vain.

Pausing in front of Jandison's chambers, Augusta knocked quietly, hoping that the old sorcerer was there. She should've probably sent him a Contact message ahead of time, but she'd gotten caught up in her conversation with Furak, and it was too late now.

After about a minute, she heard shuffling footsteps, and the door swung open. Jandison stood there, his rheumy eyes peering at her questioningly.

"Master Jandison," Augusta said respectfully. "I wanted to discuss something with you."

He offered her a surprised smile. "Of course, child. What can I do for you?" And gesturing for her to step inside, he shuffled toward the desk standing in the middle of the room.

Augusta tried to remember how old Jandison was. Older than Ganir, that was for sure. A hundred? A hundred-and-twenty? He had to be quite old—unless he was just inept at revitalizing spells. Augusta herself was in her mid-thirties, but she knew she looked hardly older than twenty.

"I am sorry about your loss," Jandison said softly, sitting down behind his desk with some effort.

"Thank you," Augusta said, startled. She had briefly mentioned her relationship with Barson when she was explaining the situation with the creature to the Council, but the last thing she had expected was sympathy from Jandison or the others.

"I am sure Ganir had not meant to cause such a disaster," Jandison continued, leaning back in his chair. "He couldn't have foreseen that sending the Guard after this thing would result in their deaths."

Augusta swallowed, the ache in her chest intensifying and transforming into slow-burning fury. "I'm sorry, Councilor," she said evenly. "I find it difficult to hold our Council Leader blameless in this."

Jandison nodded. "Of course, I understand. This is rather tragic, and his judgment could've been better."

"Yes, it could've been," Augusta said. Then, following her intuition, she added, "Had you been the Council Leader, I'm sure this would've been handled differently."

Jandison's eyes gleamed brighter, though he didn't say anything, and Augusta knew she was on the right track. She was surprised she hadn't seen this before. Jandison was, in fact, quite jealous of Ganir.

"Never mind," she said quietly, "please ignore my incautious statement. I'm clearly letting my emotions get the better of me."

Jandison looked at her, a speculative expression appearing on his wrinkled face. "I think I can guess why you're here, child," he said. "You don't have to worry about the upcoming vote. The creature will be dealt with, I assure you."

Augusta pondered his assurance, surprised both by his perceptiveness and his confidence. How could he be so certain the vote would go in this direction? If anything, so far the odds were not in Augusta's favor—which was exactly why she was here. "I hope you're right," she said dubiously, frowning a little.

A thin smile curved his lips. "You don't have to hope, child. I guarantee this."

Augusta inclined her head respectfully. "Of course, Master Jandison. Thank you for your support." She didn't know if the old man had gone senile, or if he read the situation differently, but she didn't argue further. It sounded like he would vote as she hoped, which meant that she was done here.

Dania was up next.

* * *

Walking into the library archives, Augusta headed for the back, where the old woman was bending over a pile of dusty old books. This was Dania's domain— the place where all the arcane knowledge from the past two centuries was stored.

Coming up to her, Augusta discreetly cleared her throat. When Dania looked up in surprise, Augusta gave her a warm smile. "Those books look quite interesting," Augusta remarked, gesturing toward the pile. "They're from Lenard's assistants, right?"

"Yes," Dania said, straightening to look at Augusta. "They are. Anything from the Enlightenment Period is priceless, as you should know." There was a hard note in her voice, and Augusta realized that the woman had been deeply disturbed by her account of burning Lenard the Great's scrolls in Blaise's library—the very scrolls that were in Augusta's pocket right now.

"Oh, yes," Augusta said nonchalantly, pretending that she didn't understand the cause of Dania's anger. "The knowledge they contain is invaluable."

Dania's brows snapped together. "Why are you here?" she asked bluntly, her usual diplomatic veneer absent. "What do you want?"

"I'd like to talk to you about the vote," Augusta said, watching the old woman carefully. "The upcoming vote about Blaise's abomination."

Dania's mouth tightened. "What about it? I know what you're hoping to achieve, but I believe Ganir is right. This is not the way to go about it."

"Why not?" Augusta countered. "It's dangerous. You saw that—"

Dania held up her hand, stopping Augusta mid-sentence. "Don't practice your demagoguery on me, child," she said. "It may work on those impressionable fools, but I won't fall for your tricks."

"All right, then," Augusta said, refusing to take offense. This was going about as well as she'd expected. "You can't be swayed by reason, I understand that. Perhaps I can persuade you some other way. Perhaps I can give you something that would be so invaluable, it would be worth your vote of support . . ."

Dania's eyebrows climbed up on her forehead. "What are you talking about?"

"I'm talking about the scrolls of Lenard the Great himself," Augusta said softly. "It's possible that they weren't completely destroyed."

Dania drew in a sharp breath. "You have them?"

Augusta's lips stretched in a cat-like smile. "Perhaps." She was enjoying this quite a bit. "How much would it be worth to you to find out?" And before Dania could say anything, Augusta added, "Keep in mind that I put a little spell on these scrolls. Should they leave my possession without my consent—or if I'm feeling like they might—then they will disintegrate without a trace." Augusta was mostly bluffing, but Dania didn't need to know that. Augusta did indeed have such a spell on the notes, but she would never activate it. She agreed with Dania that some knowledge was too precious to be destroyed.

Dania's eyes narrowed. "I see. You took those scrolls from Blaise's office, and now you'd like me to vote your way."

Augusta simply shrugged in response, giving Dania a coolly amused look. "Perhaps," she said casually. "Who is to say what happened in Blaise's house? Certainly there were no witnesses either way."

Dania stared at her, a calculating look appearing on her face. "So if I vote your way, you'll give them to me? Those scrolls?"

"Yes." Augusta smiled. "In fact, I will give them to you now. All I require in exchange is your vow to keep your promise about the vote . . . and your help with locating a couple of books in this library." Taking the scrolls out of her pocket, she handed them to Dania, who accepted them with a reverent look on her face.

The old woman's hands shook with eagerness as she unrolled the scrolls and quickly glanced over them. Augusta knew she could see traces of her incinerating spell on them, so she had no fear of Dania double-crossing her. For the next minute, Dania seemed so absorbed in the scrolls that Augusta had to clear her throat again to remind Dania of her presence.

When Dania looked up, Augusta gave her an even look. "Well?" she prompted. "Do we have an agreement?"

Dania hesitated, looking torn, and Augusta knew that this was difficult for her. She wanted those scrolls, but she was also loyal to Ganir. "Keep in mind," Augusta said softly, "that these scrolls contain dangerous knowledge—knowledge that was used to create this thing that we need to destroy. If you don't take them and hide them in the depths of this library,

I may have no choice but to incinerate them. I can't leave them lying about unattended. They could easily fall into the wrong hands, you see?"

"No." The word sounded like it was torn from Dania's throat. "No, you can't destroy these. I'll take them, and I'll give you that vote."

"Good." Augusta smiled again. "I knew we'd see eye to eye on this. Now I also need a book on locator, paralysis, and energy drainage spells, as well as a few texts for the physics project I've been working on."

And with that, her mission was complete. Now all Augusta had to do was wait for the vote and hope that she had not misjudged Gina after all.

CHAPTER TEN

※ BARSON ※

Stealthily making his way through the Tower halls, Barson fixed his hood, making sure it covered his face. So far, no one had paid him any attention, making his plan of staying hidden remarkably easy to implement.

Approaching the now-empty Guard barracks, he took a look around to confirm that no one saw him, and entered the familiar quarters, lowering his hood on the way. As expected, his allies were already there, gathered in the room that typically served as the training area for the soldiers. Barson had asked Dara to send a Contact message to all of them, and it appeared they received his invitation.

There were five sorcerers standing there—three men and two women. At his entrance, the youngest, Kira, stepped forward and gave Barson a smile. "Hello, Captain," she said warmly. "We're glad to see you alive."

"Indeed," Vashel chimed in, his hands nervously playing with the hem of his tunic. "We'd heard some very disturbing rumors recently..." A short, thin man of indeterminate age, he had been among the last to join Barson's cause, and he still seemed anxious about his decision.

"You should know better than to trust rumors. I'm not an easy man to kill," Barson said, barely managing to veil his contempt. He hated weakness and indecisiveness in all its forms. Vashel hadn't been among the five sorcerers Barson had originally approached, and if it weren't for the fact that Ganir managed to get rid of two of his potential allies, Barson would've never considered working with the man. As it was, however, he had to hope that Vashel's ambition would outweigh his cowardice.

"I think we all know that," Noriella said calmly, looking at Barson. A talented sorceress, she, like Dara, was tired of being denied opportunities for advancement. She had been the first outsider to join his cause, and Barson admired her for her determination to take matters into her own hands. "That's what we're counting on, in fact."

The other two people in the room—Pavel and Mittel—remained silent. The two middle-aged sorcerers were cousins, though they looked similar enough to be twins, both possessing bright red hair and freckled complexions. From what Dara told Barson, they were as close as brothers too, having worked together on some bit of arcane research for decades. It was the Council's peremptory shutting down of that research that prompted them to ally themselves with Barson. Apparently a sorcerer denied his research was a dangerous thing—a fact that Barson noted for future reference.

In general, all five of his allies were frustrated with the current regime. Their specific reasons were different, but it all boiled down to their unhappiness with the Council and the hierarchy within the Tower. Peasants weren't the only ones who felt neglected and oppressed by the ruling body of the land; many lower-ranking sorcerers were just as upset, their feelings aggravated by the sense of entitlement all members of their class possessed. To Barson, this was yet another failure of the Sorcery Revolution. In the old days, when rightful kings ruled, everybody knew their place, and there was a certain comfort in that. In the modern era, however, the illusion of upward mobility bred discontent among lower and upper classes alike, fostering unnecessary unrest in the Koldun society.

It was a situation Barson planned to remedy when he was king.

"So," he said quietly, looking around the room at the people who were going to help him achieve that goal, "it appears that we might be able to implement our plan earlier than expected, thanks to some recent developments. Where does each of you stand on the assignments Dara asked you to complete?"

And for the next twenty minutes, he listened as they filled him in on spells that they had prepared, each one of them eager to impress him with their knowledge and skill. Barson nodded and praised them, giving them the approval they so clearly craved, and all the while his mind was going over strategies for the upcoming battle. It would not be easy, but he was confident that they would succeed. They had to succeed.

As the meeting was wrapping up, Barson instructed his allies to keep a close eye on Ganir and the general happenings in the Tower. "If the old man so much as sneezes, I want to know about it," he told them, and they promised to keep him informed.

Satisfied, Barson left the Guard barracks, pulling the hood up around his head again. As soon as the Council had a chance to complete their vote, he would go talk to Augusta.

He couldn't wait to see her again.

CHAPTER ELEVEN

※ BLAISE ※

"What is it?" Ara asked, seeing what must have been an alert expression on Blaise's face.

"I am not sure," Blaise replied. "I heard an animal of some kind. It was growling."

"What kind of animal?"

Blaise listened closer. He didn't hear a growl again, but now he heard something heavy moving through the forest. "I think there is more than one creature."

She frowned, looking disturbed.

"They must be quite large," Blaise said, closing his eyes to better focus on his hearing. "I can hear their footsteps. It almost seems like they're trying to tread lightly, but their bulk hits branches and bushes, giving them away."

Opening his eyes, he saw the girl standing there, her face pale. "We need to wake the others," she said urgently.

"What is it?"

"I don't know, but if it's anything from the Dark Woods, we need to prepare immediately."

They hurried back toward the tents, approaching Kostya first. As soon as Ara explained the situation, he ordered all the rest to be woken up. Only Maya, Esther, and Gala were allowed to sleep uninterrupted.

"How far away would you say were the noises you heard?" Kostya asked Blaise, his voice tense.

Blaise thought about it. "About half a mile away, I think."

"What? There is no way you can hear that far," Shram said derisively. "Are you sure you didn't fall asleep and dream the whole thing?"

"We were both awake," Ara said sharply, looking at Shram with annoyance. "And he could hear that far because he did a spell to enhance his hearing. And be glad that he did. If there is even the slightest possibility that there is something from the Dark Woods here, this close to the village . . ."

The other men nodded. "She's right," a blond man said. "We have to check this out, and if it's a threat, deal with it."

"You don't have to come, Blaise," Kostya said, apparently reaching a decision. "This might be dangerous."

"I want to come," Blaise said. "But we should leave someone behind to guard that tent." He pointed at where Gala and the old women were sleeping.

"Yes, and we need to make sure someone can warn the village, should something go wrong with our hunt," Ara added.

"Then it's settled," Kostya said, ordering four of his men to stay behind. The rest gathered their weapons and quietly headed in the direction of the noise.

Letting the hunters walk ahead, Blaise spoke the words of the shielding spell again, casting a protective bubble around the tent. It wouldn't last long, but it was better than nothing.

Then he hurried to catch up with the others, looking through his spell cards on the way. He was not prepared for encounters with wild creatures, but he was sure he could improvise.

As they got closer to the source of the noise, Blaise held up his finger, warning the hunters to be careful. "I can only hear one of them now," he whispered to Kostya. "Maybe the other ones left?"

"Let's see what we're up against," Kostya whispered. "How far is it?"

"Not far now. It sounds like it's heading in our direction."

The hunters got their bows ready.

Two minutes later, a powerful roar split the air. Blaise felt a chill skitter down his spine. Whatever this creature was, it sounded big and vicious.

It was also running straight at them.

The hunters spread out in a semi-circle and drew back the strings of their arrows. They looked scared, but determined.

And then the creature was upon them.

Bursting through the bushes, it was a blur of dark fur, claws, and teeth, with small yellow eyes that had some kind of a reflective sheen.

It was also massive. For a second, Blaise thought it was a bear—but the creature was even larger, with a thick tail, long pointed snout, and movements reminiscent of a jackal or a fox.

The archers released their arrows.

Only two reached their target, and the hide of the beast seemed too thick for the arrows to penetrate. One of the arrows fell harmlessly to the ground, while the other one got lodged in the creature's massive paw.

The sound it made was hair-raising. And before anyone could react, the thing jumped onto a nearby tree, making a leap over the stunned hunters' heads, and disappeared into the forest.

"We must go after it," Kostya yelled, apparently emboldened by their success. Before Blaise could object, the hunters took off at a run, forcing him to sprint after them to keep up.

"What was that?" Blaise managed to ask, catching up to Ara. He had no idea how the hunters were able to move so quickly through the dark forest. Even with his enhanced vision, he found it difficult to keep such a fast pace.

"It's a bearwolf," she panted in response, ducking to avoid a low-hanging branch.

"A bearwolf? Do you mean a wolf-bear hybrid? I

didn't know those things still existed." Blaise remembered the old stories about the sorcerer who had done experiments on living creatures. Augusta had been obsessed with those tales at some point, using them as an example of the dangers of hubris in sorcery.

"Oh, they exist," Ara muttered, breathing heavily from the run. "The Dark Woods swarm with them. I think a couple of those things got there at some point, and they bred like rabbits. That's partially why so few people get through those forests—that and all those poisonous plants."

"How did you and the others get through it, then?" Blaise jumped over a thick tree root, barely managing to stay upright as his foot sank into a hidden hole. Yanking it out, he hurried after Ara, who continued running at a breakneck pace.

"Long story," she panted, apparently reaching the limits of her endurance. He could see beads of sweat glistening on her forehead.

At that moment, they reached a large clearing. Bursting through the bushes, they stopped abruptly when they reached the middle.

The other hunters were already there, standing frozen in place.

The creature they followed was not running anymore. It had turned to face them, standing its ground on the other end of the meadow.

And all around the edges of the clearing, Blaise could see more of its kind standing in a circle around the hunters, their yellow eyes gleaming in the moonlight.

The bearwolf had led them to an ambush.

* * *

The cool, rational part of Blaise involuntarily admired the creature's intelligence. This was long-term planning in action. Like its more commonplace wolf relatives, bearwolves apparently hunted in packs—and were quite good at coordinating their actions.

They also seemed to know how to hunt humans.

"We are so dead," Ara whispered, standing next to him. Blaise could hear the fear and resignation in her voice, and some of his own shock faded.

The archers were frantically preparing to release their arrows, their hands shaking, but Blaise could see the lack of hope on their faces. All around them, he could hear low, furious growling and see the reflective sheen in the creatures' small yellow eyes.

At most, they had seconds before the bearwolves attacked.

His heart pounding, Blaise grabbed his Interpreter Stone and began reaching for his spell cards. Out of the corner of his eye, he could see Shram pulling out a long knife.

"What are you doing?" one of the men hissed at him.

"I'm going to die on my own terms," the scarred man gritted out, gripping the knife tightly and starting forward. Before he could take more than a few steps, there was a blur of motion, and Shram was on the ground, a large snarling mass on top of him.

"No!" Ara let out a shrill scream just as Blaise loaded a card into his Stone, releasing the fireball he prepared earlier.

The flash of light was so bright, it hurt Blaise's enhanced vision. However, it appeared to hurt the beast more, singing its fur. With a roar, the bearwolf jumped off Shram, rolling on the ground in pain.

It was a big creature, Blaise noted with that cool part of his mind. Bigger than the rest. Perhaps it was the alpha of this pack. His hands shaking, Blaise desperately searched his cards again. There was nothing he'd be able to write in time. He only had moments to improvise something else, before the creatures would recuperate and attack in full force. "Buy me a little time," he barked at Kostya, beginning to chant the shield spell.

At Kostya's command, the archers released their arrows. Many hit their targets, but as before, few penetrated the animals' thick hide. Maddened, the bearwolves sprang at them, and at that moment, Blaise's shield spell manifested. Instead of reaching the hunters, the beasts' massive bulk hit the shimmering wall of the protective bubble Blaise had managed to erect.

"How long is this going to hold?" Kostya asked, his voice tight with anxiety. Two of the men were dragging Shram away from the bubble's edge. He looked to be in bad shape, his arm ripped to shreds.

"Not long," Blaise said tensely. "I have an idea,

but I need to concentrate."

This idea hinged on a lot of assumptions. The biggest one was that an illusion spell designed for human beings would work on these animal hybrids. Blaise thought it might, just because many of these spells were initially tested on animals, but there was no guarantee.

His other assumption was that these creatures were indeed like wolves in their behavior.

Frantically writing his spell, Blaise could hear the creatures attacking the bubble over and over again, growing more maddened with every attempt. He knew he had almost no time, as pressure applied to the spell bubble tended to weaken it faster. It was as though the creatures knew it too, because they kept pouncing, clawing at the invisible wall.

His hands slippery with sweat, Blaise loaded the spell as soon as it was done. Then he looked up, waiting to see if it worked.

Visibly, nothing had changed about himself and his companions. However, the bearwolves stopped attacking the bubble. Instead, they appeared confused, their thick tails swinging from side to side.

At that moment, the bubble shimmer began to fade as the shield spell ran its course. If Blaise's illusion spell didn't work correctly, they would all be at the creatures' mercy.

"What's happening?" Kostya asked, sounding fearful.

"I used an illusion spell," Blaise explained quietly. "If I did it right, they should see us as a rival pack of bearwolves. Essentially, they see what we see, a mirror image of their own selves. And they hear us growling instead of talking."

"So what now?" Ara whispered, her entire body trembling.

"Now we need to threaten them into leaving us alone," Blaise replied, hoping that his idea would work. It might've been effective with wolves, but he didn't know if it would be with these creatures.

"All right," Kostya said, immediately understanding the task in front of them. "Let's all spread out and walk toward them. Show no fear."

They all slowly started forward, two of the men in the back supporting Shram.

The bearwolves snarled threateningly as the humans began to approach. The alpha of the pack—the one who had attacked Shram before—took a step toward them, letting out a loud growl. As the hunters continued moving forward, however, the creature slowly began to retreat, apparently intimidated by the approaching 'pack.' Blaise had purposefully used the alpha's own image for the illusion, making all of the human 'bearwolves' as large as the pack's leader. There were also nine humans, including Blaise, versus eight bearwolves.

Still, the animals seemed hesitant to leave. The one thing Blaise hadn't been able to do with the spell was mask the people's real scent. While the animals saw and heard others of their own kind, they undoubtedly still smelled humans in the vicinity and were loath to give up their prey.

Blaise and the hunters needed to do something more aggressive before the illusion spell began wearing off.

"Start screaming," Blaise told the others. "Scream as loudly as you can—as if your life depends on it. Because it does." And he let out a war-like yell, which he hoped would sound like a powerful roar to the animals' ears. The hunters joined in, their voices mingling in a furious cacophony of sound.

The bearwolves took a step back . . . one, then another. Blaise could see their ears twitching and their tails swinging in displeasure from side to side. He continued screaming, even though his throat was sore and his ears were ringing.

And just when he was sure the plan would fail, the bearwolf leader let out a loud growl and turned around, disappearing into the bushes. The rest of the pack followed, and Blaise could hear them running through the forest to the east—back toward the Dark Woods.

The hunters and Blaise stopped screaming. Shaking in the aftermath, they looked at the now-empty meadow with stunned expressions on their faces.

The hunters could hardly believe they survived—and Blaise knew exactly how they felt.

* * *

After everyone had a chance to calm down a bit, Blaise walked over to Shram—the only one who had been wounded during this encounter. The scarred man was sitting on the ground, clutching his torn arm. Blaise could see blood seeping out of the wound despite a makeshift bandage of someone's shirt pressed against it.

Crouching next to the man, Blaise pulled out his Interpreter Stone and a few spell cards, and began preparing a healing spell.

"What are you doing, sorcerer?" the man asked harshly, watching Blaise's efforts.

"Planning to heal your wound, of course," Blaise replied, continuing to write. "We need to get back to the camp, and your injuries will slow us down."

Shram frowned, but didn't voice any objections as Blaise finished writing and loaded the appropriate cards into his stone. As soon as the spell began working, Shram gasped, his eyes opening wide. Blaise knew what he was feeling—immediate relief from the pain. Pain that must've been quite bad, judging by the size of the wound. The bearwolf had literally torn out a chunk of Shram's flesh—flesh that was now healing.

A few minutes later, the bleeding had stopped, and the injury was gone.

Slowly rising to his feet, Shram touched his arm, the expression on his face oscillating between wonder and resentment. Blaise got up too, and was about to walk away when Shram reached out and grabbed his arm.

"Thank you, sorcerer," he said gruffly. "For this and for saving my life earlier."

And before Blaise could react, the man walked away, apparently as uncomfortable with this scene as Blaise himself.

CHAPTER TWELVE

※ AUGUSTA ※

On the morning of the vote, Augusta woke up groggy and with a massive headache. She had scarcely slept, tossing and turning all night long, thinking of the impending vote. Every time she drifted off, she dreamed of Barson, images of his death dancing in front of her eyes.

Crawling out of bed, she forced herself to write a healing spell for her headache, so she could get a semblance of a clear mind. Sleep deprivation was one of the few things they hadn't quite figured out how to combat with spells; nobody fully understood the physiological process behind sleep and how it helped the human body.

Once her temples were no longer throbbing, Augusta dressed and got ready. Walking through the Tower halls, she could see the apprentices looking at her with curiosity. The entire Tower was buzzing with rumors and speculation about the upcoming meeting. As she approached the Council Hall, she heard the gong that announced the start of the meeting.

Most of the Councilors were already gathered inside, and Augusta nodded at them in greeting as she walked over to sit down on her throne. Ganir was already there; as usual, he was the one who had used the gong. Dania was there too, looking uncomfortable and guilty. Augusta guessed that she was not happy about her task.

Once Kelvin and Furak arrived, the vote began.

It was a custom as old as the office of the Sorcerer Council itself. Each Councilor had a voting stone that would need to be teleported into one of the voting boxes—red box for Yes, blue one for No. The boxes stood on the Scales of Justice in the middle of the large marble table. When the vote was complete, the weight of the stones would force the Scales to tip in whichever direction the vote was leaning. Afterwards, each of the voting stones would get summoned back to its original owner.

The process was supposed to be both fair and anonymous, and Augusta wondered again how Blaise had learned how she'd voted at his brother's trial.

Ganir sat there silently instead of addressing everyone like he usually did. Looking away from him, Augusta caught Jandison's gaze. He gave her a barely perceptible nod and got up.

"Those in favor of taking action against the

creature, vote Yes," Jandison said, addressing the Council in a loud voice. "If we get a No vote, we will discuss what the next option will be."

Perfect, Augusta thought. The choices were something unknown versus a clearly defined action. It was human nature to avoid uncertainty. Jandison really was completely on her side, and for the first time, Augusta wondered if he did have what it took to lead the Council in Ganir's stead.

At Jandison's signal, she teleported her voting stone into the red box and waited, holding her breath. A few seconds later, the Scales of Justice tipped, the red box lowering under the weight of the stones.

The fate of Blaise's abomination was sealed.

"It's done," Jandison said. "We'll reconvene to decide what our next move should be."

The expression on Ganir's face was frightening in its stillness. Augusta could sense the fury burning within him, but he didn't say anything to anyone.

Instead, the Council Leader got up and left the room.

* * *

Exhausted but triumphant, Augusta made her way back to her quarters. Entering her bedroom, she began to disrobe wearily, desperately needing some rest. There was still a lot to be done—spells to be written, plans to be solidified—but right now, Augusta was only capable of collapsing on her bed.

Suddenly, out of the corner of her eye, she caught a flicker of movement. Whirling around in panic, she stared at the dark shadow in the corner, her heart climbing into her throat.

Before she could even begin to chant a protective spell, the figure stood up and stepped into the light.

It was Barson—the man she'd thought she lost.

CHAPTER THIRTEEN

✳ GALA ✳

Waking up the next morning, Gala tried to remember her dream, but the specifics of it eluded her. All she could recall was a feeling of curiosity and awe, as though she'd learned something amazing.

Getting up, she became aware that she was alone in the tent—and that she could hear excited chatter outside. Straightening her hair and clothes, she stepped out of the tent, intrigued by the little tidbits she'd managed to overhear.

"Did you say 'bearwolves?'" she asked, approaching a small group that included Maya, Esther, Blaise, and a few of the hunters.

"Oh, yes, Gala, you will not believe what happened," Esther exclaimed. "We were attacked last night by these . . . these creatures!"

"What creatures?" Gala stared at them in surprise.

"These wolf-bear hybrids that some sorcerer

created a long time ago. They apparently prospered in the Dark Woods," Maya said, her voice filled with fearful excitement. "From the way the men described them, we are lucky that Blaise was standing watch and heard them before they got to our camp—"

"I'm sure they wouldn't have attacked such a large camp," Blaise broke in, looking uncomfortable. "And besides, everyone participated in scaring them off."

"Yes," Kostya said, coming up to the group. "But it was your spell that made it possible. And I wouldn't be too sure that they wouldn't have attacked the camp. We've had interactions with these beasts before, and it's never ended well. They're bold, these creatures, and a single animal has been known to kill upwards of five men. With a pack that large, they could've destroyed half of our village."

Blaise still appeared reluctant to take credit for whatever it was that occurred last night. "I'm just glad I could help," he told Kostya. "And if there is anything I can do to help protect your village from future danger, please let me know. Maybe there are some spells I could implement to keep these beasts away from your settlement."

"That would be great," Kostya said, apparently no longer as wary of sorcery. "We would appreciate it."

Burning with curiosity, Gala looked at the group. "What are these bearwolves?" she asked. "What happened? Please, tell me the whole story."

And for the next twenty minutes, she listened in shock as the hunters described their nighttime adventures and the inventive way Blaise defended them from the creatures. "Why didn't you wake me?" she asked Blaise. "Surely I could've helped—"

"No." He shook his head. "You've been through enough. I was not about to put you in danger again— not if I could help it."

Gala stared at him, unsure how she felt about Blaise's protectiveness. "But you were in danger yourself," she protested. "You and the rest of the people here—"

"Gala . . ." Blaise stepped closer to her and placed his hands on her shoulders. "I was able to handle it, all right? Please, don't worry about it. It's over. Let's just pack up and get to the village before we have to spend another night here."

And with that, he lowered his arms and walked off to join the men who were disassembling the tents, leaving Gala frowning after him.

* * *

It took them several hours to finally reach Alania. If not for the chance meeting with these men, Gala doubted they would have ever stumbled upon these dwellings. The houses were small and hidden among the trees, blending into the landscape so well that they were almost invisible. They were generally made of wood, with roofs that were covered with vines and other types of plants. There were no fields of any kind surrounding the village, and Gala didn't see any signs of domesticated animals. As Kostya had told them, hunting and gathering fed the village.

When they reached a larger dwelling in the center of the village, Kostya announced that it was his home. "That's my wife, Liva," he said, stepping inside and gesturing toward a stocky woman sitting at the kitchen table.

Surprised, Liva stood up. "Who are these people?" she asked her husband, eying them with curiosity.

"Liva, please meet Esther, Gala, Maya and Blaise," he answered. "We met them in the forest and invited them to join us here, in Alania."

A welcoming smile appeared on Liva's broad face in response. "Oh, more refugees? Excellent! Glad you were able to make it through the woods. The last time someone came here was that lovely young woman, Ara—and that was almost two years ago."

"They're not exactly refugees," Kostya said. "You've heard of Blaise, haven't you?"

Liva frowned. "Blaise? As in, the sorcerer?"

"That's the one," Kostya said. "These people are his companions."

"Oh." Liva seemed nonplussed for a moment, then recovered quickly. "Well, regardless, welcome. We are pleased to have you here. I trust that you had a good journey?"

"We did," Blaise said, smiling at her. "And thank you for offering us your hospitality. I can assure you that I mean you no harm."

"I figured as much," Liva said calmly. "Otherwise Kostya wouldn't have brought you here. Can I offer you something to eat?"

"I'm not hungry, thank you," Blaise said. "But I'm

sure Gala, Esther, and Maya would appreciate a meal."

"Thank you, we would," Esther said. "And you should eat too, Blaise. Liva, can I help you prepare something?"

"Wife, I need to go out on a hunt again," Kostya interrupted. "Is it all right if I leave our visitors with you?"

"Of course. I'll take care of them." Liva made a shooing motion toward the door, and Kostya swiftly exited the house. Gala got the impression he was uncomfortable dealing with so many guests and preferred to leave that task to his wife.

As soon as he was gone, Liva turned toward Esther. "I would welcome some help," she said with a smile, answering Esther's earlier question. "I never turn down an offer of another pair of hands in the kitchen."

"Excellent," Maya jumped in. "Then let me offer my services as well." And before a minute had passed, all three women were companionably cutting up some roots and vegetables and throwing them in a skillet coated with something that smelled like fried meat.

Gala remained silent, quietly observing everything. She was fascinated by these people and their way of life. There was also something in the house that made her feel strange. It wasn't long before she realized that she was sensing a spell of some kind. She didn't know what the spell was supposed to do, but she could feel it in the room.

"What's that spell you're using?" she asked Liva, speaking for the first time. She assumed it was Liva doing it, since Blaise hadn't had a chance to write or say anything.

Liva turned toward her slowly. "Whatever do you mean, child?" she asked, as though she didn't know. However, her pupils were dilated, and Gala saw her fingers twitch slightly. These were signs that she wasn't being truthful, Gala guessed. Did Liva feel uncomfortable with the topic?

Gala thought about changing the subject to accommodate the woman, but she was too curious. "Is the spell intended to lift people's spirits or cure minor ills?" she persisted, trying to figure out what exactly she was feeling.

Liva looked both amazed and scared. "How do you know this?" she asked, staring at Gala in awe.

Gala shrugged, uncertain of how to explain it. She could feel spells sometimes, as if a part of her was attuned to the changes in the fabric of the Physical Realm that resulted from sorcery.

"Are you a sorceress?" Blaise asked Liva, regarding their hostess with surprise.

"I'm not a sorceress," Liva denied. "I just dabble with some spells, that's all. No one knows about it— not even my husband." She paused, giving Blaise and Gala a pleading look. "And I would like to keep it that way, if you don't mind. Sorcerers are not exactly liked around these parts."

"Oh, don't worry," Maya said reassuringly. "We'll keep your secret. I don't know why you feel the need to conceal your gift, but we respect your right to do so."

"Yes, we do," Esther chimed in, and Gala and Blaise nodded their agreement.

"Good." Apparently considering the matter closed, Liva went back to chopping the vegetables.

Now it was Blaise who couldn't restrain his curiosity. "But how did you learn?" he asked, studying Liva. "I've never met anyone who simply dabbles in sorcery."

"I learned from my father," Liva explained, stirring the vegetables in the skillet. There was a hint of nostalgia in her voice. "He was an apprentice who got his arm blown off during his first test in the Tower. He also injured another apprentice. To punish him, they made him perform menial tasks around the Tower, and he chose to leave instead. He had a lot of pride, my father did. He continued learning some spells on his own, and even though he wasn't very good, he still taught me some things in secret."

"Why didn't your father take you to the Tower then?" Blaise asked, frowning. "If you had an aptitude for sorcery, then you could've become an acolyte."

"By the time he started teaching me, we were already here, far away from the Tower. Besides, he hated them, and he wouldn't have been happy if I'd left to go to Turingrad. Not that I would have—it's a miracle we made it here safely in the first place." And she busied herself with food preparations, looking uncomfortable with the topic.

"Can I help?" Gala asked, approaching the woman. From her time at the inn, she knew how to cook, and she wanted to lend a hand if Liva allowed it.

Liva shot her a wary look. "If you want, child. Are you a sorceress, like this one here?" She jerked her chin toward Blaise.

"Something like that," Gala murmured, starting to chop up mushrooms. "I'm not very good, though—"

"Not very good?" Esther snorted. "Right, sure."

"I'm still learning," Gala insisted, and Blaise frowned at Esther in warning, causing the old woman to fall silent. Blaise didn't want these people to know about Gala's unpredictable powers, Gala realized, and she was in agreement with that decision. Given what had happened before, she understood the importance of discretion now, and she was determined to do her best to fit in at this new place.

"So you gathered all these plants in the woods?" Maya asked, changing the subject, and the older women began discussing the best ways to find edible mushrooms. Listening to them, Gala worked quietly, not wanting to draw any more attention to herself.

Before long, the meal was ready.

They sat down to eat at a large wooden table. "Your house is quite large for the two of you," Blaise remarked, noticing that the table had room for six people.

"It seems large now—" Liva smiled, "—but when

our three sons lived with us, it was quite crowded. The boys have now grown up and married, living in houses of their own, so we have some extra room."

"The food is wonderful," Gala said as they began to eat. "I've never had anything so delicious before." And it was true—even Esther's stew paled in comparison to the rich, hearty mix of flavors she was tasting now.

"The food is fresher than what you would get back in the territories," Liva explained. "The soil here has not been abused as much."

"Plus she's probably famished," Esther muttered, shooting Gala a frosty look. Gala blinked, startled, and then she realized that she had inadvertently offended the woman who had fed her several times.

"Your stew was delightful too," she reassured Esther, trying to make up for her blunder. "And you're right—I'm very, very hungry."

Esther's expression thawed out. "I know, child. And the food here is pretty good, I must admit. Look, even Blaise is eating."

Turning to look at her creator, Gala noticed that he was wolfing down the dishes with signs of obvious enjoyment.

When they were done, Gala felt comfortably full and relaxed. Before long, she began to get sleepy and was overcome by a yawn.

"You must all be tired from your journey," Liva said. "I have two extra rooms." She paused, looking at Blaise and Gala. "Perhaps the two of you can share one, and Maya and Esther can take the other?"

Blaise looked taken aback, but Gala liked that idea quite a bit. "Sure," she said brightly. "I'd love to sleep with Blaise." The idea of sleeping near her creator was very appealing to her.

Maya and Esther burst out laughing, and Blaise looked uncomfortable for some reason. Liva grinned. Gala frowned at them, unsure what she'd done wrong this time.

"Sure you would, child," Maya said after a bit, wiping away tears of laughter. "If I were young like you, I would too."

"Of course you would, you strumpet . . ." Esther looked like she would die from laughter.

"Strumpet?" Gala asked, her frown deepening— and then it hit her. In the books she'd read, sometimes 'sleeping' was used as a euphemism for sexual relations. They must've thought she wanted that with Blaise.

They weren't necessarily wrong, but that wasn't what she meant. She had a feeling, though, that if she tried to explain herself, she would just make things worse. One didn't admit to wanting sex so bluntly, she knew that much, and she felt slightly embarrassed that she had inadvertently broken that societal taboo.

At that moment, Blaise stepped into the conversation. "That's enough," he said quietly, his serious tone cutting through the hilarity that reigned in the room. "Gala is tired, and we need to rest. Liva, thank you for your hospitality, and we'd love to take you up on your offer of the room."

And with that, he followed Liva toward the back of the house, with Gala gratefully trailing in their wake, even as Maya and Esther resumed laughing at the kitchen table.

When they reached the room, Liva pointed out the bed—a straw-filled mattress on the floor—and quickly departed, stifling a smile.

Gala yawned again, feeling tired, and Blaise turned toward her. "Gala," he said softly, reaching out to touch her cheek lightly with his fingers, "let's go to sleep, all right?"

She nodded, her lids growing heavy. As intrigued as she was by the possibility of sex with Blaise, at the moment sleep was quite appealing too.

Blaise stepped away, taking off his shoes and outer tunic, then sat down on the bed. Gala followed his example, joining him there. Yawning, she lay down and saw Blaise stretch out beside her. In the last few moments before she was overcome by sleep, she felt him put his arm around her, drawing her closer . . . and then she slept, warm and content in his embrace.

* * *

When she woke up, Blaise was already gone. Entering the kitchen, Gala saw him sitting at the table, talking to Liva.

"Good morning," he said warmly, seeing Gala come into the room. "Come have breakfast, and then we can maybe go for a walk, see the surrounding areas."

Gala grinned at him, excited at the idea, and began eating the berries Liva had prepared for breakfast. Now that she wasn't so tired, she couldn't wait to spend more time with Blaise.

A few minutes later, she was done with breakfast and ready to explore.

Exiting the house, Gala and Blaise walked down a broad path made by the villagers. It was a street of sorts, the only street in the village. After passing a few houses, they turned off the main path and headed into the woods.

As they walked through the greenery, Gala stared at the gorgeous nature surrounding them. "This is beautiful," she said as they entered a small clearing in the woods. "Not as beautiful as yesterday's lake, of course, but still quite nice."

Blaise smiled at her. "Would you like to go back there?"

"Sure," Gala said, smiling back at him. "But isn't it far away now?"

"Not if we fly there," he said and began chanting the words of a spell. When he was done, he explained, "This will summon the chaise to us. It should get here shortly."

Gala grinned at him. "Great. What should we do while we wait?" She had one idea . . .

"How about I try to teach you how to control your magic?" Blaise suggested.

It wasn't exactly what Gala had in mind, but she wanted this too. "Of course, I'd love that," she said earnestly. Maybe if she had better control of her abilities, Blaise wouldn't feel like he needed to protect her all the time.

"I have a couple of ideas for how to go about it," he said, sitting down on the grass. "I think, for starters, I can teach you how to do sorcery our way, with verbal and written spells. It might help you understand it better, so you can gain control over that part of you that does something similar."

That made sense to Gala. She sat down beside him and gave him her attention.

"I do wish I still had access to my house," he said ruefully. "It would make things a lot easier." He seemed sad for a moment, then shook it off. "Regardless, I should still be able to show you verbal spell casting, and I also brought some written spells with me when I rushed to your rescue. Those will have to do for now."

Gala nodded, an idea beginning to form in the back of her mind. Perhaps Blaise wouldn't need to be without his house for long . . .

"Another thing we could try is for you to learn to control and understand your emotions, since you seem to do magic when you experience strong feelings," Blaise continued. "This might be a bit harder. Unlike the sorcery code, emotions are very imprecise."

"I would love to learn more about human emotions in general," Gala said, giving him a warm look.

He smiled. "Well, why don't we begin with spells," he said, "and see where we go from there. As you probably already know, both verbal and written spells require that you learn a new language. Two related languages, strictly speaking. One builds on the other, so once you master speaking spells, learning the written part will be easy."

"I find it strange that oral casting is harder, but written casting lets you create more complicated spells," Gala observed, remembering what Blaise had told her once.

He nodded. "The best analogy is to compare doing complex arithmetic in your head, which would be like using the spoken spells, to writing out equations on paper. Doing math in your head is much harder, and the complexity of the math you can do is much less."

Gala cocked her head to the side. "Actually, I'm not sure if that's true for me . . ."

He laughed. "Right, of course. I almost forgot that your mind can do any kind of math. But I can assure you, for most people, my analogy would work. You see, with written spells, because the coding language is simpler and more powerful, one can weave greater complexity into the spell. For verbal spells, the longer and more complex they are, the greater the risk of error—of saying something wrong. There have been a lot of accidents and unfortunate deaths as a result of that." He paused, then added wryly, "Spells have gone awry because of something as simple as a sneeze."

"A sneeze?" Gala found that absurdly funny.

He grinned briefly. "Indeed. Also, another

powerful feature of written spells is that you can mix and match existing spell components—or even short, simple spells that had already proven themselves. That allows one to prepare ahead of time instead of always having to recreate the spell from scratch by speaking it—and that obviously saves time as a result."

Gala nodded. This all made sense to her. She was impressed that Blaise had been the one to come up with the simplified language that enabled them to do the written form of sorcery. She recalled him telling her about himself and Augusta inventing the Interpreter Stone, and she felt an unpleasant twinge of some dark emotion. She didn't like the idea of him being so close to that woman, she realized—of having worked with her . . . having loved her.

"Why don't we start with teleportation?" he said, interrupting her thoughts. "Over short distances, it's actually a fairly simple spell. You have done this without conscious control, but I will teach you how to do it using a verbal spell."

"That would be amazing," Gala said eagerly. Of all the feats she'd done, she had the least understanding of how she'd been able to get herself from one place to another in a blink of an eye.

"Great." He smiled. "Before we go into the details of the actual language, let me tell you the spirit of what you would be doing. You need to be thinking of the world surrounding you as a set of coordinates. Think of the three-dimensional space around you as little cubes or spheres, whichever suits you, and establish a mathematical convention for naming each location."

Gala visualized a grid ahead of her, picturing the meadow covered by evenly placed, tiny pebbles, where each pebble had its own unique name. The names were not fancy: pebble one was next to pebble two and so on a million times around the area of the meadow. She could also easily picture a whole meadow filled up with these imaginary pebbles and name them around the volume of the space. If she wanted what Blaise called a coordinate, she just needed to name the right pebble.

"I have it," she told him. The entire process took her only moments.

He raised his eyebrows, looking impressed. "I was just beginning my explanation."

Gala grinned at him. "Well, you can move on. I understand these coordinate things."

"All right then, teleporting requires you to pick a coordinate you want to end up at. You need to plan your spell carefully. If you are going someplace outside your line of vision, you had better plan for what happens if there is an object already at that coordinate. That's why long-distance teleportation is so dangerous." He took a breath, then continued, "You need to picture your own body split into the same sub-units as the coordinates, so you can specify exactly the space you will occupy when the spell is done."

This also made sense to Gala. She imagined her own body made of pebbles. If she wanted to put the pebbles that made her body somewhere, she needed to decide which pebbles it would displace. She nodded to show her understanding.

"When all that is done, you use the words that someone had already invented for this task, and just fill in the variables that I explained. This is a simple task, because you're not inventing a new spell. Someone, long ago, already did that. You're just tweaking it, so it works the way you want. And then you just need to say the Interpreter spell—"

"What exactly is the Interpreter spell?" Gala interrupted. "I know you've mentioned it before . . ."

Blaise smiled. "Well, I can explain to you what it does, but I can only guess at how it does it. From what we understand, it takes the logic of the spell and transmits it to the Spell Realm in some form—and then the spell acts upon our Physical Realm."

"I see," Gala said thoughtfully. She had more questions, but those could wait for now. "Can you please teach me what to say for the teleportation spell?"

Blaise proceeded to give her a language lesson. It was long, but Gala found every aspect of it fascinating. Blaise kept saying how amazingly quick she was to pick up all of the nuances of the arcana and how she was leapfrogging years of study. Gala accepted his praise with pleasure, even though this way of doing spells didn't appeal to her as much as doing them directly.

The language itself was very natural to her. It was precise and logical. There were things like

conditional statements—if A is true, then B follows—
that existed in regular speech. However, with verbal
spells, these statements had formal definitions and
always had to be spoken in a specific way. There
were a lot of words for formulas and quite a bit of
formal mathematical constructs with their own
version of grammar.

After hours of drilling, Blaise decided she was
ready.

Closing her eyes, Gala recited the spell, followed
by the Interpreter litany. It was supposed to teleport
her a short distance. When she was done speaking,
she opened her eyes and saw that Blaise's face was
much closer to her. Before the spell, they were sitting
about an arm's length apart, but now her knee was
touching his. Even though she had planned it exactly
this way, the sense of wonder was overwhelming.

Filled with joy, Gala looked into Blaise's eyes. He
held her gaze, and she could feel the growing
connection between them. The joy immediately
transmuted into something else—something that
only Blaise could make her feel. Her heartbeat picked
up, and she unconsciously moved toward him, her
body beginning to ache with a strange longing.

"Gala . . ." There was a soft, deep note in Blaise's
voice. It made her skin prickle with heat, as though
she was burning from within. "Are you sure about
this?"

Gala stared at him, and then, without saying a
word, she placed her hands on his shoulders. "I'm
not as naïve as you think," she murmured before

pressing her lips to his. She could hear the catch in Blaise's breathing, and then he encircled her in his arms, pulling her into his embrace and deepening the kiss. The fire burning inside Gala spread until she couldn't think, overwhelmed by the sensations. The intensity of her feelings was too much, too sharp, almost as it was when she lost control before . . . and then she suddenly felt unbearable heat—heat that was coming from outside herself.

Gasping, she drew back . . . and saw that the meadow around them was ablaze.

She must've accidentally set it on fire.

CHAPTER FOURTEEN

✳ BARSON ✳

"I hear you thought I was dead?" Barson said, stepping forward when Augusta just continued staring at him, seemingly frozen in place.

"You're..." Her face was pale, her lips barely moving. "You're not dead."

"No, I'm not," he said gently, pulling her toward him. He could feel her beginning to shake, and fierce satisfaction surged through him. She cared. She genuinely cared about him. Nobody could fake that kind of physical response. He also felt an unwelcome twinge of guilt for putting her through this—a guilt that he immediately suppressed. As he had hoped, the Council had voted to confront the threat of the young sorceress, and he strongly suspected that the Guard being 'dead' was a factor in that decision.

"How?" Augusta whispered, reaching up to touch his face with a trembling hand. "I thought I saw you die . . . Is this real? Are you real?"

"Oh, I'm real," Barson assured her, picking her up and carrying her over to the bed. "Why don't I show you just how real I am?" he murmured, starting to take off her remaining clothes.

And for the next couple of hours, he proved to her that he was fully alive and well.

* * *

When they were lying spent in each other's arms, Augusta began crying. Surprised, Barson stroked her glossy hair, not knowing what else to do.

"I'm sorry," she said after a minute, wiping away the tears. "I think I'm just exhausted and . . . and so relieved that you're alive. I still can't believe it. How did it happen?"

Barson hesitated for a moment, then decided that he had nothing to lose by telling her about the battle. As he explained how the young sorceress had healed many of them, he could feel the growing tension in Augusta's body.

Pulling back from him, she stared at him through tear-wet lashes. "Such power," she whispered, and there was horror in her voice. "Such inhuman, unnatural power . . ."

"Yes," Barson said, "I've never experienced anything like it before. It was euphoric, amazing . . . and the way she wielded the sword . . ." He couldn't hide the admiration in his voice, which seemed to upset Augusta. Her expression darkened, her eyes narrowing into golden slits, and he quickly added, "Of course, she's dangerous and needs to be dealt with."

"She needs to be wiped out of existence." Augusta's voice was low and furious. "This kind of creature cannot be allowed to live."

"Creature?"

Augusta nodded, and then she told him the most incredible story he'd ever heard. When she was done, he stared at Augusta in disbelief. Only a sorcerer would've done something so foolish—creating life without a thought to possible consequences. Their hubris knew no bounds.

"Does everybody know that the Guard has survived?" Augusta asked, interrupting that train of thought.

Barson understood where she was heading immediately. "No," he said, looking at her. "I rode ahead of my men." He'd suspected that this might be Augusta's reaction, and he was glad that she was taking the conversation in this direction.

"I don't know how to put it delicately," she said slowly, holding his gaze, "but do you think your men could take a well-deserved vacation for the next couple of weeks?"

"Oh?" Barson arched his eyebrows. She was doing exactly what he'd hoped.

"Your survival could . . . change things," Augusta said quietly. "It could cast the validity of the vote in doubt, since it was based on potentially faulty information."

"I understand." Barson hid his satisfaction. "We'll do as you ask and stay dead for now. Though, of course, this won't be easy on my men's families . . ." He added that last touch to give the appearance of reluctance. It wouldn't do to seem too eager.

"I know." Augusta frowned a bit. "I don't want them to suffer, but this is too important to be left to a re-vote. We need the Council to take her out. You understand that, right?"

"I do." Barson sighed, pretending to be thinking about this. "Perhaps we can have my men dress as peasants for now and visit their families in secret."

"That's a great idea," Augusta said, giving him a quick smile. "Thank you. I really owe you for this."

"Of course, if Ganir finds out about this . . ." Barson let his voice trail off.

"Don't worry. I will handle Ganir if it comes to that," she said, and there was a hard glitter in her eyes.

"In that case, we'll do as you ask," Barson promised, leaning down to kiss her again.

This had gone even better than he'd expected. Everything was falling nicely into place.

* * *

"There's something I have to tell you," Dara said, greeting Barson with a hug as he stepped inside her house.

"What is it?" Barson asked curiously, following her toward her study.

"Actually, it might be best if you see this for yourself." She led him toward the desk in the middle of the room and held out a needle. "Here, prick your finger. You'll want to record this."

"All right." Not bothering to question Dara, Barson held the needle to his finger, letting a droplet of blood well up. Then he pressed it to the Life Capture Sphere that sat on the desk.

"Good. Now take this." She handed him a droplet, and he realized that she wanted to retain the information on this droplet, to have his experience of consuming it recorded. Whatever was on this droplet had to be fairly important.

Putting the droplet in his mouth, Barson felt it overtaking his mind.

* * *

Picking up the droplet, Dara put it under her tongue, curious as to what it contained. She'd found it on the floor of Jandison's office, lying carelessly under his desk. It helped that Jandison was such a slob. He would never notice its absence, she thought right before she was pulled under.

* * *

Jandison watched the final stages of the voting process with a strange mix of satisfaction and regret. He didn't like Louie—the boy had always been Ganir's puppet, treating Jandison without any respect—but

Jandison regretted upsetting Louie's brother. And Blaise would be very upset when he found out the results of this vote.

Of course, that could only benefit Jandison at this point. He needed some way to reduce Ganir's influence on the Council, and this was the first step in that direction. Ganir and Dasbraw's sons were close, but they wouldn't be for much longer. If all went according to plan, Louie would be gone, and Blaise would hate Ganir very shortly.

Jandison would need to speak to Blaise, to apologize for his role in Louie's sentencing. He would tell Blaise that he'd changed his mind, but it was too late. He would explain how he had been persuaded to vote along with the rest of the Council, how everybody but Blaise voted the same way.

And everybody would end up voting the same way—at least once Jandison was done moving the voting stones into their proper place.

* * *

Regaining her sense of self, Dara stared blankly at the Sphere. She had never been so surprised in her life. Before she could analyze this further, she quickly touched the Sphere with her bloody finger, creating a new droplet.

* * *

"What was that?" Barson asked in shock, staring

at his sister. "Did I understand it correctly? Jandison had something to do with fixing a vote?"

She nodded, her eyes shining. "Yes. And I doubt Louie's trial was the only vote he'd tampered with."

"But why?" Barson asked, frowning. "Why do something so treasonous?"

"Because I think this is his way of taking what he feels is his rightful due," Dara said with an undertone of admiration. "Because, by controlling the vote, he—not Ganir—becomes the true leader of the Council . . . and I have long suspected this is something Jandison wants."

"Of course," Barson said slowly, "he's the oldest, but most dismiss him as only a teleportation expert, nothing more. But that's what the vote is, right? They teleport those stones in there?"

"Yes, exactly." Dara beamed at him. "He must've come up with some way to move the stones from one box to another as it suits his purpose. I don't think he teleports them, since I read that the boxes are made impenetrable to that kind of magic, but perhaps he created some kind of pathway or a portal between them to bypass this restriction—"

"The particulars of how he does it are not relevant," Barson said, cutting short her excited lecture. Like all sorcerers, Dara could ramble about spell details for hours on end. "What we need to figure out is how we can use this information."

"I've already thought about it," Dara said, grinning. "I think it would be quite helpful if Ganir knew about this."

Barson considered that for a moment. "Yes, I think you're right. Divide and conquer might be the way to go here. We just need to make sure we don't cast the validity of the latest vote into question."

She appeared thoughtful. "Yes, we want to plant the suspicion in Ganir's mind, but not arm him with damning evidence."

"How about an anonymous letter?" Barson suggested. "We could have it delivered to Ganir's quarters. It would make him suspicious, but won't be enough for him to go public with his accusations."

"Right." Dara looked excited. "And if he did, everyone would assume he's being a sore loser because the last vote didn't go his way. But the letter would be enough for him to distrust and suspect Jandison—and that could take his attention away from us and cause some additional rifts within the Council."

"Excellent." Barson gave his sister an approving look. "Let's do it."

CHAPTER FIFTEEN

※ BLAISE ※

At the realization of what was happening, Blaise jumped up, cursing. The meadow around them was on fire, the flames devouring the bushes with startling speed. The smoke was thick and noxious, choking them, and he heard Gala beginning to cough. There was no time to waste.

Acting on instinct, Blaise began to chant the words of the spell he'd used to put out the fire in his house during Augusta's visit. He could hear his own voice growing hoarse from the smoke, and he wondered fleetingly why all the women in his life tried to burn him lately. By the time the spell was complete, he could barely speak—but foam began streaming from his hands, putting out the fire with record speed. Within minutes, the blaze was out, and they were standing in the middle of the soggy clearing, looking at the ashes of what used to be a beautiful green meadow.

"I'm so sorry!" Gala wailed, covering her face with her hands. "Oh, Blaise, I'm so sorry . . . I lost control again. I could've really hurt you—"

"Gala, stop it . . ." Blaise took her hands and gently pulled them down to her sides. "You didn't do anything wrong. It's not your fault that you can't control your emotions yet—it just means we need to expedite your training." She still looked upset, so he added, "And besides, I have a feeling you would've teleported us out of here if things got too hot." He grinned at her, inviting her to share in the humor.

She shook her head, still looking distraught. "Maybe . . . but there is no guarantee of that. My magic is still too unpredictable." She sounded frustrated.

"Look, Gala, I was flattered," Blaise said, framing her face with his hands. "That was quite a reaction to my kiss."

She started to respond, and then he saw her looking up behind him. Letting go of her, Blaise turned quickly, ready to battle whatever might be there—but it was just the chaise, finally arriving from the lake.

"I think we need a change of scenery," he said, looking around the burned meadow. "Let's go back to the lake now."

"Yes, please." She sounded eager, and he knew she was as anxious to leave this place as he was.

"Let's go then." Leading Gala to the chaise, Blaise did a spell to get it back to its normal size, and then they got on it. Thinking back on the fight with the bearwolves, he wished he'd insisted they fly to the village the night before, instead of walking with the hunters. It took no time at all to reach the lake this way.

"This is as good a place as any other to try to have some more lessons," he said as they descended on the shore of the lake. The place still took his breath away with its beauty. Looking at the still waters, he remembered swimming there with Gala, and a wave of warmth rolled through him. He definitely needed to teach her how to control her emotions, he thought wryly. It wouldn't do to have her burn down the entire forest if they became more intimate.

They walked to a small grassy area on the edge of the forest. Gala sat down on a fallen tree, and Blaise joined her there.

"Please sit comfortably," he said, noticing that Gala was perched in an awkward manner.

"Does my posture matter?" she asked, looking at him.

"The key is that you are comfortable," Blaise explained.

She adjusted her legs, folding them underneath herself, and pulled back her shoulders. There was a sensuality in her posture now, and Blaise shifted a bit in reaction. Focus, he told himself. Don't think of that kiss.

"I am by no means an expert at this," he began, taking a few deep breaths to relax himself. "All I know is that these techniques helped me focus when

I was a child. My mother taught them to me. You see, I was overly active and had trouble concentrating on some tasks, so she thought that this, along with some spells, would help me relax and clear my mind. Later on, when I was in a very dark place after Louie's death, I practiced these relaxation methods to help me regain some equilibrium."

She sat there listening, absorbing his every word.

"Close your eyes and focus on your breathing," Blaise told her. "Think of nothing else."

She closed her eyes, her face assuming a serene, introspective expression.

"Now follow your breath," Blaise told her, trying to make his voice as soothing as possible. "Don't try to control it, but just focus your conscious awareness on it. In and out, in and out . . . Try to feel the exact moment when the 'out' breath ends. Can you feel it? Can you tell when the 'in' breath becomes the 'out' breath?"

From his own experience, he knew that it was very hard to pinpoint that moment, but trying to do so quieted the mind tremendously.

"Now try to gently slow your breathing," he said after a couple of minutes. "Start counting in your head to five on the 'in,' and to five on the 'out.'"

She nodded, continuing to breathe as he'd instructed, and he could see that she was doing exceedingly well for a first-timer. That was good; if she mastered the technique, it would enable her to calm down if she needed to. He could see all the tension in her face and body ebbing away until she was as relaxed as he had ever seen her. Instead of her customary expression of excitement and curiosity, she looked serene, beatific. It almost seemed like she was—

Blaise's jaw dropped. No, it didn't just *seem* like it. Gala actually *was* beginning to float upward. So far she was only a few inches off the ground, but he had no idea how high she would go if allowed to continue. "All right," he said gently, not wanting to startle her, "now slowly start getting back to your regular speed of breathing."

She followed his instructions, and he could see her slowly descending. When her folded legs touched the tree, he told her to open her eyes.

"That was wonderful," she said, beaming at him. "I felt very even and calm. Then I started feeling a lightness as well."

"Yes, I could tell." Blaise smiled.

"You could?"

"You started floating upward," Blaise explained, his smile widening.

"Oh." She frowned a little. "Does it mean that I failed?"

"No. You seem to start getting into trouble when you are at extreme points of any emotion or sensation. I think this floating happened because you were maybe too calm and relaxed. It doesn't make the technique any less useful, however. If you are overwhelmed with a stressful emotion, using this strategy should help you get closer to a safe, neutral state," he said, hoping he was actually right.

"Truth be told, I am not surprised that I floated," Gala said, looking at him. "I think I wanted to. I was feeling so good and so light . . ."

"Good." Blaise was glad to hear that. "Now we need to figure out how you can use some of what you learned to control your spell casting."

"I want to try something," she said with a mischievous expression on her face, and before Blaise could respond, she started walking toward the water. Blaise figured she wanted to go for a swim, but she didn't move to take off her clothes. It was only when she took the first step that he finally understood what she was doing.

She was walking on the calm waters of the lake, her feet barely creating any ripples.

Grinning at her achievement, Blaise pulled out his Interpreter Stone and quickly wrote a spell for himself—and then he headed toward the water, joining Gala in walking on the surface.

Apparently hearing something, she looked behind her, toward Blaise, and immediately started sinking. She broke her focus, he realized. Concentration was critical for her, it seemed. She was up to her shapely calves in the water when he grabbed her hand.

With his support, she seemed to recover quickly, her feet once again gliding on the water as they walked further. Blaise knew his spell would only work for a limited time, so he tried to enjoy the thrill of it. It had been ages since he had done something like this—simply using magic for the sheer fun of experiencing something no one else could do.

After a couple of minutes, Gala slowed down and reached for his other hand, facing him as they stood in the middle of the lake. He could feel the familiar pulsing heat rising between them, and he lowered his head, kissing her again. She kissed him back fiercely, her arms coming up to wrap around his neck. Their bodies moved and swayed together, almost as if they were dancing . . . and then Blaise felt his spell end. He began to sink, and Gala gasped, losing her focus again.

They fell into the water with a splash. Out here, away from the shore, the water was much cooler, and Blaise could feel it seeping through his clothes. The heated moment was over. Cursing and laughing, they swam to the shore.

Emerging from the lake with their clothes dripping, they quickly headed back to the chaise. "I think that's plenty of training for now," Blaise said, grinning at Gala. "You did what you set out to do for today."

She beamed back at him. "I did, didn't I? I finally controlled a spell!"

* * *

After they came back from the lake, Gala joined Maya and Esther, and the women went to check on a pregnant woman in the village. Blaise was left alone in the house with Liva. This was his opportunity to implement an idea that had been hovering in his mind ever since his and Gala's semi-dance on the lake.

Going to the room he was sharing with Gala, he laid out a few spell cards and his Interpreter Stone. He wanted to give Gala a gift, and he knew just the thing she would like. As he was writing out the spell, he caught himself grinning. He was looking forward to Gala's reaction to this.

As he was finishing up, he heard a tentative knock on the door.

"Come in," he called out, not bothering to put away the evidence of his work. Given what he'd learned about Liva, he didn't think she would mind him doing a little sorcery in her house.

The older woman entered the room with an uncertain expression on her face. When she spotted the cards and the Stone, her eyes widened. "Is that the Interpreter Stone?" she asked reverently. "I heard about this new invention from some of the recent arrivals, but I've never seen it before."

"Yes, this is the Stone," Blaise said. "Would you like to take a look at it?"

Liva's face lit up. "Oh, may I?" She reached out and picked up the black object with trembling fingers. "This is amazing . . . Is it true that you can do all kinds of complex spells with it?"

"Yes, it's true," Blaise confirmed, and he repeated some of the things he had explained to Gala earlier in the day. Liva listened intently, hanging on his every word. There was an expression of longing on her face, and he realized that she was as hungry for arcane knowledge as he was himself.

"What do you use your spells for?" he asked Liva, wondering how she managed to do magic in a place that seemed to frown upon sorcery in all its forms.

"Oh, I only use it for things that will not be attributed to spell casting," she said, looking at him. "When someone is sick in a way that nothing else would help, I sometimes use a spell to make them feel better. I can't always cure them, but I try to take some pain away."

"That's quite impressive," Blaise said, studying the woman with newfound respect. Healing spells were not easy, particularly when done in verbal form. Her knowledge base was more extensive than he had thought.

"I also help out with food in the winter months," she added, looking pleased at the praise, "and when the storms hit."

"Does that happen frequently?"

She shook her head. "Fortunately, no. But when it does happen, it's brutal. People die, and we have to rebuild our homes. The worst ones can do severe damage to the local forests, destroying edible plants and causing animals to hide in other areas."

"So what do you do then?" Blaise asked curiously. "How does the village survive?"

"There are a few fruit trees at the very edge of the village, as well as some that bear nuts," she explained. "I figured out a way to help those trees thrive, even in tough times. It's not that different from doing a healing spell. The rest of the village think the trees are just unusually sturdy. So between that and some of the meat that we cure, we usually make it through."

"That's amazing, Liva," Blaise said, impressed by the woman's ingenuity. He'd never heard of anyone using a variant of a healing spell to make trees stronger. He himself had worked on this type of problem, but his approach relied on modifying the seeds to produce more resilient crops. As he thought about it, he made a mental note to offer these types of seeds to the villagers, given the problems they seemed to have with the storms.

There was also another thing that he could do to help the villagers, Blaise realized. "How would you like to learn written sorcery?" he asked Liva. With a more powerful tool, he knew this woman would be able to do more good for her people.

"Oh, I would love that," Liva exclaimed, a wide smile appearing on her face. Then the smile dimmed. "But wouldn't I need an Interpreter Stone for that?"

"Yes, you would." Blaise smiled at her. "Luckily, I have a very good idea how to make one. I could create one for you, given enough time. For now, you could practice with mine."

"That would be amazing," Liva said, "but I don't know if I could afford such a treasure—"

"Liva, please . . ." Blaise gave her an exasperated look. "You are offering us your hospitality. This is the least I can do in return." And before she could protest, he added, "Why don't you join Gala and me for a lesson tomorrow? As it so happens, I plan to start introducing her to written spells."

CHAPTER SIXTEEN

※ AUGUSTA ※

The white mouse ran around its cage as Augusta prepared the latest version of her spell. When it was ready, she fed the cards into the Interpreter Stone and waited. The results were almost instantaneous.

Within seconds, the mouse collapsed, appearing dead.

Reaching into the cage, Augusta pulled out the little animal and studied it closely, feeling its heartbeat. It was not dead after all; the spell had worked as intended. Dania's books had turned out to be quite helpful.

Sighing, Augusta placed the mouse back in its cage and began to prepare the next spell in her arsenal. That one, if successful, would likely kill the mouse, so Augusta intended to try it on a cockroach instead.

She was also making progress on her physics

project, and the results of what she was uncovering were breathtaking—and frightening. She had been thinking about this theory for months, but only since Barson's 'death' had she realized the destructive potential of what she was studying. If she was right, then she could use this previously unimaginable power to destroy the creature if all other measures failed. What she needed was a viable spell to go along with the theory.

After a few minutes, she realized that her attention was drifting again. For the first time in her life, Augusta had difficulty focusing on her work. Ever since she woke up alone in her bed this morning, she'd been gripped by a sense of unreality. It was difficult for her to believe that after everything, Barson had survived—that he was as alive and vital as ever.

Everything she'd done since that awful battle was based on the assumption that he was dead, that the creature had killed him and other members of the Guard. Had Augusta done the right thing in committing the Council to this course of action? At the time, she'd had no doubt, but now she wondered if there had been something else she could've done instead. If there was some way she could've destroyed the monster without endangering Blaise in the process.

Her gaze turned toward a small droplet lying on her desk. It was the one she had picked up in Blaise's house during her last visit there—the one that had been lying discarded on the floor. She suspected that this droplet most likely contained a memory of her and Blaise's time together... a memory that her former lover clearly didn't value anymore.

She hesitated for a moment, then her hand reached for the droplet, almost involuntarily.

Closing her eyes, Augusta placed it under her tongue.

* * *

Blaise sat with Augusta in a large auditorium, watching the show of light unfolding in front of them. It was a spectacle unlike any other, with every color of the rainbow meshing together and separating in large spheres. The spheres looked like gigantic soap bubbles moving in fractal patterns, flowing with the serene music that accompanied the show.

"I always thought sorcery could be beautiful," Blaise whispered, leaning closer to Augusta, "but this is truly amazing."

She gazed up at him, her amber eyes reflecting the lights. "You're right—it's gorgeous."

Blaise felt a familiar warmth in his chest, a type of tenderness mixed with overwhelming desire. Even after seven years together, Augusta was still the most beautiful woman he had ever seen—not to mention, the most intelligent. Minor philosophical disagreements aside, she was everything he had ever wanted.

It was time, Blaise decided. He had waited for the perfect moment, and it wasn't ever going to get better than this.

Reaching out, he took her hand, holding it gently. Then he lifted her palm to his lips, kissing each finger in the traditional declaration of intent. Her eyes rounded with wonder, her soft mouth parting in surprise, and he quickly spoke the words: "Augusta, my love, will you be my bride?"

She blinked, staring at him, and then a smile of sheer joy lit her face. "Yes . . . Yes, Blaise, of course."

He had never been so happy in his life.

* * *

Regaining her senses, Augusta opened her eyes, feeling the burn of tears. She hadn't known that Blaise had captured the memory of their engagement; he must've been recording it without telling her. She recalled that he did have a big bag with him that day, but she hadn't known he was lugging around the new Sphere his brother gave him.

The ache in her chest was almost unbearable. For a moment, she felt like she had lost Blaise all over again. Seeing herself through his eyes had been devastating. In recent months with Barson, she had managed to convince herself that she was fine, that she had moved on from the wreck of her eight-year relationship, but the truth of the matter was that she would never be able to fully erase Blaise from her memories.

Getting up, she walked over to the window, gazing out at the streets of Turingrad far below. She could feel her cheeks getting wet from the tears running down her face, and she wiped them with the sleeve of her silk dress. More than ever, she wished that she could go back in time and undo everything that had happened in the last two years, but that was not even a theoretical possibility.

She had to live with the consequences of her actions . . . and so did Blaise. She couldn't let her emotions get in the way of doing the right thing again, no matter how much it hurt.

Blaise's creature could not be allowed to live, and this memory changed nothing.

CHAPTER SEVENTEEN

※ BLAISE ※

At Blaise's request, Liva took them to a more deserted part of the mountains. It was a safety precaution on his part—he did not want Gala to accidentally destroy half the forest with some spell gone awry. He didn't explain his rationale, not wanting to hurt Gala's feelings, and he knew she thought that he simply wanted them to enjoy the scenery—which did turn out to be truly breathtaking.

It took them about an hour to fly there, and Blaise used the time to teach Liva how to operate the chaise. As he'd suspected, she was a quick learner, mastering the new oral spells with ease. By the time they arrived at the location, she was directing and landing the chaise on her own, reveling in the freedom of using sorcery out of sight of her fellow villagers.

Gala sat quietly on the trip, seemingly absorbing

the sights. As they got deeper into the mountains, the green of forest and grass was replaced by the yellow and orange of naked stones. The wind also picked up, blowing from the ocean side.

"The storms are more likely to reach here," Liva explained when Blaise questioned her about the strange-looking rocks. "And even when it's calm, like today, the winds tend to be pretty fierce, stripping away all life from these rocks over time."

As they approached what looked like a large gash in the ground, Liva directed them to fly lower. They were going to a canyon, Blaise realized as they descended. Up close, the canyon was massive. The mountains were like walls, rising up all around them. It was desolate and majestic, and all three of them were silent as the chaise touched the ground, awed by the magnificence of nature.

After they explored the area a little, Blaise began his instructions. "I am going to teach you a very basic elemental spell," he said, looking at the two women. "You will manipulate the power of fire, the way our apprentices usually do."

Gala and Liva nodded, watching him intently.

"First and foremost, I need to teach you the language for written sorcery. It's similar to the verbal arcane language—you still have the conditional statements that you both know—but it also contains some powerful extensions and mathematical constructs that don't exist in the spoken language. This, for example—" he drew a symbol for loop on the card, "—is a repetition construct we call the 'loop.' It allows your spell to repeat an action many times without having to write it out more than once."

"So it lets you say 'do this one hundred times?'" Gala asked, looking fascinated.

"Yes, but it also lets you say things like 'Raise the temperature of this water by one degree until it starts boiling,'" Blaise explained, and wrote out the spell version of what he just said. It was much more elegant and precise on the card than it would be if spoken.

For the next couple of hours, he continued going over the basics of the language, explaining how to use formulas and calculations on paper instead of doing complex math in one's head. They took a short break to eat some of the food Liva had brought, and then Blaise continued the lesson.

"There are two paths to every spell," he told them. "The hard way is to start from scratch and specify in code exactly what you want to happen. There are infinite ways of doing that, just as there are infinite ways of writing a poem using words. It's also very time-consuming. An easier way, the way I am teaching you today, is to use something someone had already written in the past and modify it for your own purposes."

Liva frowned. "So does that mean a commoner could learn to do some spells by just copying the symbols without understanding them?"

"Yes," Blaise said, trying to hide the bitterness in his voice. "That had been my hope originally—that the Interpreter Stone would allow people to do this.

But unfortunately, it didn't quite work out that way. Theoretically, one could indeed do a spell by just copying something already in existence, but it still requires access to an Interpreter Stone—and the Council doesn't let that happen."

"And I would think many spells require at least some basic understanding of the language," Gala said, looking at Blaise, "to change the variables and so on."

"Yes, indeed," Blaise confirmed, and moved on to the demonstration of the spell itself. Just thinking about the way sorcerers tried to keep this knowledge to themselves made him furious.

Taking a few deep breaths to calm himself, he pulled out a blank card and started writing, explaining every word and symbol along the way. Here, at least, he could make a difference by teaching sorcery to someone who needed it.

The spell he chose to demonstrate was a simple one. It would just burn some of the dried bushes near them. When he was done, he slid the finished card into the stone.

As expected, the bush to his right flared up, burning quickly in the dry air of the canyon.

It was Liva's turn next.

Blaise watched as she carefully wrote out her spell, changing the variables to target a different bush. At first, it looked like she wasn't going to provide enough kinetic energy for the bush to ignite, but then she caught her omission and fixed it before feeding the cards into the stone.

Within seconds, the targeted bush caught on fire as well, causing the older woman to squeal in excitement. Gala clapped, and Blaise grinned at them, pleased with his students' progress.

"Now let me try," Gala said, clearly eager to get started, and Blaise handed her the writing implements. To his surprise, the code that she began writing was different from what he had taught them. Apparently she had decided to improvise. While she was busy, Blaise surreptitiously wrote out a protection spell for Liva and himself, just in case anything went wrong.

When Gala was finished with her code, Blaise looked over her cards. He was pretty sure he knew what would happen when the spell was cast, but he was still glad for the protection around them. "Go ahead," he told Gala, and watched as she fed the cards into the Stone.

The targeted plant started to smolder, slowly and gracefully, one branch at a time. The pattern of this fire was unusually complex. Somehow Gala had managed to raise the temperature of the bush in parts, focusing on branches of specific length and dryness. And then, in what seemed like a coordinated way, the entire plant burst into flames.

"Beautiful," Liva said, looking deeply impressed.

"Amazing," Blaise agreed, echoing her sentiment.

"Thank you." Gala's cheeks glowed at their praise.

They kept discussing written spells until Liva confessed that she was tired. Gala and Blaise were not ready to quit yet, but Blaise graciously told Liva that they were done with lessons for the day. Gala looked slightly upset, and Blaise guessed that she wanted to stay in this starkly beautiful area for a while longer. "Why don't you take the chaise?" he suggested to Liva. "Gala and I will remain here for a bit, look around. You can land it in the forest right next to the village, so the others won't see you."

Liva frowned. "But how will you get back?"

"I'll summon the chaise when you're done with it," he told her, and spent the next couple of minutes convincing her to use this opportunity to practice her verbal spells. Liva finally gave in, climbing onto the chaise, and Blaise and Gala were left alone.

"I have a special spell I wrote for you," he told Gala when the chaise disappeared into the distance. "It's a gift."

"A gift? Why?" Gala's face brightened with excitement.

"Because you're wonderful," Blaise said softly, "and because I wanted to do something nice for you."

"Oh, thank you—"

"First experience the gift, then decide if you want to thank me," Blaise interrupted, smiling.

Taking a batch of cards, he loaded them into the Stone. He had conceived of this gift on the lake, when he was holding Gala in his arms. As the first strains of music sounded and Gala's face took on a rapturous expression, he knew it had been a good idea. The spell was designed to vibrate the air in exactly the right way, to imitate the sound of instruments playing a tune.

"I wrote this melody for you," he explained, watching as Gala closed her eyes, swaying to the music.

"It's so beautiful," she breathed after a few moments, opening her eyes to meet his gaze. "I heard your music before, in the village, but it was played with instruments. This seems more pure, somehow, and moves me even more. Can we dance to it?"

"Of course," Blaise said, walking up to her. He had to agree with her in regard to the purity of the music. It was as though the dry yellow mountains decided to sing for them, as if nature itself wanted to express its love. The melody he created was meant to show how Gala made him feel, but it transcended something as simple as human feelings, resembling no earthly instruments.

Putting his hands on Gala's waist, he slowly began moving to the tune. The beats of low frequency sounds echoed his racing heartbeat. She seemed to melt in his arms, their movement perfectly matching the slow, careful turns of the melody. It was as if they were attuned to each other, their bodies moving as one.

As the music reached a crescendo and started winding down, he leaned down and kissed her again, his breathing quickening as he felt the softness of her lips. His hands encircled her waist, pulling her even closer, when he heard something behind him.

Turning swiftly, he stared at the intruder, instinctively holding Gala pressed against his side.

"I am truly sorry to interrupt such a lovely dance, but we must talk, now," the Council Leader said, looking directly at Blaise.

CHAPTER EIGHTEEN

✳ GALA ✳

"Gala, run. It's Ganir, from the Council," Blaise told her, pushing her behind him. His face was tight with anger. "Teleport away if you can. He might be the first of many." As he was speaking, he pulled out his Stone and several cards, beginning to write on them with incredible speed.

The old man stepped toward them. "I am here by myself and with only peaceful intentions," he said, opening his hands to show that they were empty. He sounded genuine to her, but she could see that Blaise was not convinced.

Deciding to humor Blaise and, at the same time, do something she'd wanted to do for a while, Gala looked inside herself. Learning to do sorcery using the code had indeed changed things for her, enabling her to better understand how she had accidentally been doing magic before—and, more importantly, how she might be able to control it. This was her chance to try a simple spell. If it didn't work, then she intended to do as Blaise asked.

The spell she had in mind was quite different from anything she'd seen before, but it seemed fairly intuitive to her. She would be here, but neither man would know it—and for that, she needed to bend all the light around her in the right way.

She focused on the mathematics of the task, pretending that she was about to cast a spell using one of the methods Blaise had taught her today. It was a sham, though; deep inside, she knew that she had a direct route to achieving her goal. Going through the training made her realize that she didn't need the cumbersome spoken word or its slightly more elegant written cousin. In a way, something like the Interpreter Stone was already built into her mind, and she could now sense it.

She took a deep breath, letting her mind clear. This time it happened quicker than when she had practiced at the lake. Then she focused on what she was hoping to achieve, mentally running through the proper calculations. A second later, everything went dark, as though she'd lost her vision. For a moment, Gala panicked, sure that she'd done something wrong, but then she realized what happened.

She had done too thorough of a job of bending light. The inner workings of her eyes needed to reflect some light in order to see. To fix this problem, she needed to make her eyes exempt from this spell, but that would probably result in a strange visual of eyeballs floating in the air, defeating the purpose of the invisibility spell. Oh well, Gala decided, maybe she didn't need to see—hearing should be enough.

"She teleported?" Ganir asked, his voice penetrating the cocoon of darkness that encased Gala. "Just like that?"

"How did you find me?" Blaise demanded in a hard voice. Gala flinched, startled by the bitter anger she heard there. She'd never heard Blaise speak like that before, not even at the lake when he confronted the hunters.

"I used a locator spell on you," Ganir answered calmly. "I placed it on you during our last encounter. You know how those things are pretty much unnoticeable."

"You must've embedded it in the pacifying spell," Blaise said, his voice sounding strained. Gala thought that, mixed with anger, she could hear a slight undertone of admiration.

"Yes, of course I did." Ganir's voice sounded like he was smiling. "You always were bright, my son."

"Don't call me that." Blaise's voice turned hard again. "Why are you here? Give me one good reason why I shouldn't kill you on the spot."

"Because I'm here to tell you something important." Ganir paused, and Gala heard him take a deep breath. "The Council voted to move against you and your creation. They are preparing now, and it's only a matter of time until they find you."

Gala felt an unpleasant sensation that she identified as fear and resentment. Why couldn't people leave her alone? She didn't intend to harm anyone, not even those soldiers who'd attacked her before.

"Of course they'll find me now," Blaise said bitterly. "You're here, aren't you?"

"I have no intention of telling the Council anything," Ganir said. "Isn't it clear to you by now that I'm on your side?"

"Nothing is clear to me," Blaise said harshly. "If you think I'm going to trust you this easily, you've got another thing coming."

"Blaise . . . there's something you should know." Ganir's voice sounded heavy now. "I have strong reason to believe that the vote during Louie's trial— and on many other occasions—may have been subverted."

"Subverted? What are you talking about?"

"Can you tell me how you learned about the vote being unanimous? Who told you that the entire Council, except you, voted in favor of Louie's execution?"

Blaise snorted. "You think I'm going to tell you my source?"

"Was it Jandison?" Ganir persisted. "Blaise, please, this is very important. I think Jandison has been manipulating the Council vote for years. Ever since you and I spoke about Louie's trial and you told me you thought I voted to kill him—when I knew full well that I hadn't—I have been deeply suspicious of the voting procedure. And then I got a letter, an anonymous letter claiming that the vote during Louie's trial had been rigged."

"You think Jandison rigged the vote?" Blaise sounded incredulous. "Why? What would he have to gain by it?"

"Was it he?" Ganir sounded frustrated. "Blaise, was it Jandison who spoke to you after the vote?"

"What proof do I have that you're not lying to me right now, trying to get me to betray something that I was told in confidence?" Blaise asked, and Gala could hear the simmering anger his voice.

"I can give you proof," Ganir said. "I had a thorough look through my Life Capture archives, and I want you to take this." Gala heard shuffling footsteps as Ganir presumably approached Blaise.

"If I take that droplet, I will be at your mercy," Blaise said, still sounding uncompromising. Gala wished she could see what was happening, to better understand her creator's emotional state.

"You are welcome to use it later to verify my words," Ganir said. "This droplet contains my recollections of Louie's trial, including my memory of voting against the execution."

For a few moments, there was silence. Then Blaise spoke again. "All right, I will watch this later. But tell me one thing. If this is true, why haven't you gone to the Council with this information?"

"Because at this point, all I have are your words, my suspicions, and this anonymous letter," Ganir explained. "It's not enough to publicly accuse one of our own, let alone call for a trial."

"So what do you plan to do?"

"I have some ideas of how I can prove this," the old man said. "The next time we hold a vote, I will know more about the breakdown, and I will record it as proof."

"How can you do that?" Blaise sounded curious now. "The process is designed to be anonymous."

"I wrote an intricate spell, similar to the locator one, which would be embedded in my voting stone. This should show me where my stone is after I place it into the voting box. I plan to vote in a way that would not suit Jandison. If he is indeed behind this, then my stone will shift, and I will have my proof."

"That would be proof indeed," Blaise said, sounding thoughtful.

"If you could replicate the droplet when you take it, I would be grateful," Ganir said, sounding mildly relieved. Gala guessed he was glad Blaise was less angry now, though she had no idea what the man meant by his request.

"What do you mean, replicate?" Blaise voiced Gala's unspoken question.

She listened in fascination as Ganir explained how one could preserve the information contained in Droplets. Blaise appeared quite interested too, asking several questions to clarify the simple process. "So promise me you will take the droplet as soon as you can," Ganir said finally, concluding the Life Capture lecture.

"How do I know you didn't tamper with the droplet itself?" Blaise asked. "If anyone could manipulate Life Capture, that would be you, its creator."

"I am honored you think so highly of me." Ganir sounded amused now. "But I assure you, what you describe is impossible."

"Nothing is impossible if you come up with the right code," Blaise said derisively.

"You're right. It would be theoretically possible, but extremely difficult in practice. So much so, it might as well be impossible," Ganir responded. "Ask yourself this: even if I could do it, why would I go through that much trouble?"

"Because you want Gala for your own purposes." There was renewed anger in Blaise's voice.

She could hear the old man sighing. "It's true that I'm curious about her," Ganir admitted, "but all I want is to learn about her. She's important to you, and because of that, I want to help you save her." The old man sounded so sincere that Gala felt touched by his words.

"Is that why you sent the Sorcerer Guard after her?" Blaise said sarcastically. "So they could save her with their swords and arrows?"

Gala shuddered, remembering the fight. Maybe Blaise was right to distrust Ganir; those soldiers certainly hadn't had peaceful intentions.

"I only sent a few men after her so they could bring her to Turingrad." Ganir sounded defensive now. "I don't know how the entire Sorcerer Guard ended up going—I certainly didn't authorize it."

"Right, of course. They acted on their own."

"They did," Ganir insisted. "Either that, or your

former fiancée had a hand in it. You do know she was seeing the Captain of the Guard, right?"

"Augusta?" Blaise sounded surprised. "She was with Barson? No, I didn't know that. Are you saying she got the Guard to come after Gala?"

Ganir let out a heavy sigh. "I can't say for sure, since I don't know the depth of her involvement with the plot. It's possible that Barson was responsible for this himself."

"What plot?" Blaise sounded as confused as Gala felt.

Another sigh from Ganir. "It doesn't matter now. They're all dead, thanks to you and your creation."

Gala bit her lip to remain silent. Everything inside her wanted to protest the unfair accusation. The soldiers were not all dead—she'd healed many of them.

"All dead?" Blaise echoed her thoughts. "What do you mean, all dead? The majority were alive and well when I last saw them."

There was dead silence. "I see," Ganir said after a few moments. "Barson is smarter than I thought. Is he alive too?"

"I don't know," Blaise replied coldly. "I was more concerned with helping Gala than paying attention to the individual soldiers trying to kill her."

"Well, it's my problem now," Ganir said with resignation. "I guess I will have to deal with them directly after all."

"What are you talking about?"

"Blaise, my son, come back to Turingrad, please."

Ganir's voice turned cajoling as he issued his request. "There's trouble brewing, and I could use your help . . . your help and that of your creation—"

"Her name is Gala," Blaise said icily, "and trouble for the Council sounds like good news for me. I wish you all the best in dealing with Augusta and her Captain. It sounds like she finally found someone ruthless enough for her tastes."

Gala frowned, detecting an unfamiliar note in Blaise's voice. He sounded angry with Augusta, and Gala could tell that the news that she was with someone else bothered him—and that bothered Gala for some reason.

"I must go now," Ganir said, interrupting Gala's thoughts. "Take care of yourself and Gala. Once you've had a chance to view the droplet, please contact me and let me know the name of the informant. It's very important, my son."

"All right." Blaise sounded curt. "Now go."

Gala remained silent until she heard the old man leave. Blaise called out her name, but she remained silent and hidden. She needed to digest what she had just learned—and she also wanted privacy for what she planned to do for Blaise.

After a few minutes, she heard the swooshing sound of a chaise returning. Blaise must've gotten on it, because she heard him saying the oral spells that directed the flight of the chaise. When there was silence again, Gala undid her light-bending spell, turning visible again. She could see Blaise's chaise flying over the canyon in the distance, but for now, she was alone.

It was the perfect opportunity to do what she intended. From what she'd read, gift-giving required reciprocation, and she had an idea of what Blaise might want.

She began by trying to calm her mind, as Blaise had taught her. When she was sure that she had her emotions under control, she began doing the calculations for a complex teleportation spell. The mathematics behind this were quite intricate, though she had no doubt that she could do them correctly. She'd had a good look at the object she was thinking of, and had been inside it, too. Mentally double-checking everything, she let the spell loose.

When it worked, she was overwhelmed with glee. This was her first serious attempt at controlled magic, and the result of it was quite spectacular. She knew Blaise would not believe his eyes when he saw what she had done for him.

He'll love this gift, she thought, gazing at the immense object in front of her.

Emboldened by this success, she looked at Blaise's chaise flying in the distance. If she was able to do the prior spell, this should work too. The complication came from the fact that the chaise was moving—but that speed was fairly constant, and she was able to account for it in her mental calculations. It took no time at all before she was sitting on that chaise next to him.

"Blaise, I did it, I teleported myself here from the ground," she told him, looking into his startled face.

CHAPTER NINETEEN

※ BARSON ※

Barson frowned, looking at the map of the Tower spread out before him. The place was, quite literally, a fortress.

"Are you sure this is the right time?" Dara asked, looking worried.

"I don't think we'll be able to find a better moment," Larn replied, giving his future wife a reassuring smile.

Larn and a few of Barson's closest lieutenants had finally arrived in Turingrad disguised as peasants. Barson was glad to see them there, even if it increased the risk of exposure. At this point, no one outside their immediate families knew that the majority of the Guard were alive, and they needed to keep it that way for a while longer.

"I have some interesting news concerning Ganir," Larn said, turning toward Barson. "We had Mittel follow him again. It looks like Ganir took a long trip."

"A trip where?" Barson asked, looking up from the map.

"To the mountains in the west." Larn reached for the larger map of Koldun lying on the other corner of the table. "Mittel flew behind him, and he saw Ganir land right there." He pointed at a mountainous area beyond the Western Woods.

"Interesting," Barson said thoughtfully. "I remember seeing Blaise and his creature flying in that general direction. I wonder if there is any connection."

"Even if there isn't, you might want to share this information with Augusta," Dara said. "There is already tension between her and Ganir, and I think it might not be a bad thing if she accuses the old man of trying to undermine the Council's latest mission."

Barson mulled it over. "Yes," he said after a few moments. "That is a good idea, indeed. In fact, I think it's time I bring Augusta up to speed on everything."

Dara looked taken aback. "Are you sure she'll side with us?"

"No," Barson admitted truthfully. "I'm not. But at this point she's in too deep. The fact that she wanted us to remain dead and her prior request to go up against the creature . . . Well, let's just say she wouldn't be too eager to reveal her involvement with those matters to the rest of the Council. If nothing else, self-interest will keep her from betraying us."

That, and the fact that Augusta cared for him—or so Barson hoped, at least.

CHAPTER TWENTY

※ AUGUSTA ※

Hearing the door open, Augusta looked up from the spell she'd been working on—the powerful spell that was starting to finally come together. Barson's broad-shouldered frame appeared in the doorway. Instead of his usual Guard uniform, he was wearing a merchant's hooded garment.

For a moment, they regarded each other silently, then Augusta got up and walked toward him. He pulled her into his embrace and kissed her with the usual urgent hunger. Before they could get carried away again, however, he pulled back.

"Augusta . . . there is something you should know," he said quietly, still holding her in his arms. "A sorcerer friend of mine saw Ganir leaving the Tower and followed him."

Augusta stared at him, surprised by the change of topic. "A sorcerer friend of yours? Who?"

"It doesn't matter," Barson said. "The important thing is where Ganir went and why he went there."

"Where did he go?"

Barson let go of her and stepped back, pulling out a rolled-up map from a bag he had hanging over his shoulder. "Here," he said, pointing at a place on the western edge of the land. "It appears he landed somewhere in this canyon."

Augusta's hands balled into fists. The old man had betrayed them after all. "I see. That must be where they're hiding. I wonder how Ganir knew . . . unless he's been helping them hide all along."

"Yes, that's what I also thought when I heard about this," Barson said. "It looks like the Council Leader has been secretly collaborating with your enemy. I don't see any other reason for him to go to the mountains. It's not exactly a short trip."

She frowned as a question occurred to her. "Why did this sorcerer follow Ganir?"

"Because I asked him to keep an eye on Ganir for you," Barson said. "Because I thought that something like that might happen."

Augusta regarded her lover curiously. She had underestimated Barson; he seemed to be as well-versed in intrigue as any sorcerer in the Tower. Why had she never seen this before? "Did your man get close enough to see Blaise?" she asked, staring at his hard features. "Did he see the creature? Do you think they're hiding in the canyon?"

Barson shrugged. "All I know is that Ganir landed. My source was too cowardly to get close. As it was, he had to use the clouds for cover the entire way and maintain a solid distance between Ganir and himself."

Augusta nodded. "I see." This wasn't quite as much detail as she'd hoped, but it was enough for her. Her every instinct was screaming that Barson's suspicions were right—that Ganir had indeed gone to meet with Blaise. She felt a burning anger at the thought. "I think it's time Ganir and I had a little conversation," she said slowly, musing out loud. "Perhaps he'll be able to answer these questions . . ."

Barson frowned. "What do you mean, 'have a conversation?' You should tell the others about this, confront him in a public forum."

Augusta stared at him, mildly annoyed. "I'll handle this in my own way." As much as she appreciated Barson's help, she had no intention of taking political advice from a soldier—even one who appeared to be smarter than she'd thought.

Her lover's expression darkened. "Augusta, don't do anything rash. He's a powerful sorcerer, and I don't want you in danger. And speaking of that, we need to talk about what happens when the Council goes to deal with Blaise's creation."

Augusta raised her eyebrows. "What do you mean?"

"I don't want you to go with them," he said, holding her gaze. "It's too dangerous."

"Too dangerous? Are you saying the entire Council can't handle this thing?"

"You weren't there," Barson said. "You didn't see

what she can do. She's this beautiful, fragile-looking girl, but she was fighting better than any seasoned warrior. Then I was all but dead, and she brought me back to life . . ." There was awe and barely concealed admiration in his voice, and a sudden ugly suspicion stirred in Augusta's mind.

"Did she touch you?" she asked quietly, her heart beginning to beat faster. "Did she do something to you?" Her stomach curdled at the memory of how Kelvin's overseer had been changed . . . and at Blaise's infatuation with the monster. Was Barson now affected by the creature too? Had it somehow messed with his mind, or was he simply reacting to its deceptive beauty?

"What?" Barson looked surprised by her questions. "I told you, she healed me when I lay there, broken from the fall. But that's not important . . . I don't want you going on this mission."

Augusta felt her hackles rising. "You don't get to tell me what to do," she said evenly, her pulse still pounding at the suspicion that the creature might've gotten to Barson in some way—or worse, that he lusted after it.

Barson's nostrils flared. "You don't understand. There are bigger things at play here—"

"I understand exactly what's at play here," Augusta interrupted, her fury growing by the minute. "You don't want this thing dead either, do you? You, Blaise, Ganir—it's gotten to you all. It's chosen its guise well, hasn't it? Men can't seem to think straight when it comes to *her*—"

Barson's eyes flashed with anger. "All I am trying to do is protect you—"

"I don't need protection from someone who can't even do a basic spell," Augusta said sharply, losing her temper. She was more than capable of looking after herself, and the fact that Barson was trying to imply that she was some weak damsel in need of protection added to her fury. She wasn't about to let some soldier tell her what to do—especially when she was beginning to suspect his motivations.

"Is that what you need—a man who can do spells?" A muscle pulsed in his jaw as he took a step toward her. "Is that what this whole thing is about for you? Is that why you want to destroy this creature so badly? Because she's with *him*? Are you still pining for your reclusive conjurer?"

Augusta literally saw red. "Get out," she hissed, pointing at the door. "Get out before I show you exactly what a 'conjurer' can do—"

"Are you threatening me?" Barson's voice turned dangerously soft. "I don't do well with threats, Augusta."

Driven beyond fury, Augusta jumped back, her hand instinctively scrambling for the Interpreter Stone lying on the table. Before she could grab it, however, she felt his hard arms close around her, whirling her around and pressing her against his muscular body. She pushed at him, but it was like trying to move a mountain with her bare hands, and the sense of powerlessness was even more enraging.

Her mouth opened to chant a spell—she didn't know which one and didn't care at this point—but his lips closed over hers, the kiss hard and filled with rage, and all she could do was hang helplessly in his embrace.

She could feel the heat of passion rising between them, but before it could go any further, his arms loosened around her and he stepped back, his chest heaving with anger and something more.

Her body shaking all over, Augusta tried to say something, but the words wouldn't form on her swollen lips. And before she could pull herself together, he turned and stormed out of the room, the door slamming shut behind him.

CHAPTER TWENTY-ONE

※ BLAISE ※

Shocked, Blaise stared at Gala who had just materialized on his chaise. She had teleported herself there—a very complex maneuver, given that the chaise was moving through the air at the time.

"I did it," she said, beaming at him. "I controlled a spell again. A few spells, as a matter of fact."

Recovering from his shock, Blaise pulled her toward him, shuddering at the thought of what could've happened if she'd miscalculated just a tiny bit and landed inside the chaise, instead of on top of it. Or inside Blaise, for that matter. His heart pounded heavily in his chest.

She hugged him for a brief moment, then pulled back, looking up at him. "Wasn't that good?" she asked proudly. "I did exactly what I set out to do and nothing else."

Blaise nodded, still not trusting himself to speak,

and her bright smile faded. "What's the matter?" she asked. "Are you upset with me?"

Blaise took a deep breath, letting the remnants of tension drain out of him. "No," he managed to say evenly. "It's just that what you did was dangerous, and I was imagining what could've happened if you'd made an error in your calculations."

Her delicate eyebrows lifted. "An error? Like thinking that two plus two equals five? I don't think I could do such a thing."

"So you're telling me you're infallible?" Blaise asked, amused at her inadvertent arrogance.

"I don't think I'm infallible." Gala frowned at him. "You know I have trouble with sorcery sometimes. But I just don't know how I could possibly get math wrong. It's so simple and straightforward. The calculations always yield the same results; it's just a matter of thinking about them for a second."

Blaise smiled at her, his pulse slowly returning to normal. "I see. Well, I can assure you that the rest of us make errors all the time."

She smiled back at him, and then a mischievous expression stole across her face. "I have something for you," she said, looking as excited as a child on her birthday. "A gift of sorts."

"What is it?"

"Close your eyes," she said, moving behind him and placing her small palms over his face. "Let's go back to where you met with Ganir."

"You expect me to navigate the chaise like this?"

"Well, I can also teleport us there—"

"No, that's all right," Blaise said quickly. "I'll navigate." And doing his best to remember where they needed to go, he directed the chaise to fly in that general direction, with Gala occasionally correcting their course.

"Stop here," she finally said, taking her palms away, and Blaise blinked a few times, letting his eyes get used to the bright light again. "There it is," she said, pointing down, and he looked in that direction.

What he saw made him stop breathing for a second. "Is that . . . is that my house?" he finally managed to ask, turning toward Gala. The large structure was sitting in the rocky canyon below, looking as intact as he had seen it the last time in Turingrad.

"It is." She gave him a huge smile. "You said you wished you still had access to your work, so I brought it here for you."

"Brought it how?"

"I teleported it, of course."

Blaise's jaw fell open. He had never heard of anyone teleporting such a large object over this kind of distance. It was possible in theory, but not doable in practice. Unless one had a mind forged in the Spell Realm, he thought with awe, staring at the beautiful young woman sitting next to him.

"Do you like it?" she asked uncertainly, her blue gaze clouding over when he didn't say anything, and Blaise shook off the remnants of his astonishment, reaching over to take her hand.

"Gala, I love it," he told her sincerely, and

watched her face brighten again.

"Do you want to go inside?" she asked excitedly. "Here, let's land."

Grinning, Blaise directed the chaise to the ground. As soon as they got down, he jumped off and headed into the house, his own excitement growing with every moment. His study was here. His archive room. All of his notes. Well, at least the ones that Augusta hadn't destroyed, he thought with a trace of anger. Pushing the unpleasant memory of their confrontation—and of Ganir's recent visit—out of his mind, he concentrated on Gala's amazing offering.

Entering the house, he gazed around the familiar surroundings, struck by a feeling of nostalgia. All of his things—paintings, statues, even the green needle-sword that had traveled to the Spell Realm—they were all here, just as he remembered. Even though Blaise had been home not too long ago, so much had happened that it was strange to be here, where he had spent so much time since Louie's death. The house had been his sanctuary from the outside world—and now he had it again, thanks to Gala's incredible abilities.

"You could watch that Life Capture now," Gala said, catching up with him. "The one that Ganir gave you."

Blaise stopped dead in his tracks. Had Gala come up with a way to read his mind?

"I was there when you had your conversation," she admitted, looking a bit sheepish.

"You were?" Blaise frowned in confusion.

Gala nodded, and began explaining how she had managed to turn herself invisible after he asked her to leave.

"You're getting much better at controlling your magic," Blaise said after she was done. He knew he should be upset that she hadn't listened to him, but he was too amazed and proud of her achievements. She was already performing feats that he'd once thought impossible.

As they walked past the library, Gala paused, looking into the room filled with books. Seeing the longing on her face, Blaise smiled. "Would you like to read some more?" he asked, and grinned when she practically jumped in excitement.

"Yes, I would love that!" Her eyes were shining. "There are still many books that I haven't read. Do you mind if I take a look at them?"

"No, go ahead," Blaise told her. "I will check on the droplet Ganir gave me in the meantime."

And leaving Gala to her reading, he walked toward his study.

* * *

As he approached his study, Blaise hesitated, his thoughts dwelling on the information Ganir had given him. He hadn't realized that the droplets could be preserved—and now that he knew, he couldn't stop thinking about one particular droplet that he'd been saving.

Turning, Blaise walked down to his storage area. Entering the room, he stared at the little jars and bottles containing memories of the past couple of years. Many were recordings of his work, but some were much more personal. Stopping in front of one particular jar—the jar that had a skull-and-bones sign on it—he reached for it, picking it up with a mingled sense of fear and reverence. As far as he knew, it was the only droplet of its kind.

It contained a recording of his brother's death— from his brother's point of view. It had been Louie's last act of defiance, capturing his own execution via the tool he'd shared with the commoners. It was also his last grand experiment. During the weeks leading up to his beheading, Louie had bribed a guard to bring him a Sphere. The blood splattering onto that Sphere during his execution was what allowed the recording loop to close, creating the droplet that Blaise had later retrieved.

Blaise had never dared to view it before. It was too precious to use up on a whim. Now, however, he knew he could preserve the droplet—but as he stared at it, he knew he still wasn't brave enough to ever do it. It would be too devastating to feel his brother's agony and know that Blaise had been unable to save him.

Drawing in a calming breath, Blaise picked up another droplet instead—the one that Ganir had just given him. As interesting as it would be to experience some memories from the past, Blaise needed to focus on the here and now—and to do that, he needed to learn if Ganir was telling the truth.

CHAPTER TWENTY-TWO

※ GALA ※

The pile of books at Gala's feet grew quickly. With each book she read, her speed seemed to increase, until she was swallowing a whole book in a matter of seconds.

Blaise had quite the collection when it came to subjects that interested Gala. She tackled verbal spell casting first, devouring texts both modern and ancient. It seemed that every sorcerer, every author, had his or her own approach to coding, yet there were patterns in common as well. When Gala couldn't find any more books on this subject, she moved on to written spell casting.

There were fewer books on this topic, since it was a new invention, but there was still enough material to keep her occupied for a number of minutes. As she consumed the texts, she found it amusing how much less variability there was in the code for written spells. It seemed that now that spells could be reused, sorcerers just copied the same component spells over and over, instead of trying to improve on existing offerings or starting from scratch.

Depleting the books on sorcery, Gala went for anything that could give her a better understanding of how the world worked. Chemistry, physics, mathematics, biology, psychology—she knew that these were as important to sorcery as the code itself. Though her ultimate goal was to control her spells, she enjoyed learning about how the natural world functioned. Oxygen, for instance . . . Gala found it mind-blowing that it was an element in both the air that she breathed and the water that she drank. It was also crucial for controlling fire spells.

After she was done reading, the pile of books surrounding her was waist-high.

Examining herself for a moment, Gala realized that she could now say or write many spells. There wasn't anything in the books that she would not be able to do. However, she wanted more. She knew that her way—how she'd sporadically done sorcery before—was more direct and more powerful. More pure, in a sense. With the new knowledge she'd absorbed, she felt like she was on the cusp of understanding how her mind worked. In a way, it was like the Interpreter Stone, except it used her thoughts and emotions as inputs, rather than cards. All she needed to do was shape those thoughts and emotions properly.

She decided to try something—a feat of

teleportation, something she was already beginning to master. She saw in her mind how a verbal spell would sound that would teleport all the books on the floor to their original place. She then visualized how that would read as written code. And then, clearing her mind with slow breathing, she tried to do it directly.

At that moment, Blaise entered the room. "What—" he began saying, but stopped mid-sentence, mouth agape, as the books began to disappear off the floor and reappear back on the shelves. Within a few moments, the mess was gone and the shelves were as neatly arranged as before.

"That was amazing, Gala," he breathed, staring around the room. "I've never seen anyone perform such a well-coordinated spell before."

Gala felt her cheeks warm at the praise. "Thank you," she said softly. Then, remembering the droplet, she asked, "So did Ganir tell the truth?"

"He did," Blaise said, his smile disappearing. "The droplet did indeed show him voting against Louie's death—and I felt his pain at the outcome of the vote." He paused, his lips tightening. "I was wrong about Ganir. I let my anger and hatred cloud my judgment, and that made it easier for Jandison to deceive me."

"So what does that mean?" she asked, her heart aching at the pain she saw on Blaise's face.

"It means Jandison has a lot to answer for." Blaise's voice was flat, and Gala saw something frightening in his eyes. "Both to the Council and to me."

"Are you going to tell Ganir that it was Jandison who told you about that vote?"

Blaise nodded. "I already sent him a Contact message. I'm sure he'll take it straight to the Council."

"Do you think this changes anything as far as the Council coming after us? After all, if Jandison has been fixing the vote, could their latest decision be considered invalid?"

"Yes, it could. Ganir said he'll keep me abreast of the developments on that front. I think I can trust him, but I wouldn't bet our lives on it. If Ganir found us, so can the others. It's unfortunate, but I think we still need to leave this place."

"What? No!" Gala couldn't contain her disappointment. "We just got here, and Liva said she'll introduce us to everyone in the village. I'd like to stay and meet more people."

"Gala . . ." Blaise sighed, looking at her. "It really wouldn't be wise."

"Please, just for a little while longer?" Gala pleaded. "It will take Ganir some time to get back to Turingrad. It's not like they'll come after us tomorrow, even if they somehow learned we were here."

Blaise hesitated, visibly wavering. "All right," he finally said. "We'll stay, but not for long. I won't have you in danger again."

CHAPTER TWENTY-THREE

✳ AUGUSTA ✳

Trembling with fury, Augusta stared at the closed door before beginning to pace up and down her room. How dare Barson treat her like she was his possession? And how dare Ganir betray the entire Council by consorting with Blaise and that abomination?

The old man had to be dealt with. Now—before he did any harm. She would think about what to do about Barson's suspiciously unreasonable behavior later.

Grabbing her Stone and the cards she'd prepared for another purpose, Augusta stuffed them in her bag and hurried out of her room. As she walked, a plan began forming in her mind.

She had to get Ganir away from his study, as he would have an advantage there. The big question was how to accomplish that. There was one way, but it would be a risky maneuver. Stopping for a minute, Augusta sat down on one of the stone benches lining the hallways and started scribbling. When she was done, she double-checked her calculations.

The idea should work, she decided.

Getting up, she hurried toward Ganir's chambers, and as she rounded the corner, she saw Barson's right-hand man Larn and two other soldiers pass by. She stared after them in disbelief, her fury spiking. Barson had not kept his promise to her. He was supposed to have his men in hiding, and yet here they were, strolling through the halls of the Tower right next to Ganir's quarters.

Taking a calming breath, she put the matter out of her mind for now and focused on the task at hand. Stopping a few feet away from Ganir's door, she fed a few cards into her Stone to implement some defensive spells, paying particular attention to mental defenses.

Then she knocked decisively. Once. Twice.

The door swung open. Ganir stood there, his face calm and expressionless.

"Did you go see Blaise?" Augusta asked sharply, not bothering with any niceties. "Was the creature there with him?"

The old man's eyes widened almost imperceptibly, and Augusta knew that it was true— that Barson hadn't lied. Ganir had indeed betrayed her and the Council.

"Don't bother to deny it," she said when Ganir opened his mouth. "I know the truth. You're nothing but a traitor—"

"You dare call *me* a traitor?" Ganir sounded incredulous. "You, who consort with your 'dead' lover? I gave you the benefit of the doubt, but now I see that you must be in league with him—"

Augusta's eyebrows snapped together. So Ganir already knew the Guard were not dead. Had Barson betrayed her to the Council Leader? Was that what the old man meant by her being 'in league' with her lover? Her anger intensifying, she saw Ganir taking a few steps back, and she realized that, in a moment, he would be near his desk, where his Interpreter Stone lay.

There was no more time to waste.

Loading the card she'd prepared earlier, Augusta closed her eyes and braced herself. When she opened them, she and Ganir were standing on the roof of the Tower, with all of Turingrad laid out far below.

Without giving Ganir a chance to get his bearings, Augusta went for her first prepared spell.

It was pure kinetic energy, focused all on one spot. It should've caused him to fly off the roof—yet Ganir barely flinched. He must've had a defensive spell on himself, she realized, watching him fumble as he took out cards from his pockets and began changing a spell at the same time.

Seeing those cards, she clutched her own stone, her biggest advantage right now.

Ganir's first verbal spell was an elemental fire attack. It hit the shield Augusta had prepared, and waves of fire spread around the roof. It was the most powerful spell of this kind she had ever encountered.

Swiftly loading the pre-written card into her Stone, Augusta retaliated with a lightning bolt. It hit Ganir's defense, causing the smell of ozone to permeate the air. The old man, however, was still unharmed.

He was also still attempting to write something on his cards. Why would he do this, when he had no Stone? There was no way he would be able to get Augusta's Stone—and it wouldn't work for him, anyway, since she had it customized for herself.

At the same time as he was writing, Ganir was saying the words to some verbal spell. The fact that he could do both at the same time was impressive; Augusta didn't know anyone who could do two such concentration-intensive tasks at once. It made him even more dangerous, she thought as she loaded more cards into her stone.

Her next spell was designed to blast Ganir with sudden changes in temperature. As the spell began working, the air around him shimmered, turning from boiling to freezing and back to boiling within seconds. His shield held, but Augusta knew it would begin to weaken soon.

Suddenly, a triumphant expression appeared on Ganir's face. To her shock, Augusta saw that he was now holding his Stone. He must've summoned it with that verbal spell he was chanting earlier, she realized with dismay, even as she quickly loaded more defensive spells into her own Stone.

It didn't help. All of a sudden, she felt a

debilitating fear—a nebulous, undefined fear of anything and everything. When she was a young girl, she had been dreadfully afraid of spiders, and it was like that fear, only multiplied a thousand fold. There was a silent scream in her throat, her panic irrational, yet overwhelming. Her vision darkened, her heart pounding like a drum, and cold sweat broke out over her body. She couldn't even scream, her vocal cords paralyzed by terror. If she hadn't had her shield in place, this would've been a thousand times worse, she realized dimly, battling the nauseating terror that crippled her thinking.

Ganir was literally trying to frighten her to death.

The fear intensified, waves of it washing over her at the knowledge that if he succeeded, the Council would think she died of natural causes. They wouldn't even look for her killer. Fury, sharp and healing, seized her at the thought, giving her the strength to move her arms. Out of the corner of her eye, she could see Ganir writing something else on a card.

She didn't have much time. His next spell would be the end.

Gathering herself, Augusta reached with trembling hands for a spell she'd prepared for another purpose. A new wave of fear hit her, causing her to nearly drop the card, but she managed to fit it into the Stone before collapsing to her knees.

Time seemed to slow. She could hear her own ragged breathing and the heavy pumping of her heart. Somewhere at the back of her mind she registered the fact that Ganir swayed on his feet and then sank down to the floor, and that the waves of fear battering her abated slightly.

Struggling to her feet, Augusta approached Ganir's fallen body to make sure her spell had worked.

Then she began to work on a spell to calm and heal her shattered mind.

CHAPTER TWENTY-FOUR

✳ BARSON ✳

Barson was doing what he always did when he was angry: channeling it into practice. Three sacks with sand now lay in a shredded mess on the floor, destroyed by his fists, and he was moving on to training with his sword. He knew it was risky, remaining in the Tower, but no sorcerer ever visited the Guard barracks, and Barson needed to let off some steam before he went back to Dara's house.

Augusta was impossible, he thought between ragged breaths, swinging his sword in a wide, furious arc. He'd had every intention of telling her about his plan, but she'd twisted everything, throwing out accusations that made no sense. And then to imply that he couldn't protect her because he couldn't cast spells? He'd always admired her strength and independence, but she took it too far this time. He would not stand for that kind of disrespect—and certainly not from a woman whom he'd wanted to be his companion in the new order.

His intention today was to pass out from exhaustion in this training room, and he was making good headway when the sound of footsteps caught his attention. Turning, he saw Larn walking his way, accompanied by Zanil and Pugan, two of his best lieutenants.

Breathing heavily, Barson lowered his sword. What were they doing in the Tower when they were supposed to stay hidden? Had they come here for exercise as well? "Why are you here?" he yelled as they came closer. "Didn't I tell you to lie low?"

Strangely, they didn't respond, just continued walking.

As they got closer, Barson noticed the blank expressions on their faces. Their eyes were glassy and unfocused, as though they were out of their minds with exhaustion or drink. But if that was the case, what were they doing in the training room? And why had they not answered him?

"Larn, stop and explain what's going on," Barson commanded. There was no reaction, but Barson could see the muscles in Larn's right hand tense as his fingers tightened on the hilt of his sword.

This had to be some kind of prank Larn dreamed up. "I am in no mood for levity," Barson told them sharply. "Explain yourselves. Now."

They unsheathed their swords instead.

Puzzled and annoyed, Barson assumed a defensive posture out of habit, gripping his sword tighter—and in that moment, they attacked.

They moved with a fury that took him completely by surprise. This was no training.

For some unknown reason, Barson's best friend and his two trusted soldiers were out to kill him.

Parrying the first thrusts, Barson frantically thought about this situation. There had to be an explanation. "Is someone keeping Dara hostage?" he yelled at Larn, blocking the second wave of attack. "Is that how they are making you do this?"

A cut to his left shoulder was his only answer.

The cut was not deep, but its effect was sobering.

If Barson didn't focus, he would die.

CHAPTER TWENTY-FIVE

✳ BLAISE ✳

Entering Liva's house with Gala, Blaise saw Esther and Maya sitting at the table with their host.

"There you two lovebirds are," Esther exclaimed with a wide smile on her face. "Liva tells me that was quite a lesson today."

Gala grinned, her face lighting up. "Liva did a great job with her spell," she said, looking at the woman.

Liva flushed, both pleased and embarrassed by the praise. "Oh, I'm nowhere near as good as this girl right here . . ." She pointed at Gala. "Now, she's got real talent."

"Oh, we know," Maya said drily. "Believe me, we know."

"So when is the celebration?" Gala asked, looking excited at the thought. "I'd love to meet everyone."

"We were just waiting for the two of you to get

back," Liva said, smiling. "Now that you're here, I'll let the others know, and we can start."

* * *

Everybody gathered at a large clearing near the edge of the village. A big fire was blazing in the middle, with a boar roasting on a spit. "The hunters caught it today," Liva said proudly as they approached the gathering. "It's not often that we get such a feast, and we're happy we can welcome you to the village properly."

Blaise counted about a hundred people, ranging in age from toddlers to elders. It was a sizable settlement, he realized, watching them.

"Here, Blaise, have a drink," an attractive dark-haired woman exclaimed, coming up to him and handing him a clay cup. She looked vaguely familiar, and the way she was talking made it seem like they knew each other.

"Thank you," Blaise said, and then he realized that the woman was Ara—the female hunter he'd met earlier. He almost didn't recognize her in a feminine blue dress, with her long hair unbound and streaming down her back. She'd looked so much like a boy before that the transformation was startling. Taking a sip of the drink she handed him, Blaise choked and made a face. "What is this?"

She laughed, patting him on the back. "Fermented berries. Not as fancy as the wine you're probably used to, right?"

Blaise grinned at her. "I don't typically drink, but the wine I had before was indeed very different."

At that moment, Gala came up to them, a strange expression on her face. She looked almost angry. Looping her arm through Blaise's elbow, she gave Ara a haughty look. "I don't think Blaise likes that drink of yours," she said sharply.

Blaise stared at his creation in shock. He'd never seen her be purposefully rude. Did she dislike Ara for some reason?

Ara shot Gala an equally disdainful look. "I think as a former Council member, Blaise can decide for himself what he does and does not like," she began, and Blaise saw Gala's free hand curling into a fist. The truth dawned on him. Gala was jealous. He needed to diffuse the situation and quickly.

"Gala," he said evenly, "why don't we take a walk right now? I think the fresh air would be good for us. Ara—thank you for the drink. It was actually quite good." And before Gala could protest, he led her into the woods, trying not to notice the disappointed expression on Ara's face.

"Gala, were you jealous?" he asked when they were out of the earshot of the villagers. "Was that why you acted this way with Ara?"

Gala looked at him, a stormy expression on her face. "Do you like her?" To his surprise, there was a hurt note in her voice. "Do you want her? Because I think she wants you—"

"What? No!" Blaise couldn't believe someone so beautiful was feeling insecure. "You're the only one I want. How can you even think otherwise? Ara was just being friendly—"

"No, she wasn't," Gala said quietly. "I've seen her looking at you before. She doesn't act this friendly with the others—only with you."

Blaise took a deep breath. "Regardless of what Ara may or may not feel, what matters is how I feel," he said, holding Gala's gaze. "And I can assure you, you have nothing to worry about. I don't think of her that way."

A faint flush stole across her face. "I'm sorry," she said, looking away. "I don't know what came over me. It's not logical, but I don't like the thought of you with some other woman. Even Augusta, although I know it's in the past—"

"Gala . . ." Blaise reached for her hand, clasping it between his palms. His heart was beating faster, and a feeling very much like euphoria spread through him. "Believe me," he said softly, "I can't think of anyone but you."

She looked up at him again, her expression unusually vulnerable. "And I can't think of anyone but you," she whispered, her eyes large and liquid in the fading twilight.

Unable to resist, Blaise bent his head and kissed her, his hands sliding around her back to press her closer. It was only the knowledge that the entire village was less than fifty feet away that enabled him to stop with just a kiss.

"Come," he murmured, taking her hand again. "Let's go back. And please, don't be upset with every woman I speak to. I can promise you, they mean nothing to me."

Gala gave him a soft smile. "All right. I will try."

When they got back, the boar was ready, and the women were starting to slice off thick pieces of meat dripping with fat. Liva handed Gala and Blaise two misshapen wooden plates loaded with meat and roasted vegetables, and they sat down to eat next to the fire.

An old, white-haired man was sitting near them, with a few children gathered around him. He was telling the children a story. As Blaise listened closer, he realized it was one of the myths from the western lands.

"In the beginning, a thousand years ago, the world was all water," the elderly man began, his voice deep and sonorous. "There was nothing there except two brothers—the Sea Monster and the Thunder Creature. They lived together, in the water and the sky, until one day they had a big fight. The Thunder Creature was envious of the Sea Monster's freedom to swim, and in a fit of jealous rage, he ripped the Sea Monster's heart out. That heart became the land of Koldun, and the Sea Monster's flesh became its people. With his brother gone, the Thunder Creature went insane from loneliness, his howls creating the storms that surround our land to this very day."

The old man paused, and Blaise saw that the children were looking at the old man in wide-eyed fascination—and so was Gala.

"That's not what I read," she told the old man,

looking puzzled. "And what I read sounded much more plausible."

Blaise smiled at her confusion. "Gala, these are just old stories . . . legends. They are not meant to be taken literally."

The elderly storyteller frowned at Blaise. "What do you mean by that, sorcerer? These are the stories passed down for generations. Do you have some other explanation for how we came to be?"

"Well, yes, actually," Blaise said slowly. He didn't want to offend these people and their beliefs, so he needed to proceed carefully. "We don't have all the answers, but we know a couple of things for sure. The world is very old. A thousand years is but a moment compared to its true age. In fact, there are trees that are older than that—you can tell their age from the number of rings inside their trunks. Sorcerers studying weather patterns have found a couple of pine trees that are over five thousand years old."

The old man stared at him in shock, and some of the children giggled, enjoying the adults' disagreement. "Over five thousand years?" one little boy asked, his eyes round with wonder. "That's a long time for a tree to be alive."

"Indeed," Blaise said, smiling at the child. "But that's not the only proof of our land's true age. There are stalactites in the caverns of these very mountains that grow at a rate of about four inches every thousand years. Given how long some of them are, they must've been growing for hundreds of thousands of years. And, of course, there are the mountains themselves. The canyon that's nearby has been formed by erosion from water and the other elements—a process that has most likely taken millions, not thousands, of years."

The elderly man still looked skeptical. "If that's true," he said, "then where did Koldun and all of us come from? How did we come to be?"

"That's a good question, and one that wise men have been pondering for ages," Blaise said. "One theory right now is that nature shaped people, not unlike how people bred wolfhounds and shepherd dogs from the primordial wolf."

He was about to continue his explanation when a loud boom shook the ground. At the same time, the sky lit up with a blazing white-and-purple light before going dark again.

Everybody froze, and one of the younger children began to cry. Only Gala looked more curious than alarmed.

"Was that thunder?" Blaise asked, looking at the frightened faces around the fire. "I've never heard it be so loud."

The old man rose to his feet, his hands trembling. "Yes, sorcerer, that was thunder. It sounds like a storm is heading our way."

CHAPTER TWENTY-SIX

❈ AUGUSTA ❈

Once she stopped shaking from the aftereffects of her battle with Ganir and the debilitating fear left her mind, Augusta began considering the consequences of what she'd done.

Ganir's limp body was lying on the floor. She knelt beside it and pressed her fingers against his neck to feel his pulse. It was there, still going strong. The Council Leader was alive, but his mind was deep in a coma, just as she had intended. Of course, she hadn't planned to use this particular spell on Ganir, but she was glad she'd had the cards on her. The spell had saved her life. And now that she knew it worked on people as well, she would definitely need to prepare new cards before leaving Turingrad.

Now that she had rendered the old man unconscious, Augusta wasn't sure what to do with him. Ideally she should kill him, but the thought of snuffing out another sorcerer's life was repugnant to her. Despite their differences, she'd always respected Ganir's abilities, and the idea of killing him in cold blood bothered her.

She couldn't let the others find him, though. They would immediately suspect sorcery, and since Augusta's differences with Ganir were public knowledge, that would not bode well for her. Even though she knew she was in the right on this, she had no doubt there would still be a trial—a trial that could delay the upcoming mission to destroy Blaise's creation.

No, she couldn't let that happen. Ganir needed to disappear.

After pondering the problem for a minute, Augusta began working on a complex and highly risky spell. There was a chance that it could kill Ganir, but that was better than murdering him outright.

When the spell was done, she loaded the cards and watched the old sorcerer's body disappear. If her calculations were correct, it would reappear in Ganir's mansion in his territory, far away from Turingrad. She knew the location because Ganir had hosted a party there several years ago, and she and Blaise had been invited. Of course, if Ganir had changed anything in that room of his house—or if she had miscalculated even a tiny bit—he could easily end up dead. She didn't feel too guilty about that, though, not when he had been planning to kill her with that fear spell of his.

Taking one last look around the empty roof, Augusta opened the door leading to the rooftop and began to climb down the winding staircase. She needed to make her way back to Ganir's study, and she wasn't about to risk teleportation again.

Walking through the hallways, she made sure that no one saw her as she approached Ganir's quarters. She needed to find something, anything that would give her more information about where Blaise and his creature were. It seemed unlikely they would live in a desolate canyon, though that canyon could still be a good place to start looking for them.

Opening the door quietly, Augusta surveyed the room. Ganir was almost impossibly neat. She couldn't find any recently written notes lying about, or jars of Life Capture droplets. As she looked around, however, she noticed a single droplet inside his Sphere.

Without hesitation she walked over to it, sat down in his chair, and brought the droplet to her mouth.

* * *

Ganir observed the three men who were tied up in his study—Barson's soldiers who had been captured in a tavern in Turingrad. The binds were not necessary, strictly speaking, as he had already pacified them with a spell. Still, it paid to be cautious. Some stronger minds could snap out of the lethargy of the spell prematurely, which could be a problem with these men. He had to concentrate on the key spell, the spell that would finally rid him of the nuisance that was Barson.

At that moment, a Contact message reached his mind.

"Ganir, this is Blaise. I wanted to confirm your suspicions. Jandison was indeed the one who told me what the vote breakdown was."

Hearing that, Ganir was overcome with a fury so strong, he actually shook with it. Because of Jandison's treachery, he had lost Louie and then nearly lost Blaise. Ganir had never had children of his own, and Dasbraw's boys had been the closest he'd gotten to having sons. And now Louie was dead, and Blaise hated him.

Jandison would pay for this. Ganir would make sure of that.

In the meantime, there was another, more urgent problem that required handling. Barson made a fatal error by pretending to be dead . . . because now Ganir would make sure that the lie became reality.

Stepping toward the captured men, he pulled out his Interpreter Stone and began loading the cards he'd prepared earlier. This was a spell he was quite proud of; it was unfortunate that nobody would ever learn of it. This degree of mind control was the most advanced psychological sorcery, and Ganir didn't know anyone else who could do something of this magnitude.

No, that wasn't true, he corrected himself. Gala, Blaise's creation, could do this and more. She had literally changed the brain of Davish without forcibly controlling his thoughts, as Ganir was about to do with these soldiers. And the effect of her spell was permanent in nature, while Ganir's was temporary at best—though a few hours was all he needed to achieve his goal.

He desperately wished he could talk to her, to learn about how her mind worked and how she had come to be. He wanted to delve into the mystery that was this Spell Realm-born creature, and it was frustrating to him that Blaise was so overprotective of her. The young man saw her as a desirable woman—which Ganir could still understand on some level—but her beauty blinded Blaise to her true potential. With someone like Gala at his side, Ganir would be unstoppable. He would never need to use intrigue or subtlety with the Council again. One touch of her pretty hands, and they would think whatever he wished them to think.

As the spell he'd unleashed on the soldiers finally took effect, Ganir could see the glazed look in their eyes. It was safe to let them go. Their programming was simple: kill Barson and then themselves. If, by some chance, the last part didn't work out, they would not remember any of it anyway, as the spell was designed to suppress their memory of this mind manipulation.

Untying the soldiers, Ganir ushered them out of his room, taking a look outside first to make sure nobody saw them leave.

Then, just as he was about to sit down and figure out how best to solve the Jandison issue, he heard a knock on the door. Annoyed, he pricked his finger and *touched the bloody spot to his sphere, ending the current recording.*

* * *

Coming out of the Life Capture, Augusta felt the heavy pounding of her own heart. So that was why she'd encountered Barson's men in the hallway; Ganir had set them against her lover. Her blood ran cold as she remembered seeing them in practice; as good as Barson was, his men were also well-trained—and, most importantly, he would not be expecting any treachery from them.

Jumping to her feet, Augusta ran out of the room, desperate to find Barson. Regardless of their differences, she needed to warn him about this. She didn't know why Ganir hated Barson so much. Her lover had once hinted that the Council Leader had purposefully misinformed them about the larger-than-expected peasant rebellion, but she'd forgotten about it, too distracted by Blaise's creature. It didn't matter now, though. She had to find Barson before Ganir's plan could come to fruition.

She couldn't stand to lose him again.

CHAPTER TWENTY-SEVEN

※ GALA ※

As soon as they heard the word 'storm,' the villagers sitting around Gala jumped to their feet with panicked expressions on their faces.

Gala stared at them curiously. "A storm? Are you talking about one of the ocean storms from beyond the mountains?" She had seen a regular storm before—had, in fact, inadvertently created one—and it hadn't seemed all that bad to her. The upcoming weather had to be something different to warrant such reactions.

"Yes," Liva said tersely, bending down to collect the remnants of the food. "We need to take shelter in our homes and hope that we don't get a direct hit."

"What happens if you do?" Blaise asked, looking more intrigued than worried. "Are these storms truly as bad as they say?"

"Worse," the old man said succinctly. "Far worse

than you can imagine, sorcerer. You may not believe in the Thunder Creature, but you are about to witness its power."

Within minutes, all of the villagers left the clearing, heading back to their homes. Blaise took Gala's hand, and they hurried after Liva, who was all but running at this point. "We need to close the shutters and board up our windows," she told Blaise. "I don't know when the storm is getting here, but we might have less than an hour, given how loud that thunder was."

"Why don't I help?" Blaise suggested. "If you can gather everybody, I should be able to put a protective shield around them. It would be more effective than just boarding up the windows."

"How strong is your shield?" Liva asked doubtfully. "These storms tend to be very, very powerful."

Blaise considered it, a thoughtful expression appearing on his face. "All right, how about this?" he suggested after a moment. "We'll board up the windows, and I will strengthen the walls of a couple of houses. Everybody can gather there, and then I will also put a protective shield around those houses."

Liva nodded. "That's a good idea. I'll go tell the others, get them to come to my house. It's one of the larger ones, and between my house and that of my neighbor, we should be able to accommodate everyone. I'll meet you back home."

Gala watched as the older woman disappeared

down the street, then looked up at Blaise. "Have you ever seen one of these storms?" she asked, wondering about the phenomenon. "Is it truly that much worse than regular lightning and thunder?"

"I've never seen one," Blaise told her, reaching out to take her hand as they walked toward Liva's place. "I've heard stories, though, and read about them. There is a good reason why the mountains are not considered a habitable location."

At that moment, a blinding flash of light illuminated the purple-streaked sky, and the thunderous boom that followed was so loud that Gala literally felt the ground shake beneath her feet. "It sounds like it's getting closer," she commented worriedly, looking up. The villagers' fear was starting to rub off on her, even though she still didn't understand how some rain, wind, and lightning could be that dangerous.

"It does, doesn't it?" Blaise stopped at the entrance to Liva's house and looked up at the sky himself. "You know, I never thought I would get an opportunity to see one of these in action. It should be fascinating—particularly if we make sure that no one gets hurt."

Gala nodded, hurrying inside the house as a light rain began. Blaise followed, already taking out his magic supplies. She watched as he spread out his cards on the table and began to write what looked like a series of complex spells.

"Can I help?" she asked. "Maybe I can do something too."

Blaise hesitated for a second. "Do you understand all the spells I'm writing?"

"Of course," Gala said, surprised that he would even ask. "In fact, I think I can do it even more efficiently—if I wrote those spells, that is. I'll do it my way, though. I could use more practice."

He gave her a rueful smile. "Sometimes I forget how advanced you've become in such a short time. In that case, why don't you take the neighbors' house and strengthen its defenses as much as you can? I will put a protective bubble around both houses."

"Why don't you put a protective bubble around the entire village?"

"Because that's a much more complex task, and the bigger the bubble, the less stable it is. It's easiest to shield something small, like a person."

Gala nodded and hurried outside. Another flash of lightning nearly blinded her, and she could feel the wind picking up as the rain intensified, the cold water lashing at her face.

The storm was on its way.

CHAPTER TWENTY-EIGHT

※ BARSON ※

The seriousness of his situation was beginning to dawn on Barson as he continued fighting Larn and the two other soldiers. He was already tired from practice, and Larn was one of his best; they had trained together since childhood. To make matters worse, Zanil and Pugan, though not the best archers, were both excellent with the sword.

Larn made a triple feint, and Barson barely managed to block what would have been a lethal blow. As they circled around the room, their feet kicking up the sand from the bags Barson had decimated earlier, Barson's mind was racing. Why was Larn doing this? Was this a power play? It was hard for Barson to believe that, though he knew military history was rife with instances of second-in-command trying for the top. Larn was practically family, about to marry Barson's sister; surely it wouldn't make sense for him to do this.

As the fight continued, Barson did his best to defend himself without killing his soon-to-be brother-in-law. Although it made the fight more challenging, he could not bring himself to do that. It helped that the three men seemed to be fighting without coordinating their movements. It was odd, but he was grateful for it. He was also confused. They all knew how to fight as a team, and the fact that they were not using such a powerful advantage was strange. Was this some sign of what was really going on? If so, Barson was still not sure what that was.

Zanil came at him next, leaving Pugan and Larn behind.

Barson made a split-second decision. Pretending to go for Zanil's left shoulder, he switched tactics as the man blocked, and thrust his sword deep into his opponent's thigh. Blood gushed from the wound, but to Barson's dismay, Zanil didn't stop. Instead, he continued to attack Barson, each step causing more and more blood to spill from the leg wound. It was as if Zanil had lost all reason, all sense of self-preservation.

An ugly suspicion stirred in Barson's mind. Sorcery. His men were somehow being controlled.

Cursing, Barson took advantage of Zanil's clumsy movements and punched him in the face, knocking him out. At that moment, Pugan and Larn reached him again. Though they still didn't act in a coordinated fashion, they attacked together, forcing Barson to retreat as he parried their furious onslaught.

Everything seemed to happen in a blur of motion. Pugan sliced at Barson's forearm, inflicting another wound. The pain was sharp and sobering. Spotting an opening in Pugan's defense, Barson swung his sword at the soldier's exposed throat, dodging Larn's attack at the same time. Out of the corner of his eye, he saw the young soldier falling to the ground, his blood seeping into the spilled sand.

There was no time for guilt or regret, as Barson felt himself weakening from his own loss of blood. If he didn't bring this fight to a swift conclusion, he would die.

Whatever was done to Larn seemed to have actually made him a better fighter in some ways. Larn's usual problem was letting his emotions get the best of him, but right now he appeared to be fighting with deadly precision—methodically, without passion. A thrust followed by a block, followed by a counter attack, over and over again.

As the fight continued, Barson began to feel his blood loss more acutely. A wave of dizziness washed over him, blurring his vision. Larn lunged at him in that moment, and their swords clashed together. Gathering his last strength, Barson punched Larn in the stomach, hard, desperately hoping that the pain would snap the man out of whatever spell he was under.

It did not. Instead, Barson felt a fire explode in his right shoulder as Larn's sword penetrated his own defenses.

Despite the injury, Barson's right hand instinctively moved to block what would've been a killing blow. At the same time, his left hand grabbed Larn's sword arm with all his might. Everything depended on disarming his friend. Almost dislocating his own shoulder, Barson ripped at Larn's sword, causing the object to fly across the room.

Disarmed, Larn still didn't make a sound. Instead, he hit Barson's wounded shoulder, causing an explosion of agony to spread. Cursing, Barson felt his sword slip from his numb fingers. As it hit the ground, he managed to kick it across the room.

They were both weaponless now, except for their fists—but that didn't diminish the danger one bit. Larn fought like a man possessed, and Barson did his best to remain conscious while trying to knock him out with his still-functional left hand.

It was a futile effort, and Larn kept landing blow after blow to Barson's injured flesh. His vision going gray, Barson pretended to stumble, as if he was passing out, and as Larn lunged at him, Barson swung his right hand in a vicious uppercut, ignoring the agony in his wounded shoulder. Dimly he thought he heard a crunching sound of bone breaking, but it wasn't clear if it was his fist or Larn's jaw ... and then Barson's world went dark as his consciousness finally fled.

CHAPTER TWENTY-NINE

✳ BLAISE ✳

As Blaise continued working on the protective spells, people began coming in, one family at a time. Before long, every room of Liva's house was crammed full of villagers. Small children ran around, squealing in excitement, while most of the adults were somber and frightened, tense with anxiety.

In the meantime, the weather outside kept getting worse with every passing second. Rain lashed at the windows, and the wind picked up, its gusts buffeting the house with startling force. Every lightning strike seemed to be getting closer, every boom of thunder more deafening than before.

"Has everyone made it in?" Blaise yelled, trying to be heard over the chaotic din of voices, wind, and rain. "Once I put up the shield over the houses, no one will be able to come through."

"I don't know," Liva yelled back, shoving aside a

couple of boys to get closer to him. "Many of them are in the other house—the one Gala is working on."

Blaise quietly cursed. Given the speed with which the storm was approaching, they needed to get everyone to safety before it was too late. He had no idea how bad the storm would get, but if it was anything like the stories said, he knew it could be deadly.

As if to lend credence to his thoughts, the wooden shutters on the boarded-up kitchen window began to shake, the wind rattling them with such force that a panel broke off, flying into the room. A child cried out, then began to scream, and Blaise saw a little girl with her arm bleeding. He hesitated for a second, wanting to heal her, but there was a more important task he needed to accomplish first. If he didn't get the shield up and strengthen the house walls promptly, they would all be in trouble.

As Blaise was finishing the last lines of his spell, he heard a loud thump, then another and another. It sounded like rocks were falling on the house, each hit more frightening than the next. He could hear the wood above them creaking and breaking, and he knew he had to hurry before the roof caved in on them. A cold fist squeezed his chest as he realized that Gala could be out there—that she might be facing the storm on her own.

"It's hail," someone yelled. "The hail has started . . . Mom, look at the size of those ice pieces!"

Forcing himself to ignore the panicked shouts, Blaise wrote the last line of the spell and quickly checked his work before loading the cards into the Stone.

A minute later, the worst of the racket ceased, the shield dampening the sound of the battering hail. Jumping to his feet, Blaise ran to the door, eager to retrieve Gala from the other house.

"Blaise, where are you going?" Liva screamed. "It's too dangerous out there!"

"I'll be right back," Blaise yelled back. "I just need to check on the neighbors' house." And opening the door, he stepped outside.

* * *

The sight that greeted Blaise was surreal. The sky was a deep, violent purple, the clouds heavy and stretching as far as the eye could see. Flashes of lightning intermittently bisected the sky, and the smell of ozone was sharp in the air. Beyond the barrier, the deadly hail continued, icy rocks falling from the sky like boulders in a mountain slide.

Looking down in disbelief, Blaise saw that some pieces of ice underneath his feet were bigger than his head. If he hadn't gotten the shield up in time, the roof would've been destroyed. As is, his barrier would not last for long under that kind of assault, he realized, staring up at the flickering shimmer of the bubble surrounding the two houses.

His heartbeat picking up, he ran across the street, the walls of the bubble providing protection from both hail and wind. Nonetheless, he could feel the crackle of electricity in the air, and the fine hair on the back of his neck stood up in response.

Suddenly, a bright flash of light blinded him, and the ground vibrated under his feet. Sparks flew just outside the barrier, and Blaise realized that a tree nearby had been struck by lightning, the force of the blast splitting it apart.

Almost immediately, there was another flash, followed by another clap of thunder. Still running, Blaise realized that the lightning struck the village again, this time setting one of the houses on fire.

The storm was worsening.

Frantically knocking on the door of the neighbors' house, Blaise stared in disbelief as the deadly force struck the village again and again, the ice melting wherever lightning touched the ground.

"Blaise!" The door opened so suddenly that he jumped, startled. Gala was standing there, a worried expression on her face.

Tremendously relieved to see that she was all right, he hugged her for a quick second. "Come," he said, stepping back. "We need to get back to Liva's house. I left my Stone there without thinking, and I need to create a new shield, as this one will not hold up for long. Did you finish everything?"

She nodded. "I just got done strengthening this house. A woman got hurt trying to get here, and I healed her—that's what took me so long."

"Good, let's go," Blaise said tersely, grabbing her hand. Lightning struck the barrier, sparks flying everywhere, and he saw the bubble flicker even more.

"We have to get back there, now."

They ran to Liva's house as the barrier flickered again and again, the shimmer fading in spots as boulder-sized hail continued to pound against it, and bolts of lightning struck over and over again.

"Quickly, inside!" Blaise pushed Gala into the house just as the shield gave way under the assault.

He was less than a foot away from the door himself when he heard a sickening crack, followed by an agony so intense that his entire world went black.

CHAPTER THIRTY

❊ AUGUSTA ❊

Running through the hallways, Augusta ignored the startled looks she was getting from the apprentices and other sorcerers. All that mattered to her now was finding Barson. Where could he have gone?

As she'd expected, his quarters were empty. Her breathing fast and uneven, she stopped to think for a second. There was a spell she could do to aid her in the search, she realized after a moment. If Barson was anywhere in the vicinity, perhaps she would be able to hear him.

Pulling out her cards, she frantically began scribbling. Two minutes later she could hear the mice squeaking in the distant hallways and the chatter of conversation on the other side of the Tower.

She also heard a sound that nearly made her heart stop: the ding of metal clashing against metal. It was coming from the Guard's training barracks.

Augusta ran there with all the speed she could muster.

Rounding the corner, she saw Barson locked in a deadly combat with his friend Larn. Two other men were lying on the floor, surrounded by sand and blood. As she opened her mouth to scream Barson's name, she saw both men slump to the floor, a pool of blood spreading out from under their bodies.

"No!" Augusta had no idea how she had ended up across the room, but suddenly she was there, kneeling next to Barson. She could hear his ragged breathing, and tears of gratitude ran down her face. He wasn't dead. Not yet, at least. Her hands shaking, she pulled out her cards and began working on a healing spell.

It was a race against time. The spell needed to be precise, but with every second that passed, Barson was losing more and more blood. With her enhanced hearing, Augusta could hear his heart laboring harder and harder as his lungs struggled to draw in enough air. She tried to focus, to concentrate, but tears kept blurring her vision, her cards getting smeared with blood that seemed to be coming from everywhere.

With one last stuttering beat, Barson's heart stopped.

Augusta wanted to scream. *No.* She wouldn't let this happen. She couldn't. The spell was not yet complete, but she began loading it into the Stone anyway, using one hand to feed the cards and the other to write the last few lines.

The spell was finally complete.

She waited with baited breath for the wounds to begin to heal, but nothing happened.

Her entire body began to shake. Crawling on top of Barson, Augusta began pressing methodically on his chest with her hands, trying to get the heart muscle working again. Leaning down, she placed her mouth over his and began to blow air into his lungs. Push, blow. Push, blow. Augusta had never done this sort of healing by hand before. She wasn't sure if she was doing it correctly, but that didn't matter. She couldn't give up, couldn't let Barson die. She felt like she was doing it forever, but only moments must've passed before she heard a faint heartbeat.

Laughing and crying, she sat back and watched as the spell began to take effect, the wounds slowly mending as the damaged tissue began to knit together from the inside out.

When Barson was fully healed, she turned her attention to Larn. The soldier was sprawled unconscious on the floor, his jaw broken. Feeling utterly drained, Augusta nonetheless managed to write another spell for him—both to clear his mind of Ganir's influence and to heal his injuries.

When she was finished, she had no energy left for the other two men. One of them appeared to be long dead, anyway, while the other one was simply knocked out. Feeling like she was going to pass out herself at any moment, Augusta headed wearily back to her quarters. There was a Council meeting coming up in a couple of hours, and she desperately needed to get some rest. She couldn't afford to be less than her best at that meeting.

Her last thought before she collapsed in her own bed was that she should've killed Ganir after all.

CHAPTER THIRTY-ONE

※ BARSON ※

Barson woke up on the floor of the training room covered in bloody sand. To his surprise, nothing hurt too much—or at all, he realized, rising slowly to his feet.

Hearing a groan, he turned and saw Larn crouched over Zanil, who appeared to be slowly regaining consciousness.

"Explain yourself," Barson said hoarsely, looking around for his sword. Spotting it on the floor, he walked over to pick it up, even though it seemed like Larn had come to his senses.

Larn turned toward him. "Barson, I don't know what happened." His eyes were wide, his face unusually pale. "Were we attacked?"

"*I* was attacked." Barson gave his friend a narrow-eyed glare. "What were you thinking? Were you insane?"

"What do you mean?" Larn looked confused now. "The last thing I remember was drinking some wine in the tavern. Did I have too much? How did we end up here in the Tower, and what happened to us?"

Barson inhaled deeply. It was as he had suspected. Somebody—and he had a very good idea who—had turned his own men against him. His insides churning with anger, Barson proceeded to explain everything to Larn, including his suspicions about mind sorcery.

"So what now?" Larn asked when Barson was done. His eyebrows were drawn into a worried frown. "If Ganir knows that we're alive, that changes everything."

"Not necessarily," Barson said. "There is a Council meeting coming up tonight. Vashel figured out how to listen in on it. I don't want to do anything rash until we know more."

As they were walking out of the room, with Barson aiding Zanil and Larn carrying out Pugan's body, it occurred to Barson that he should still be bleeding right now.

Someone had healed his injuries.

The question was: who?

CHAPTER THIRTY-TWO

※ GALA ※

Gala stumbled into Liva's house, pushed by Blaise. Quickly catching herself, she turned to say something, and saw Blaise collapse as a large piece of hail slammed into the side of his head.

Her heart appeared to stop beating. She was not fully cognizant of reaching for him and dragging his body into the room, but she must have—because she found herself crouched over Blaise's unconscious form in the middle of the kitchen, surrounded by Maya, Esther, and the villagers.

He was bleeding profusely, a pool of red spreading out from the wound on his head, and Gala knew she had to do something to help him. However, her panic didn't allow her to think clearly, her emotions chaotic and out of control. The hail battered the house with deadly force, and she could hear the women screaming as some parts of the roof started caving in. She knew she needed to calm down, to pull herself together, but all she could see was Blaise and his terrifying injury.

"Gala, I need you to focus. Do you hear me? Please, focus." It was Liva, her voice even and soothing, penetrating the fog of anguished fear clouding Gala's mind. Taking a deep breath, Gala tried to follow her advice, realizing that she was on the verge of losing control of her powers again—something that could be disastrous for all concerned.

"Gala, it's all right—he's breathing." It was Esther speaking to her this time, and Gala felt her panic recede further. Reaching deep within herself, she called upon everything she'd learned thus far and everything Blaise had taught her, and simultaneously began working on two spells.

A minute later, the barrage of deadly hail stopped as Gala's replacement shield went up. At the same time, Blaise's injured head began to mend as she implemented a more targeted version of the healing spell she'd inadvertently used on the soldiers before. He still remained unconscious, but she knew he would soon be all right.

Shaking, Gala rose to her feet. She hadn't realized that fear could be so paralyzing—that nearly losing Blaise could cloud her mind to such an extent. She never wanted him to be in danger again. She would never allow him to be in danger again.

"Gala, do you remember approximately how many people were in the other house?" Liva asked, her tone filled with anxiety now that the immediate danger to Blaise was over. "Did everyone make it to safety?"

"There were twenty-eight adults and five children," Gala replied, instantly recalling the layout of the house she'd just left and mentally counting the people there.

"Are you sure?" Liva asked, a worried frown on her face. "Only thirty-three people there?"

Gala nodded. She was sure. "How many should there have been?"

"At least forty," Liva said in despair. "I think there must be a family or two still out there, beyond the protection you and Blaise set up for us."

Gala's blood turned to ice. There were people outside the shield? If they were still alive, they wouldn't be for much longer—unless she could get them to safety right away.

Running to the front door, she opened it again and stepped out. She could hear Blaise starting to wake up, but the last thing she wanted was to put him in danger again—or to have him prevent her from helping those people. She had to act, and she had to do it now, before it was too late.

Stepping out into the street, Gala cast a quick glance at the village. Several houses nearby were on fire from the lightning strikes, while many others were in shambles from the wind and hail. Thunder and lightning struck over and over again in an endless assault on the senses, but worst of all was something she could see in the far distance—a wide, funnel-like column connecting the ground to the sky.

A tornado. She'd briefly read about them in one of the books.

She could feel it coming closer, sensed its destructive power. Even with the noise from the relentlessly battering hail, she could hear the roar of the approaching monster.

Two monsters, in fact, she realized with a bone-deep chill as she saw another twister further to the east. Then she spotted a third one and a fourth . . . It was a wall of tornados—and they all seemed to be headed straight for the village.

A strange clarity settled over Gala's mind. She began doing calculations—the air pressure, the temperature, the direction and speed of all the different winds . . . Everything pointed to one conclusion. Once the tornadoes reached them, the shield would be destroyed in seconds—and so would any subsequent ones she could put up.

Unless she came up with another way to protect them, they would all die.

Sitting down on the ground, Gala began to breathe the way Blaise had taught her. As her heartbeat slowed, she could feel herself starting to float like before, but this time she did not stop it.

Instead, she focused on her first spell.

She began by trying to change the temperature. It required making the molecules of air move faster in a given space—except the space had to be quite large to make any difference to the storm. As she worked on it, she floated closer to the shield, and her mind enabled her to open it and close it within seconds, letting her body pass through. Now she was fully exposed to the elements, and she could feel the effect of the temperature change in the air. Instead of striking her skin, the hail was melting, turning into cold water all around her. It was already an improvement, but her work had just begun.

She was now high enough in the air that she could see the village laid out far below, with the twisters rapidly approaching it. To stave off fear and solidify her concentration, Gala closed her eyes. She could feel the sizzle of electricity in the air, smell the ozone from the lightning strikes, but she ignored all that, focusing only on the task at hand.

This was going to be difficult, yet it was the only way to save the village. Swiftly running through the thousands of necessary calculations in her mind, Gala opened her eyes and unleashed the force that was needed to counter the storm.

The air began moving around her, each current and counter-current melding in perfect harmony. Each blast of the storm winds encountered one of her own, the forces neutralizing each other until it was as if the wind wasn't there. It was a slow and laborious process, but Gala could feel it working. Within minutes, the heavy clouds shifted, creating an opening in the storm—an opening that encompassed the area around the village.

Everywhere else the storm raged as before, but the skies above the village began to clear, a sliver of star-dotted sky peeking through the darkness.

CHAPTER THIRTY-THREE

❋ AUGUSTA ❋

"Where is Ganir?" Jandison asked loudly, addressing the rest of the Council. It was their regularly scheduled meeting, and no one was ever late without a good excuse.

Augusta sat quietly, not wanting to draw attention to herself. The last thing she wanted was to be implicated in Ganir's disappearance in any way.

"Does anyone know where he is?" Jandison repeated, looking around the room.

"I might," Dania said, fumbling with her bag. "I have a locator spell on him. We placed those on each other a few years ago just in case. I don't ever check it, but I should be able to do so."

Augusta felt all blood drain from her face. There was a good chance that Ganir had died during her teleportation experiment. And if so, Dania would find out, as the locator spell was only active while the person it was placed on was alive.

"Does anyone have a map of Koldun?" Dania asked, looking up from her bag, and Augusta watched in horror as Moriner handed the requested object to Dania.

The old woman immediately began muttering the words of a revelation spell—a quick oral spell that was required to show the location on the map. A few minutes later, a bright blue dot appeared on the map, right in the middle of Ganir's territory.

Augusta let out the breath she'd been holding. Ganir was alive after all. Her teleportation experiment had worked.

"It looks like he went home," Dania said, looking puzzled. "Why would he do that without telling anyone?"

"Maybe because he disagrees about the latest vote, and he's showing his disdain for the Council by not showing up?" Kelvin suggested, leaning forward in his chair.

"I'm sure Ganir has a good reason for not being here," Augusta said graciously, recovering from her earlier panic. In a way, Dania had done her a favor. Nobody should suspect any foul play now.

"Either way, the protocol dictates that in the absence of one of the members, the meeting shall proceed as normal," Jandison said, his eyes gleaming. "We can't let Ganir's reluctance deter us from doing the right thing."

"No, we cannot," Kelvin concurred. "We need to take care of this threat once and for all."

"We don't even know where this creature is," Dania objected, "so what are we supposed to do? Scour all of Koldun looking for it?"

"Dania," Augusta said slowly, thinking about how to best bring this up, "can you modify the time parameter of the revelation spell to show Ganir's location last week? Perhaps there is some other reason he's not here today."

Dania frowned. "What are you trying to imply?"

"She's right," Jandison said, apparently catching on. "We all know how close Ganir was to Dasbraw's sons. Why don't you modify those parameters, Dania, as Augusta suggested?" Augusta noticed that Jandison seemed to be sitting up straighter, his posture and demeanor more confident than usual. He was assuming the role of the Council Leader, she realized with some amusement.

Still, she could see that Dania wasn't about to give in. The old woman needed some nudging. "Be careful with the map when you do it," Augusta said softly, knowing that Dania would be the only one who would understand the reference. "Old documents can be so fragile."

Dania opened her mouth, then closed it. She understood all right. If she didn't do as Augusta asked, the scrolls given to her by Augusta—the ones with Lenard's writings—might suffer. It was quite a dilemma—violate Ganir's privacy or let the precious scrolls be destroyed—and Augusta waited to see what the old woman would do.

"Fine," Dania said, abruptly giving in. "Let me see

what I can do."

Another revelation spell later, the map showed a series of blue dots mapping Ganir's location. There was a clear trail to the mountains in the west, a trail that stopped in what appeared to be a canyon.

"How interesting," Kelvin said, a wide smile splitting his face. "Looks like Ganir has done quite a bit of travel lately."

"Indeed." Jandison looked positively gleeful. "I can't think of any reason for Ganir to leave Turingrad . . . except one."

"He must've been in contact with Blaise all along," Augusta said, as though the idea was just occurring to her. "And if that's the case, perhaps that's where the creature is hiding. Right there, somewhere around that canyon."

Dania pursed her lips in irritation, but didn't say anything. Augusta knew she'd put the old woman in an untenable situation, but she didn't care. The important thing was that the Council had arrived at the exact conclusion Augusta had been hoping they would reach: that Ganir was a traitor who knew the location of their enemies.

"So what do we do now?" Moriner asked, glancing at Jandison. "If that's indeed where they are, then we need to figure out a plan of action. We all saw how powerful the creature is. We can't show up unprepared."

"No, we can't," Augusta agreed. "In fact, I've already started thinking of some spells."

"We need something powerful, and we need a

good plan for coordination," Kelvin jumped in, stating the obvious.

"I have something we could use," Augusta said, barely able to suppress her nervous excitement. "I call it the fusion spell. It's powerful—much more powerful than anything you've seen before. If done correctly, it would allow us to split water into oxygen and hydrogen, and then make the hydrogen fuse with itself, becoming helium . . ." She then proceeded to explain what such an event would mean, and how the power unleashed would be akin to the power that fueled the sun and the other stars.

The silence that followed her explanation was deafening.

"But wait," Gina said, staring at Augusta, "given your own math, the energy released at such an event would be unfathomable. Surely it would kill us along with the creature."

Augusta nodded. She couldn't fault her young colleague for being afraid. Unchecked, this spell could do more than kill them. If her calculations were correct, this kind of spell was capable of destroying half of Koldun. "I have a way to contain it in a small area," she told Gina. "It would be a complex defensive spell, but I'm confident that it could be done, and we could ensure our safety."

"We need to study this more," Jandison said. "Given the magnitude of the destructive power unleashed by this fusion spell of yours, we should only use this measure if we have no other choice."

"Agreed," Moriner said.

"Of course," Augusta said. "I would be happy to use more conventional means against the creature. Does anyone have any suggestions?"

"Well," Jandison said, "here's what I would propose . . . "

They proceeded to work out a plan that sounded like it should succeed, and Augusta departed the meeting feeling much more confident about their prospects. If all went well, her fusion spell might not be necessary, and she certainly wouldn't need to implement her plan C.

CHAPTER THIRTY-FOUR

※ BARSON ※

"Were you in the training room of the Tower?" Barson asked Dara, sitting down at her table. "Or did you put some kind of a protective spell on me, something that can heal injuries as they occur?"

"What? What kind of spell would that be?" She gave him a surprised look. "I've never heard of a preemptive healing spell. Why do you ask?"

Frowning, Barson told her what happened with Larn and the others. As he continued talking, her face turned pale.

"One of you could've died," she whispered, her gaze filled with horror. "Barson, thank you for not killing him. I've heard rumors about Ganir's mind control tricks, but I never thought he could be capable of something like this."

Barson waved his hand dismissively. "Of course. I would never kill Larn. But if you didn't heal me," he said, returning to his original concern, "then who did?"

"Augusta?" Dara suggested. "Or maybe one of our allies—though I don't know what any of them would be doing in the Guard barracks."

"Well, it certainly wasn't Vashel," Barson said, thinking of the conversation he'd just had with his ally. "He told me what he overheard from the Council meeting, and I'm sure he would've mentioned it if he'd done me such a huge favor—"

"What did he say?" Dara interrupted, and Barson filled her in on Ganir's absence and the Council's plans regarding the creature.

"The spell Augusta came up with sounds very dangerous," Dara said, her eyes wide with awe and reluctant admiration. "But I have to say, your lover is bright. Very, very bright."

"Also very stubborn," Barson said, beginning to get angry again as he remembered the fight he'd just had with Augusta. "And very arrogant when it comes to her own abilities."

At Dara's questioning look, he filled his sister in on what happened, explaining how their argument had spiraled out of control before he could talk to her about his plans for the Tower.

"So what are you going to do about her?" Dara asked when he was done.

"I don't know," Barson admitted. He hated the fact that he couldn't make Augusta stay in the Tower, where he could ensure her safety. Like it or not, with the way things currently stood, he couldn't force her to do anything. "I don't like the idea of her going after this creature, but I don't know how to prevent her," he said in frustration. If Augusta were a regular woman, it would be easy; he could lock her in a room and keep her here. But with a sorceress, things were more complicated.

Dara gave him a sympathetic smile. "That's what you get for falling for a sorceress," she said, echoing his thoughts. "If she wants to go, you have to let her . . . and hope for the best. If anyone can land on her feet, it's Augusta. Besides, there is no other choice. We're too close to our goal for you to get distracted by this matter."

Barson nodded, his jaw clenched tight. He knew his sister was right. He couldn't waste his energy fighting with Augusta right now, not when they had so much at stake.

"Yes," he agreed, forcing his thoughts away from his lover. "We don't have any time to waste. According to Vashel, the Council is departing for the mountains tomorrow—which means we need to finalize our plans tonight."

CHAPTER THIRTY-FIVE

※ BLAISE ※

Slowly regaining consciousness, Blaise became aware of the fact that he felt amazingly good—a fact that surprised him, given that his last memory was that of the storm. Opening his eyes, he saw Maya, Esther, and a number of villagers crowded around him, their faces full of concern.

"What happened?" he asked, becoming aware of an unusual silence. The deafening din from the storm was gone. He could still hear an occasional rumble of thunder, but it was distant now, as though the storm had passed. His heart jumped as he realized that Gala was nowhere to be seen. "Where is she?"

"You should take a look outside, Blaise," Maya said, a strange expression on her face.

Frowning, Blaise rose to his feet. The people stepped back, letting him pass, and he made his way to the front door. Carefully opening it, he peered outside, expecting to be slammed with rain or wind, but all was calm. Had Gala managed to put up the shield?

Stepping outside, he looked up at the sky—and what he saw there made him stop breathing for a moment.

The skies directly above were clear—but on the edges, the storm continued to rage. He could see the lightning bolts piercing the dark clouds in a never-ending assault and the twisters in the distance—but none of that touched the village or the area immediately surrounding it.

The only mark in the moonlit sky was a small dot near the edge of the black clouds.

Hearing footsteps behind him, Blaise turned to see Maya and Esther standing there, looking up at the sky. "Where is Gala?" he demanded. "What's going on?"

"Don't you see?" Esther said reverently, pointing up. "She's there."

Looking up, Blaise peered closer at the dot he'd noticed before. He couldn't tell what it was from here—but that was an easy fix. Rushing back into the house, he grabbed one of his prepared spells and loaded it into the Stone. A second later, his vision was eagle-sharp, and his hearing was magnified.

Running out onto the street again, he looked up at the sky, his heart hammering in his chest.

The dot was indeed Gala. She was floating in the air, a calm, almost blissful expression on her face.

Her eyes were closed, and her lips were curved in a small smile. She looked beautiful and strikingly peaceful—and she was the one who was controlling the storm, he realized with a chill running down his spine.

His mind reeled from the magnitude of what he was witnessing. The complexity was beyond his comprehension. She wasn't merely creating weather patterns; she was directly counteracting the storm. It seemed . . . impossible.

For a moment, the urge to go to her and bring her down to safety was almost overwhelming, but Blaise restrained himself, knowing that breaking her concentration now could be deadly. She was in control at the moment, and she needed to stay that way for everyone's safety, his own concern for her notwithstanding.

Bringing his attention back to the ground, he saw the same awe and shock reflected on the faces of villagers who had come out of the house. "She's amazing, isn't she?" Liva breathed, staring up at the sky, and Blaise nodded.

He knew that a new legend had been born.

* * *

With the immediate danger from the storm averted, Blaise focused on helping the village manage the devastation left behind. They started off with a search for survivors among those who hadn't made it to safety before the worst of the storm hit. With his enhanced hearing, Blaise was able to locate five people buried beneath the rubble of their homes and heal their injuries. In the meantime, the villagers found an old couple that were already beyond his help, having been crushed by their falling roof.

Once everyone was accounted for, they began assessing the damage done to the homes. Aside from Liva's house and that of her neighbors, no other dwelling was habitable. Several houses had burned down from the lightning strikes, while hail had destroyed the roofs of most others.

It was an utter disaster.

"It will take us years to recover from this," Liva whispered, her eyes swimming with tears as she gazed at the piles of rubble where houses once stood. "In all my years here, I have never seen a storm that bad. Usually there is some damage, but we've never lost so much."

Blaise's heart squeezed with pity. He couldn't even imagine what these people had to be thinking, how devastated they must be. What bothered him the most was the defeated look on these stoic people's faces. They had survived so much, only to be forced to start all over again.

As he looked around, an idea began to brew in his mind. He and Gala would not be able to stay for much longer, but before they left, there was something he could do to ensure the villagers wouldn't suffer like this again. He could use sorcery to help them rebuild—and make sure that the resulting houses were far stronger than the weak structures they just lost. The houses in Turingrad were usually made of stone, and they were much sturdier because of that.

It didn't take much time to gather the rocks of just the right size and shape. The spell to hollow them out was fairly easy—the inside hole was a half-sphere, the code for which was straightforward. The door opening was trickier. Still, though far from a stonemason, Blaise managed to spell a fairly even opening leading to the empty space inside every rock.

What he now had were miniature rock houses.

It was time for another spell. This one was more nuanced, as he had to have the molecules of the rocks multiplied in just the right amount and alignment. After an hour of concentrated coding, Blaise walked over to what used to be the village square, placed his rock in the middle, and stepped back, loading the spell card into his Interpreter Stone.

A minute later, a large stone structure stood there. It was not the most aesthetically pleasing house, but it was made of solid rock—and thus far more durable than anything made of wood. A few more spells took care of carving out the windows.

The first house was done.

Now Blaise had only about twenty more to go.

* * *

Several hours later, exhausted from non-stop coding,

Blaise looked up to check on Gala. She was still floating there, her eyes closed. However, the storm around the village was beginning to ease, the black clouds slowly dissipating and the lightning strikes becoming less frequent.

He had no idea how she must be feeling or the amount of effort that it took to control such a powerful force of nature. She looked peaceful enough, but he was still worried about her. At this point, however, all he could do was wait for the storm to pass and for her to descend.

As he continued making progress with the stone houses, the villagers started to gather around him, watching in amazement. "Blaise, these houses of yours are like fortresses," Ara exclaimed, walking through one of the structures. "I think they could even withstand a storm like the one we just had."

"That's the idea," Blaise replied, giving her a tired smile. "Of course, you'll still need to put up some walls inside to create multiple rooms, but at least the basic outer shell will be there. I also added a few scent markers to the outer walls of these houses, so that should hopefully keep the bearwolves and other creatures of their ilk away from Alania."

Thinking about that reminded Blaise that he still needed to give the villagers a few spell-enhanced seeds, so they could plant some fruits and vegetables that would survive these storms. Luckily, he had a small stash of them in his house in the canyon; he'd have to remember to pick up that stash the next time he and Gala went there. He also wanted to give Liva an Interpreter Stone. That would take a while to make, but he had the materials back in the house as well.

"You're leaving soon, aren't you?" Esther asked quietly, coming up to him. He'd explained to her earlier about Ganir's visit, and she knew that he and Gala couldn't stay in the village for long.

"Yes, we have to." Blaise hesitated for a moment. "You and Maya are staying here, right?"

Esther nodded. "We're getting too old for traveling from one end of the mountains to another," she said regretfully. "And I think we could be of use to these people. They don't have any proper midwives here."

Blaise smiled at her. "Of course, I understand." He would miss the two women, but he didn't want to drag them along on their travels. As it was, they had left their comfortable lives behind because of him. "I wish we could stay as well, but I'm afraid we would be putting everyone in danger by being here. If they come looking for us, we won't go quietly, and things could get violent."

Esther's chin quivered. "Why won't they just leave you alone?" she said in frustration. "It's not like you're hurting anyone."

"They're afraid," Blaise said. "Of Gala, of the unknown."

Esther's lips tightened as she glanced up at the sky. "If they truly knew her, they would realize that it's foolish," she said vehemently. "She may be the most powerful sorceress out there, but she would never hurt anyone on purpose—especially now that she seems to know what she's doing."

Blaise nodded. "I know, but they won't listen to reason—which is why we must leave."

"When are you going to go?"

"As soon as we can," Blaise replied, looking up at Gala's tiny figure in the sky. "As soon as we possibly can."

CHAPTER THIRTY-SIX

※ GALA ※

Gala's mind was at ease. She focused on her breathing and the storm for what seemed like years, but it could just as easily have been minutes—it was hard to tell in this state. Eventually, she felt her concentration ebbing, and she slowly opened her eyes.

The storm was all but gone, with just a few stray clouds remaining in the distance. Exhaling in joyous relief, she allowed her body to slowly descend.

Looking down, she was shocked to see the village transformed. There were some kind of new structures—buildings that looked like the round pebbles she had noticed all around the village, only they were gigantic, house-sized. The villagers themselves were out on the street, watching her descend.

As she got closer, she could hear them cheering

and clapping. Blaise was standing there silently, an unreadable expression on his face.

When her feet touched the ground, he was already there, pulling her into his embrace. She could feel the tremors running through his body, and she realized that he had been afraid for her—that he worried about her as much as she worried about him. For a minute, he simply held her tightly, not saying a word, but then his arms loosened and he pulled back to meet her gaze. "How do you feel?" he asked quietly, looking at her. "You must be exhausted."

"Actually, I feel wonderful," she admitted, staring up at him. She was experiencing a strange sort of pent-up energy and excitement. She wasn't tired; instead she felt powerful, like she could move mountains or battle another storm.

Of course, part of what she was feeling had nothing to do with the aftermath of controlling the storm and everything to do with Blaise himself.

"You don't feel tired?" Blaise looked shocked. "You were up there for almost twenty hours."

Gala smiled up at him. "I actually feel better than I did before."

As Blaise stared at her in amazement, she became aware that nearly the entire village had gathered around them. Sliding her arm around Blaise's waist, she turned to face them.

Maya and Esther were watching her with pride, while others seemed to be dumbstruck with awe. For a moment, she became aware of that strange human feeling of self-consciousness, but it quickly faded, and she beamed at them, happy to see that everyone she knew was well.

"Come, let's go to my house," Blaise said, looking down at her. "If you're not tired, then I'd like to gather some of my magic supplies for our upcoming trip. Tomorrow morning we'll return here to say our goodbyes."

"We're leaving already?" Gala frowned in disappointment. She felt like she was just starting to get to know the people in this village, and she didn't want to leave. "Where are we going to go?"

"I'm not sure yet," Blaise admitted, "but I don't want to put anyone in danger by staying here. You heard what Ganir told me. We might've already overstayed our welcome."

Gala stifled her disappointment. She knew that Blaise was right; the last thing she wanted was for anyone to get hurt because of her. Besides, there could be interesting things in the world out there, and she could feel her curiosity slowly awakening as she thought about all the wonders she had yet to see.

"All right," she said, a smile reappearing on her face. "Then let's go to your house."

* * *

After checking to make sure people were settling into their new homes, they got on Blaise's chaise and flew toward the canyon. On the way there, Blaise peppered Gala with detailed questions, trying to learn how she had been able to control the storm.

Gala struggled to explain exactly how it worked. If only she could somehow make Blaise experience it for himself...And then she remembered Life Capture. Perhaps with the right spell she could actually create a droplet? She tucked the idea away for later; for now, she did her best to explain how it all hinged on being calm and in control, the way he'd taught her, plus the mathematical nature of the world.

As they reached the canyon, she saw Blaise looking down at the house with a wistful expression on his face.

"You know," she said, smiling, "wherever we end up, I can teleport the house there again."

"That's true." Blaise returned her smile. "So I will only take what is absolutely necessary for our flight."

When they landed, Gala saw that the house had survived the storm essentially undamaged. It looked like the canyon walls provided a natural shield, and she guessed that the house itself was a much sturdier structure than the villagers' former homes.

They entered the house, and Blaise went to the archive room to gather his cards and take them to his study in preparation for their trip. In the meantime, Gala wandered from room to room, remembering her first days in this world. Now looking back, she could see how much she had changed. Although not a lot of time had passed, she felt like she was a different person from the girl who'd left this very house, stubbornly determined to see the world. She was still hungry for knowledge, but she would not let that hunger separate her from Blaise again. He meant too much to her now.

Walking into one of the bedrooms, she went to stand by the tinted window, gazing out at the night sky. It was almost a full moon, and everything appeared slightly surreal, with the light and shadows intermingling in strange and beautiful ways.

Hearing footsteps behind her, she turned and saw Blaise standing in the doorway, watching her. The moonlight reflected off the masculine features of his face, and there was an unreadable look in his eyes.

Slowly he walked over to her, and she could feel it—the magnetic pull of their connection, the way her skin warmed at his proximity. He looked at her, his eyes dark in the shadows, and then he leaned down to kiss her, his hands gently holding her shoulders.

It was both familiar and different, the feel of his lips on her own. She could feel her heartbeat accelerating, her breathing coming faster as heat surged through her. It was overwhelming, and she tried to calm her volatile emotions, fearing what might happen if she lost control.

Blaise raised his head, still holding her. "I love you, Gala," he said softly, and she felt like she would burst from the overabundance of emotion. She wanted to tell him how she felt, and suddenly she knew of a way—a way that resembled how Life Capture droplets worked. Her mind must've been dwelling on this process, and now in a flash, she had it. No physical droplets would be required. Reaching out, she touched Blaise's mind with her own, letting him feel her thoughts, her emotions.

Blaise's eyes went wide and unseeing for a moment, but then he appeared to come back to himself. He didn't say anything, but when he reached for her again, she felt his need, his desperation to be closer.

Without further words, Blaise picked her up and carried her to the bed. Her heart started pounding like mad. She'd read about what was going to happen, but she had no idea what it would actually be like.

Placing her on her feet, Blaise took off her clothes, his hands tender, yet impatient. She was reminded of that day when she first met him, and how the sight of her body flustered him. There was none of that now. His touch was sure and knowing, his eyes gleaming in the moonlight. Gala wanted him naked too, but she didn't bother using her hands to undress him; a wish and a moment of focus caused all his clothes to teleport onto the floor.

They kissed and caressed each other's bodies for what seemed like a long time, causing her desire to intensify further. By the time they joined as one, she couldn't think of anything but the pleasure she was experiencing. It was so beautiful that she was sure some sorcery was at play. During the most intense moments, she could also feel what he felt—and she could sense that he felt her emotions. She was not in control of this magic, but she knew she was somehow responsible for it.

Suddenly, she had a flashback to before she first appeared in his lab. She was floating effortlessly, a pure mind in the Spell Realm. She remembered it clearly, and she knew that somehow, something about what was currently happening helped increase the span of her consciousness. It was as though hidden parts of her mind wanted to fully immerse themselves in this blissful experience, and as a penance, they gave up control.

As her mind expanded, with each increment, she felt her focus on the pleasure intensifying. With each increment, she thought she'd reached the limit and would not be able to feel greater ecstasy—yet each time she was proven wrong. Another part of her subconscious mind would yield, and the feeling would, unbelievably, grow stronger.

When the intensity reached an unbearable peak, she saw a vision. She saw herself and Blaise from a distance, as though she was observing them from afar. She saw the things he was doing to her, and she to him. She saw the bed floating above ground. She saw random objects take flight all around them. And then she could see a bright, blinding light form around the embracing figures. The light got brighter and brighter, but rather than being blinding, it was filling her with a sense of beauty and awe. It radiated calm, peace, and unbelievable pleasure. The brightness of the light grew and grew, until she felt like she was staring at the blinding beauty of the sun.

Then, suddenly, the light exploded as the pleasure rose to unbearable heights—and she felt her consciousness ebb, her senses overwhelmed by the experience.

CHAPTER THIRTY-SEVEN

※ BARSON ※

Barson looked over the map of the Tower and the list of names Dara had put together. These people had been deemed useless—too stubborn or too volatile to be trusted to support Barson's cause. They would be eliminated right away, while other sorcerers would be given a chance to surrender and align themselves with Barson and his new allies.

To double-check all the logistics, he went through the plan again with Dara and Larn. "Any questions?" Barson asked when he finished.

Dara shook her head. "No. But there is something you should know—a strange thing that I heard from one of the apprentices in the Tower."

"What's that?"

"Blaise's house in Turingrad is missing," she said. "Apparently, there is only a hole in the ground where it used to stand. All the townspeople are talking about it."

"What?" Larn looked surprised. "Somebody knocked down that sorcerer's house?"

"No," Dara said patiently. "They didn't knock it down. It's just gone. Vanished."

"Do you think the Council is responsible for this?" Barson asked, puzzled.

"I have no idea," Dara replied. "It's just bizarre."

Barson frowned, trying to figure out why someone would make a house disappear. It was undoubtedly an act of sorcery, but the motivations behind it were unclear.

"Dara, are you sure none of our new allies will betray us?" Larn asked, changing the topic. "After all, it's one thing to have ambition, and another thing entirely to participate in killing people they know."

"Well, it's not like they'll be killing with their own hands," Dara retorted. "They will simply be supplying us with the spells and standing by as backup."

"She's right," Barson said, dismissing the mystery of the missing house. "Besides, they are in too deep at this point. As far as the Council is concerned, they're already traitors. From their perspective, even if they double-cross us, the Council will execute them anyway, for what they have done thus far."

Except the Council might not exist soon, he thought. Instead of glee, this idea filled Barson with dread. He should've found a way to reason with Augusta after all, to get her to stay behind. But it was too late now. The Council had just departed from the

Tower.

Dara nodded, bringing Barson out of his dark musings. "Yes, exactly. They have as much to gain as we do. In the new order, they will be the king's respected advisors, instead of bending over backwards for the little bit of recognition the Council chooses to grant them now." Her tone held familiar bitterness.

Pushing all thoughts of Augusta aside, Barson patted Dara's shoulder in a gesture of silent support. His sister wasn't unique in her feelings. There were many talented sorcerers who had trouble gaining the recognition and respect they felt they deserved. While the current system was supposedly meritocratic, two centuries of political games and the growing longevity of the current Council members meant that there was little room to move up beyond the senior acolyte level. The Council didn't help matters by treating these people as their lackeys, either. For every success story like that of Augusta, there were dozens of bitter, disappointed acolytes. For all their supposed intellect, these sorcerers knew little of how to rule, Barson thought with contempt. He had no doubt he would do a much better job.

"I also chose them carefully," Dara continued, looking at Larn. "Each of our allies was interviewed while on Life Capture, and they had no thoughts of treachery."

"Still, those cowards might change their minds now that the plan is going into action," Larn muttered under his breath, looking unconvinced.

Barson knew that his friend was fully on board, but it was just like Larn to worry right before a big event. His argumentative nature tended to surface at these times as well.

"They will not," Dara said, reaching over to take Larn's hand and give it a reassuring squeeze. "I can promise you that. Besides without the Council, these sorcerers are like children without a parent. They're not used to thinking for themselves."

"And by the time the Council returns," Barson said quietly, "if they return at all—we will be ready."

CHAPTER THIRTY-EIGHT

※ GALA ※

Waking up in the middle of the night, Gala became aware that her mind was inside her body again—and heard Blaise's quiet, even breathing. He was sleeping beside her, his long body stretched out on the other side of the bed.

She lay there silently, thinking. None of the books she'd read spoke of anything close to what she had experienced. It was mind-altering in a way—mind-expanding, even. It was as though the incredible intensity of pleasure helped her reach new, as-yet-unknown parts of herself. It was strange, yet exciting, and she couldn't wait to explore it further.

Shifting closer to Blaise, she kissed him gently on the cheek and went back to sleep, her arm draped over his waist.

* * *

The next time she woke up, it was early morning. Stretching, Gala smiled and quietly got up, not wanting to wake Blaise yet. And in that moment, she felt it.

A sense of danger—of an impending threat.

They had been found.

Her blood froze in her veins. They were coming after her and Blaise. They wanted to hurt, maybe even kill, the man she loved.

She wouldn't let that happen. She couldn't stand the thought of putting him in danger, of seeing him get hurt again.

She would protect him at all costs.

CHAPTER THIRTY-NINE

※ BLAISE ※

Hearing Gala's movements, Blaise woke up. The events of the prior night invaded his sleep-fogged mind, and a wide smile stretched his lips. The term 'lovemaking' couldn't possibly describe what took place last night. Something transcendent happened between them, something that he had never experienced before. He had felt what Gala was feeling, had joined with her on a level that went beyond the physical. He had gotten a glimpse of her mind, and he saw an incredible depth there, a multitude of layers that were overwhelming in their subtle beauty.

Her getting up interrupted his recollections. Opening his eyes, he saw a naked Gala stealthily heading for the door.

"Where are you going?" he asked drowsily, propping himself up on one elbow.

She gave him a slightly guilty look. "You should sleep some more," she said, and he caught a strange note of tension in her voice. "I'll be back soon."

"You're going out there naked?" He sat up, realizing that something was amiss.

She paused, then looked down, as though just realizing that she wasn't wearing clothes. A second later, she was wearing a simple white dress. Then, without saying another word to Blaise, she slipped out the door.

Blaise jumped out of bed and swiftly pulled on his own clothes. He had a very bad feeling about this.

As he approached the door, he felt something strange. Some spell just hit him, he realized, feeling a slight buzz in his head. He wasn't sure what it was, other than it was some sort of mental magic.

Rushing toward the door, he suddenly stopped when he reached the doorway. It was as if a block had formed, not letting him get through. His body felt heavy and unwieldy, outside of his control. Someone—most likely Gala—had cast a spell that prevented him from going outside. She must've done it to protect him from whatever was out there—a protection that he did not need or want.

Furious, Blaise tried to leave again and again, only to be met with the same results. He simply couldn't take a step beyond the room; his mind refused to let him.

And then he heard the first loud noise. The house shook from the impact, and he almost lost his footing. His stomach clenched with a mix of debilitating fear and rage. Whatever the danger was, Gala was facing it on her own, while he was stuck in the room like some helpless acolyte.

Turning, Blaise cast a frantic glance around the room, searching for his Stone. It was nowhere to be seen. He hadn't brought it with him into the bedroom last evening. Cursing under his breath, he hurried to the window, desperate to see what was happening. The tinted glass made everything appear hazy. His frustration growing, Blaise grabbed the nearest nightstand and smashed it against the window, shattering the glass into bits.

Now he could see outside. His vision was still sharper than usual from the enhancement spell he'd used during the storm, and as he peered into the canyon, a flash of colorful light in the distance caught his gaze. Frowning, Blaise tried to figure out what it was, and at that moment, he saw a familiar figure on the other side of the canyon.

It was Moriner, one of the Council members.

The Council had found them—and Gala was facing them on her own, having locked him in this room for his own protection.

Fury and dread coiled in his chest, making Blaise feel like he was suffocating. He needed to get out of the house, and he needed to do it now.

Approaching the bedroom door again, Blaise tried to clear his mind in an effort to get rid of whatever mental block Gala had placed in his way. Don't think about it, just walk out, he told himself, stepping toward the doorway.

It didn't work. He had a sense of pushing against a physical barrier—a barrier that was as impenetrable as any wall.

Seething, Blaise began to pace, occasionally pausing to glance outside.

Suddenly, he had an idea. Gala had prevented him from walking out, but had she thought far enough to prevent him from teleporting out? Looking outside, he tried to calculate the distance. This spell would be dangerous, particularly since he was going to have to do it the old-fashioned verbal way. If Gala hadn't been in trouble, he wouldn't have risked it.

Inhaling deeply, he forced himself to concentrate on remembering the complex arcane code necessary to implement the spell. He'd had it memorized before, for voting purposes on the Council, and now he was glad of that fact.

Once he had done some preliminary calculations, he began reciting the spell. He wished he had hours to triple-check everything, but there was no time for such caution. He had to act now.

As he was getting to the end of the spell, just as he was about to say the coordinates, his tongue froze. Blaise nearly growled in frustration. Gala's spell must have been thorough enough to account for the teleporting possibility.

An even louder sound came from the outside, causing his chest to tighten with fear. Were the mountains breaking apart?

Grimly determined, Blaise tried the teleportation spell again. This time he changed the coordinates from a spot just outside the house to inside the downstairs hallway.

It worked without a hitch. Just as he finished the Interpreter litany, Blaise found himself downstairs.

His intuition had been right: Gala's spell was not nuanced enough to prevent him from teleporting within the house.

Without much hope, he ran to the front door. Opening it, he tried to step outside, but the same force as before halted him in the doorway. He was still condemned to be inside after all—but at least now he had access to his Stone and much greater visibility into what was happening in the canyon.

And what was happening was his worst nightmare.

CHAPTER FORTY

✳ GALA ✳

As Gala exited the house, she assessed the situation at hand. While the canyon itself appeared empty, she was able to spot a few small figures at the top, positioned strategically all around the canyon walls.

They were surrounded by the Council.

Gala's heartbeat accelerated. She had to lead them away from the house—and from Blaise—as fast as she could.

Their first spell reached her as she half-ran, half-teleported toward the other end of the canyon. There was a powerful rumble deep within the earth, and a huge chunk of rock under her feet became liquid lava. For a moment, all she could feel was searing pain, accompanied by the sickening smell of burning flesh, but then Gala's mind reacted defensively, changing the rocks back to their original cooled state.

She was now standing on a patch of solid lava, her feet already beginning to heal.

Panting, she looked up at her attackers and saw the light of the morning sun glinting off several Interpreter Stones. She felt both angry and resolute. She didn't want to be responsible for any more deaths, but this was not a confrontation she could run from. The Council would come after them, again and again, no matter where they went. The only way to end this was to show them the futility of violence. Gala just needed to make certain she didn't lose control in the process.

She started relaxing the way Blaise had taught her. As her mind began clearing of worries, the next attack reached her.

This time, it was heat energy. Gala felt it gathering around her, about to be unleashed in a brutal explosion, and she stopped it, dissipating it with ease.

At the same time, she realized that she needed a strategy. A spell idea came to her. She would do unto them what they did unto her. Whatever someone cast upon her would get reflected and redirected toward its source. The beauty of the spell was that she would not be personally responsible for any harm that came to her attackers; they would be hurting themselves by trying to hurt *her*.

Quickly figuring out the logistics of the spell, Gala put it in place around her, like an offensive shield. She would still need to be vigilant, but now she could focus on remaining calm.

She was immediately glad she took this

precaution. The next spell was as unfair of a move as anything she could've expected.

A swarm of birds blocked out the sky. Of numerous different species, from pigeons to hawks, they were all flying her way. Gala was not sure what she would have done without her reflective spell, as she would've been loath to hurt these innocent living creatures. Now, however, whoever controlled these birds' minds was in for a surprise.

As the birds crossed a certain threshold of proximity to Gala, her reflective spell started working, and the flight path of the birds changed. At first they flew east, then northeast, then aimlessly around the canyon—as though the source of the spell was moving about. Feeling pity for the poor creatures, Gala freed them from the spell, and they began flying away.

She relaxed again, going so far as to close her eyes. Now that she was reasonably well protected, she needed to check on how Blaise was doing. Gently she reached for him, trying to touch his mind as she had last night. She had never been able to do that before, but their joining had changed something, establishing an even deeper connection between them, and she felt like reaching him now might be possible.

And she was right. Though she could not completely read his mind, she felt echoes of whatever emotions he was feeling. Blaise was not happy with her. In fact, he was so angry that she found his emotions distracting to her calm state of mind. Not wanting to lose control, she tried to dull the connection a bit. Blaise would be in the background of her mind, she decided, so she could keep a mental eye on him this way. In the meantime, she would focus on other matters.

Thinking back to the birds, she wondered why their flight pattern had been so erratic.

Suddenly, she felt Blaise's emotions changing from frustration to fear. Her heart jumping in response, Gala opened her eyes and saw a rockslide heading for her. Relieved, she realized that Blaise was afraid for *her*, that it was his worry she was sensing. It was needless worry, she thought, her mind still dwelling on the puzzle of the birds' unsteady flight.

As expected, the rockslide heading for her changed direction, Gala's reflective spell pushing it back toward its origin. Amplifying her vision, Gala watched the rocks go up the canyon wall toward a small figure—a figure that immediately disappeared from that spot.

Now it was clear to her. The person who had cast the rockslide spell had teleported to another location. The rockslide hit the original spot where her opponent had stood, but didn't do him any harm.

She had not calibrated her reflective spell finely enough to account for teleportation, Gala realized, finally comprehending why the birds had been flying so erratically. The Council members were teleporting around the canyon to avoid being hurt by her spells.

At that moment, a barrage of attacks came at Gala from all different directions, distracting her from that thought. Lightning bolts, ground shaking—it was like she was back in the middle of the storm, and it was becoming impossible to breathe calmly through it all. Gala wanted to yell at them. Didn't they realize that if they upset her, it might mean their own doom? That if she lost control, it could end badly? On some level, she understood that retaliating at them directly would not be all that different from what her reflective spell was doing, but she still preferred it this way.

All of sudden, the attacks stopped. Before Gala could relax, however, she felt echoes of Blaise beginning some kind of struggle in the house.

CHAPTER FORTY-ONE

❊ BLAISE ❊

His heart beating furiously in his chest, Blaise stared at the scene in front of him.

On the far end of the canyon, surrounded by rocky slopes, stood Gala. She looked calm and serene, the way she'd been when fighting the storm. The Council members were at the top of the canyon, spread out all around her. In a couple of places, Blaise saw the black, coal-like shine of their Interpreter Stones. They'd come prepared, and he had no doubt that their offense was planned with deadly precision.

He wasn't sure what he was going to do, but whatever it was, he would need his own Interpreter Stone.

Turning, he rushed upstairs, remembering that he'd left the Stone in his study. The spell didn't prevent him from going up. However, once he grabbed the Stone and the spell cards he'd prepared for their trip and tried to leave his study, Gala's cursed spell kicked in again.

Now, however, Blaise was better equipped to deal with it. A quick written spell, and he teleported himself out of the room in one piece. He was taking risks today, doing the teleportation spell with so little deliberation; normally, he would've triple-checked his calculations, but there was no time for such meticulousness.

Running back to the front door, Blaise saw Moriner again. To his surprise, the Councilor was in a completely different part of the canyon at this point. Blaise frowned. The only way to cover such distance so quickly was by teleporting. It looked like Blaise wasn't the only one working with this dangerous spell today. It was strange that Moriner was taking such risks, however, given his advantageous position.

Just then Blaise saw Moriner finish a spell, and slowly a giant rockslide began to move toward Gala. The weathered rocks of the canyon broke apart from the mountain and rolled down, gathering greater mass and momentum on the way. Moriner seemed to be directing and magnifying the slide, causing it to move faster and faster.

Blaise felt a wave of fear, but before he could do anything, Gala glanced up toward the rocks. A moment later, the rockslide stopped and then started moving in the opposite direction—up the mountain. Blaise was astonished. There were reflective spells that could repel attacks, but he'd never witnessed anything of this scale and potency. As the rocks slid upward, they gathered speed until they were rushing at Moriner with the same force as they had been falling at Gala. It was an eerie sight.

Right before Moriner would have gotten hit with the mass of stones, he disappeared.

Surprised, Blaise surveyed the entire canyon. Where did Moriner go? He could see the others, and then he spotted Moriner again—on the opposite end of the canyon. The mystery of the Councilor's quick relocation deepened. Blaise did not see Moriner do anything with his stone, and the Councilor hadn't had time to speak any spells. How had he teleported?

Another Interpreter Stone flashed darkly in the sunlight, and Blaise focused on its owner, Kelvin. The man's face was a mask of fury; he hated Gala, Blaise realized. True to his specialization, Kelvin was trying to manipulate the weather—an attack that didn't particularly worry Blaise, given Gala's recent encounters with the storm.

Still, he watched anxiously as a few clouds slowly gathered above Gala. Predictably, two small thunderbolts hurled toward Gala from the clouds. The thunder reverberated through the canyon, deafening Blaise for a moment.

To his surprise, Gala didn't react—and then he realized that she didn't need to. Whatever spell she used to hurl the rocks back at Moriner was still in place, and the lightning sharply reversed direction, shooting for Kelvin instead.

Kelvin also disappeared just in time.

The sky was again bright. Blaise frowned. He didn't see this Council member say or write anything either.

Continuing to observe the events in the canyon, Blaise began making his own preparations. He liked the concept behind Gala's reflective barrier, and he had an idea how to write a spell that would work similarly. It might not be as potent, but it could be quite helpful.

As he wrote the code, he continued keeping an eye on the battlefield. By mere chance, his gaze came upon Jandison. The old man was clearly trying to stay as inconspicuous as possible, hiding behind a rock.

Sharp fury rose within Blaise, nearly choking him from within. This was the man responsible for Louie's death—and for the Council moving about with such ease, Blaise realized with sudden clarity. Jandison was the foremost expert at teleportation, and he had to be the one using his skills to transport the other Council members. He was moving them around like game pieces after their attacks on Gala.

Before anger could cloud his thinking, Blaise suppressed any thoughts of Louie. As sweet as revenge would be, he needed to focus on helping Gala first.

Taking a deep breath, Blaise surveyed the field again.

No sign of Ganir. Why hadn't the old man warned him that the Council was on the way? Had he sided with them after all? It didn't seem like that was the case; Ganir's absence from the fight spoke volumes. Of course, Blaise also couldn't locate Augusta, whose loyalties were not in doubt. Though he couldn't see her, he felt her hand in this. His former fiancée had always been good at strategy, and he was certain that she had something to do with planning these teleportation moves. Where was she? What was she plotting?

Turning his attention back to the reflection spell, Blaise finished it and loaded it into his Stone. Then, deciding to use the Council's own strategy against them, he immediately began working on a teleportation spell. This could be a way to help Gala and get his own revenge, Blaise thought with grim satisfaction.

The spell worked without a hitch, teleporting a confused Jandison into Blaise's house. Now the enemy was within reach, although most likely protected by a shield.

Not giving his opponent a chance to catch his bearings, Blaise hit Jandison with a heat spell. The spell did not go through—nor did Blaise expect it to—but it did seem to weaken the old man's shield.

Finally realizing what was happening, Jandison scrambled for his own Stone. Seeing that, Blaise tried to distract him with questions while reaching for a partially completed attack spell of his own. "How did you do it?" he demanded harshly. "How did you change the vote?"

Jandison's mouth fell open. "What . . . How did

you . . ." he sputtered.

"Don't bother lying to me," Blaise said angrily, managing to write on the card at the same time. "I know the truth now."

The Councilor's expression slowly changed, a sly look appearing in his eyes. "Well, if you know, then I guess there's no harm in telling you," he said, apparently recovering from his shock. He was also multi-tasking, his hands riffling through his bag. "I created a teleportation vortex from one of the boxes to the other," he explained, and the note of pride in his voice fed Blaise's fury.

"Why?" Blaise spat, quickly scribbling the last lines of code. He wished he could rip the answer from the old man along with some inner organs. "Why lie to me before?"

"I wanted you to have a falling-out with Ganir. He's the one I have a problem with, not you," Jandison said without a hint of shame. "I always liked you—I hope you know that. I'm sorry things worked out this way, but perhaps we can still find a way to reach an understanding . . ." As he spoke, Jandison's hands were loading his own spell.

At that moment, Blaise finished his spell too, and without any hesitation he unleashed it, the rage inside him boiling out of control.

Blaise's creation hit Jandison first. It was a bone-crushing, though not lethal, spell. Had it reached its target, Jandison would be in agony, but alive. The idea behind the spell was to penetrate Jandison's shield, which might have been designed to withstand only lethal attacks.

To Blaise's disappointment, Jandison's shield held—and at the same time, Jandison's own offensive spell went into effect.

Objects started to fly at Blaise, everything from paintings to statues that stood in the hallway. As they reached Blaise, they were deflected by Blaise's recent spell, flew at Jandison, and landed at the Councilor's feet, defeated by the powerful shield the old man had at his disposal. Then they flew at Blaise again, over and over, bouncing between his shield and that of Jandison, with more objects joining in the assault with every second.

Blaise could see that his reflective barrier would not be able to take this onslaught for long. Glancing frantically around the room, he saw the green sword-like thing—the needle that had traveled to the Spell Realm and back—flying at him.

Knowing full well his reflection spell was in its last throes, Blaise readied himself for a desperate stunt. Jumping to the side, he caught the needle-sword with his right hand. It was sharp, and he could feel it slicing through his palm, seemingly to the bone. The pain was stunning, but he refused to give in to it. Without any hesitation, he hurled the needle-sword at Jandison, loading a healing spell into his Interpreter Stone at the same time. He hoped the distraction of the hurled object would give Blaise a chance to heal.

To his shock, instead of harmlessly bouncing against Jandison's powerful barrier, the sword penetrated it, spearing Jandison right in the chest.

Jandison's last expression was that of complete and utter shock. Blaise couldn't blame him. A shield that powerful should have been impenetrable to any physical attacks. Clearly, the sword was something more than a failed experiment.

Before Blaise could think about it further, however, a flash of bright light turned everything white.

CHAPTER FORTY-TWO

※ BARSON ※

The day of reckoning had arrived.

Rising from his bed, Barson swiftly pulled on his armor and grabbed his weapons. Dara was already awake and had food sitting on the table when he came downstairs. Larn was present too, his expression hard and filled with tension. There was nothing else to talk about, nothing to discuss.

It was time to act.

Though Barson was not hungry, he forced himself to eat everything Dara put on his plate, knowing he would need his strength for the bloody ordeal ahead. Then the three of them headed to the Tower, where the rest of Barson's men were already waiting.

It was close to midnight, and the entire Tower was asleep when the soldiers entered the halls. The inhabitants of the Tower relied on defensive spells to guard them at night—spells that Dara and Barson's sorcerer allies had figured out how to neutralize in recent weeks. Without those spells—and the Guard on their side—the sorcerers were essentially unprotected.

At Barson's signal, his men spread out, breaking up into small groups.

The takeover of the Tower had begun.

CHAPTER FORTY-THREE

✳ AUGUSTA ✳

Augusta hid outside Blaise's house, listening intently with her spell-improved hearing. Frowning, she tried to make sense of what she'd heard. Jandison had done something with the vote? Blaise knew about it? She couldn't even begin to wrap her mind around such an incredible story. She would have to get to the bottom of it, but for now, she needed to focus on the task at hand.

Augusta had a couple of reasons for not coming to Jandison's aid. First and foremost, with him out of the battlefield, she had to focus all of her attention on plan B, the fusion spell. She also needed Blaise weakened, as a contingency if Plan B failed, and a confrontation with Jandison was sure to accomplish that. Besides, if what she just heard was true, Jandison had made fools of her and the rest of the Council, and he deserved whatever Blaise did to him.

Turning her attention to plan B, she focused on the fusion spell. It was dangerous, and Augusta had hoped to avoid using it. Now, however, it seemed inevitable. The creature was too powerful, deflecting all of their usual spells with ease. Even the expression on its face was calm and serene, as though it didn't care.

No, they had no choice but to use the fusion spell, and to do so now. Implementing it required coordination between most of the Council. With Jandison out of the picture, they couldn't afford to lose any more Council members. Augusta had been the one to figure out the logistics behind such coordination. It involved Contact spells prepared in advance. Each Councilor had a pair of other members they would Contact—a primary choice and a back-up.

Her heart beating frantically in her chest, Augusta loaded her spell, which was to go to Moriner, her back-up for Jandison. He would Contact his primary choice—Gina—who would Contact Furak, and so on until the cards were loaded with precise timing and order.

Though she knew she'd done the calculations correctly, Augusta still felt uneasy. They were fighting hubris with hubris, and the consequences of any errors could be catastrophic. The fusion spell was a work of terrifying beauty, harnessing the power of the sun and the stars. The energies about to be unleashed were unimaginable. To Augusta's knowledge, nothing of this magnitude had ever been undertaken in the history of Koldun. But, as terrifying as the spell was, it didn't frighten Augusta nearly as much as the abomination they were fighting—and she was confident that the powerful barrier they'd built to contain the spell would hold.

Watching the battlefield, Augusta used a simple spell to protect her vision. Though the barrier was supposed to protect them from the harmful effects of the spell, she calculated that some minute percentage of light was going to escape. Given the forces at play, she didn't want to risk being blinded.

As the spell began to take effect, a shimmering sphere about a hundred feet in diameter formed around Blaise's creature. This was the barrier. Whatever earth it touched at the bottom section of the sphere was pushed aside, creating a crater underneath the creature's feet. That didn't faze Blaise's monstrosity at all. Instead of standing on the lower layer of the sphere, it was floating in the air, inside the spherical bubble, still looking inhumanly calm.

And just as Augusta noted these details, the fusion spell went into effect, and she saw a dazzling explosion of light.

CHAPTER FORTY-FOUR

✳ GALA ✳

Gala felt torn. She wanted to help Blaise, but if she rushed to the house right now, it would become the focal point of the Council's attack. The sensation of helplessness, of being unable to protect the one she loved, was unbearable. Gala could feel her calm beginning to slip, her heart starting to beat rapidly in her chest.

And at that moment, she began to feel something strange—some unprecedented spell being cast. She'd noticed she could sense magic before, but she had never felt anything of this caliber. Many people were working together—working on something big.

In the meantime, Blaise continued to fight in the house. Grimly Gala struggled for control, determined to be the master of her sorcery, rather than its puppet, but her fear for Blaise was too strong. Her mind racing, Gala felt the last remnants of her calm disintegrating as her emotions took over.

At first, she again experienced the illusion of her mind leaving her body. Only this time, it was different, more physical. She saw herself from a vantage point high in the sky. It was as if she was seeing the canyon through the eyes of a bird—and that's exactly what was happening, she realized. Somehow her subconscious mind had connected with that of the birds that attacked her earlier.

It was strange, like she was in two places at once. She could see the faces of her attackers from high up in the air, and at the same time, she saw a shimmering sphere surround her body from both her own and the bird's viewpoint. And from high up again, she saw herself floating in that glowing bubble. It was something she hadn't even realized she was doing.

There was something ominous about the bubble that surrounded her—a subtle threat that she couldn't fully understand yet. She also felt tiny changes in her body, like there was another spell attaching itself to her. She was about to examine it further when she felt the first powerful blast of energy inside the sphere that encased her.

Her reflective spell repelled the blast, pushing it outward, back toward its source, but the bubble prevented it from going beyond its walls. The energy grew, unimaginably powerful and destructive, filling the enclosed space around Gala and weakening her defenses. There was no longer any hope of retaining control, of remaining calm in the face of this maelstrom—all Gala could do was attempt to survive. She was no longer making conscious choices; instead that deep, still-unexplored part of her mind was in control.

Searing, burning pain overloaded her senses as time seemed to slow. She felt her body starting to disintegrate, each cell screaming in agony at its torturous death. The explosive energy was merciless, terrifying, yet Gala's mind systematically analyzed it, broke it down into its components. And then she knew what it was . . . knew it was the same force that powered the stars above. Hydrogen fusing with itself, forming helium—a terrible reaction that her mind could not find a way to stop.

So instead of stopping it, her mind found a different solution.

It would get rid of the energy by sending it elsewhere—to the Spell Realm itself.

As Gala's mind ran through the necessary calculations, her agony intensified until she could bear it no longer—until she found herself completely pushed out of her dying body. She was fully inside the bird now, not just seeing but feeling what it felt.

There was a momentary relief from the pain, but then Gala made the mistake of looking down at the shimmering bubble—a bubble that now shone with the brightness of the sun. In an instant, the bird was blinded, and, unable to see, it began falling.

Plummeting to the ground, Gala somehow knew she was about to leave the bird's body. With all her willpower, she tried to get the bird to fly again, but before she knew if her desperate attempt succeeded, she was brought back into her own body.

The pain was excruciating. Her flesh had disintegrated, ripped apart by the terrible forces of the fusion reaction, yet it was reforming again, somehow being fixed by the directive of her subconscious mind—a mind that seemed to reside elsewhere for now.

Crippled by the stunning agony, Gala lost connection with the mind of the bird completely. The creature was dead. Overwhelmed, she began to lose the remaining portion of her conscious control to one overwhelming emotion—anger.

Then, in a flash, she felt Blaise's mind go blank, just like the bird's.

CHAPTER FORTY-FIVE

❊ AUGUSTA ❊

Even with the protective vision spell, Augusta felt a blinding pain in her eyes. The sound of the explosion reverberated through her body, rupturing her eardrums, and the ground under her feet shook with such force that she was thrown to the ground, painfully twisting her ankle on the way. Stunned and gasping for air, she scrambled for a healing spell, her trembling fingers barely managing to load it into her Stone.

When the healing effect began, she could feel the pain in her ankle subside first. She was not sure yet, but her hearing appeared to be returning too, and she could hear some kind of shuffling inside Blaise's house. Her eyes were healing slowly, however, and she could barely tell light from darkness. She had to hurry, so she used another healing spell to aid the vision repair.

When Augusta could finally see, the first thing she looked at was the other side of the Canyon—and her stomach churned at what she saw.

With a human being, the forces unleashed would have made them disintegrate into ash, leaving the shimmering sphere empty. This creature, however, was still there. Though it was no longer floating serenely, it still existed—and was lying on its side at the bottom of the bubble, curled into a fetal position.

At best, it was maybe injured, Augusta realized with dismay. It was definitely alive, though—she knew that thanks to a hidden locator spell she'd embedded within her fusion spell. She'd hoped she wouldn't need it, but she took precautions anyway. This locator spell would allow Augusta to know where the creature was at all times, and, more importantly, whether it was alive.

She needed that location spell for her plan C—a plan she'd hoped she wouldn't need to implement.

Now, however, there was no choice.

Slowly getting up, Augusta forced herself to walk into Blaise's house.

* * *

Inside, she found Blaise lying on the floor in the hallway. It appeared that the explosion had knocked him off his feet as well. A thin trickle of blood ran down his forehead, and he looked dazed, as if he had just regained consciousness. For a moment, she had a strange impulse to heal him, to take away his pain, but that was absurd, given what she was about to do.

"You," he whispered, propping himself up on one elbow and glaring at her. "What have you done?"

Augusta could see him reaching for his Interpreter Stone and the cards, and she quickly grabbed her own spell—the one she'd specifically prepared for this occasion.

It was too late, though. Blaise's spell hit her first. Immediately, Augusta's thoughts scrambled, her mind turning to mush. A confusion spell, she realized with the small corner of her brain that remained unaffected. A confusion spell that had gotten through her weakened defenses.

Everything felt slow, every thought, every decision, requiring major effort. Why hadn't he just tried to kill her? she wondered hazily. Her eyes landed on Jandison's bloody corpse, and her vision swam for a moment. Why hadn't Blaise used a lethal spell on her as well? Did he still have feelings for her? No, that was stupid, Augusta told herself. He loved his creature now. She couldn't forget that, couldn't soften for even a moment—not if she wanted to survive.

Gathering all her strength, Augusta focused on what she needed to accomplish—the simple task of loading the prepared card into her Stone. It seemed to take hours, but finally she managed to slot it in.

Blaise slumped on the floor, his eyes closing as her spell took effect. Paradoxically, Augusta felt relieved that he hadn't been standing, that he didn't fall and injure himself further. It was ridiculous to feel that way in light of what she was about to do next.

Nonetheless, he looked still. Too still.

I didn't kill him, Augusta reminded herself, shaking off the remnants of her confusion. Like Ganir, Blaise was merely in a coma that she had induced.

Her next set of spells, however, could end up killing him—if the creature didn't act as Augusta hoped.

CHAPTER FORTY-SIX

✳ GALA ✳

No longer able to sense her connection with Blaise, Gala felt her anger turning into blinding fury.

Hardly conscious of what she was doing, she sent Blaise's house back to its usual place in Turingrad. If he was somehow still alive, he would not be safe here, not with what was about to happen.

Once that was done, she closed her eyes and focused on the most powerful force she had known prior to this explosion: the horrifying ocean storms. Mentally reaching out far beyond the mountains, Gala took a precisely measured chunk of space from the air above the ocean and teleported it into the canyon.

The sky exploded with lightning, hail, and tornados. The storm filled every inch of the canyon, with deadly lightning bolts striking every second, turning the rocky ground into glass. The howling roar of the tornados and the pounding hail combined into a deafening cacophony, sheets of rain turning the bottom of the canyon into a lake within seconds.

It was a nightmare—one from which Gala was protected by the very bubble they had used against her.

The storm lasted at peak intensity for only a few minutes and then began to dissipate, no longer sustained by the weather conditions that brought it about in the ocean. As the sky began to clear again, Gala's own fury slowly faded, replaced by the horrified recognition of what she'd done.

The canyon was all but destroyed. She had lost control again—and in doing so, she might've killed people. The Council had intended to hurt her, likely kill her, but she hadn't wanted them dead. She should've found another way.

Before bitter regret could consume her again, Gala focused on what she still had to do: find Blaise. Closing her eyes, she concentrated and teleported herself into Blaise's house—which was now back in Turingrad.

* * *

A beautiful dark-haired woman was crouched over Blaise's prone body. At Gala's appearance, she swiftly looked up, clutching her Interpreter Stone. The expression on her face was full of fear and hatred.

"If you do anything to me, he'll die," she said,

staring at Gala with striking amber-colored eyes. "He's merely unconscious now, but I joined his life to mine—and to yours."

"What do you mean?" Gala whispered, her heart pounding with a mixture of fury and dread. This had to be Augusta, Blaise's former fiancée—the woman he had loved once. The woman who betrayed him and his brother.

The woman who set the Council on Gala and Blaise.

"I used a spell on him that's tied to you," Augusta said evenly. "His life is being drained as we speak— drained by your very existence. He's dying because of you now—because you are here alive, instead of dead, like you were supposed to be."

Gala gritted her teeth, fighting the urge to lash out at Augusta. She could feel the truth of the woman's words. There was a complex spell woven around Blaise, one that indeed connected him to both Gala and Augusta. The threads that joined him to Gala seemed to be leaching something from him, killing him slowly but surely.

Examining herself, Gala realized that she'd felt something earlier—that some spell had been interwoven into that terrible explosion. The changes were subtle but noticeable, especially now that she was focusing on them. The spell ensured that she could be located anywhere; as long as Gala existed, the leaching would continue.

Gala could potentially unweave this spell, but it would take too long—and she didn't know how long

Blaise could last like this, with his life being drained by the second.

"There's only one way you can save him," Augusta said, her eyes glittering with something suspiciously resembling tears. "Your life for his—that's the only way. I know you're too powerful for me to destroy—and I know you can destroy me in a moment. But by doing that, you'll be killing him. He created you; he gave you everything, even his heart. Are you going to let him die like this?"

Gala stared at Augusta, a sick sensation curdling low in her stomach. The woman wanted her to kill herself, to snuff out her own existence. It was unthinkable—but so was the thought of Blaise dying.

Torn, she stared at Augusta, her mind running through all the possible scenarios. With the spell Augusta put on her, merely teleporting away would not help . . . and she could sense that Blaise would not survive much longer. There was no choice: Gala had to figure out a way to kill herself if she wanted to save Blaise.

She considered one morbid scenario after the next—setting herself on fire, drowning at the bottom of the ocean, cutting her flesh to ribbons with a sword—but all these had a flaw: she had no idea if she could be killed that way. She had no idea if her subconscious would end up in control, saving Gala at the ultimate cost to Blaise.

There was only one alternative she could see.

Closing her eyes, Gala remembered the spell her mind had performed when the terrible explosion was used against her. She knew that the energy of that calamity had been channeled into the Spell Realm. Analyzing it, she realized that she could replicate that spell with one difference: she would be the one to go to the Spell Realm this time.

Gala opened her eyes to look at Blaise for the last time, and then she closed them again. Taking a deep breath, she sent Blaise a brief Contact message . . . and put her plan into action.

By the time she became conscious again, she was unable to hear, see, touch, or smell.

She was back in the Spell Realm.

CHAPTER FORTY-SEVEN

❊ BLAISE ❊

Drifting in a strange blankness, Blaise suddenly became aware of an intrusion in his mind—of words that seemed to appear out of nothingness.

Gala's words, he realized, his thinking slow and sluggish.

"Blaise, my love, Augusta made it impossible for me to stay in the Physical Realm, so I had to depart this world and take a chance by going to the Spell Realm. I am not sure what awaits me there, and I wanted you to know that the last days that we spent together were the most wonderful days of my existence so far. Gala."

The message seemed to reverberate in his mind, repeating over and over again as he slowly began to digest its meaning. Recalling Augusta and her spell, Blaise realized that Augusta had done something to him, causing him to black out.

As awareness came back, Blaise became cognizant of his body lying still on the floor. His limbs felt weak and heavy, drained of all energy. A wave of helpless fury surged through him as the full meaning of Gala's words dawned on him.

She was gone.

The woman he loved more than life itself was gone from this world.

He didn't know how Augusta had accomplished that task, but that didn't matter right now. He couldn't let himself give in to the grief and hatred choking him from the inside; he needed to be able to think, to plan his revenge.

He could hear someone in the room with him, and he did his best to lie still, to pretend to be unconscious. Opening his eyes to a narrow slit, he saw his Interpreter Stone and a few cards lying spilled on the floor a few feet away. If he could only reach them quickly . . . but those few feet might as well have been miles, given the paralyzing weakness still gripping his body.

There was a sound of light footsteps and a rustle of skirts—and then the familiar scent of jasmine enveloped him as Augusta knelt next to him.

"I know you're awake," she said softly, her hand brushing lightly against his cheek. "You don't have to pretend with me. I've seen you wake up plenty of times."

Blaise opened his eyes, not bothering to hide the hatred burning within him. "What did you do?" he asked, his voice low and hoarse. "What did you do,

Augusta?"

She stared at him, her gaze hardening. "It's dead," she said curtly, and he could see her hand tightening around her Interpreter Stone. "I know because I had a locator spell on it, and the locator shows nothing. Also, you are very much alive and not losing your life's essence—which I tied to that creature."

Blaise's hatred intensified. So that was how she'd done it: Augusta had used Gala's feelings for Blaise against her.

Something of what he was feeling must've shown on his face because she grabbed a couple of cards and held them close to her Stone. "Don't even think about it," she said quietly. "You won't make it."

Cursing the aftereffects of the draining spell, Blaise let his body relax, as though accepting the truth of her words. Half-closing his eyelids, he glanced toward the cards on the floor, spotting a paralyzing spell that would have come in handy.

At the same time, he heard Augusta let out a weary sigh. "Listen, Blaise..." Her tone was conciliatory now. "I had to do it, don't you see? It was too dangerous... If you had only seen what this creature did—"

Shutting out Augusta's words, Blaise gathered all of his remaining strength. He would get only one attempt at this, and he had to make it count. Ignoring the screaming weakness in his muscles, he swiftly rolled toward the Stone, his hands scrambling frantically for the cards.

And as he blindly slotted one into the Stone,

Augusta's spell hit him in full force.

It was like being struck by lightning. Every cell in his body exploded in agony, his body jerking under the lash of the energy blast. The pain was so intense that he lost consciousness again, his mind going blank.

* * *

When Blaise woke up again, he first became aware of the heavy, slow beat of his heart. His body was one big ball of pain, and every breath he dragged into his aching lungs required massive effort. Groaning, Blaise tried to move—an attempt that sent waves of agony through him again.

Nauseous, he forced himself to lie still, willing the spinning in his head to subside. Whatever spell Augusta hit him with had been just short of lethal.

After a few minutes, he managed to open his eyes. Ignoring the pain in his neck, he slowly turned his head and surveyed the hallway.

Augusta lay on the floor beside him, her body unmoving. He had managed to hit her with the paralysis spell after all, he realized with relief. Her eyes were closed, and there was a small pool of blood spreading out from a wound on the side of her head. She must've hit her head when she fell. Probably a mercy, Blaise thought with uncharacteristic coldness; otherwise, the spell would've left her conscious, but unable to move at all—a feeling that was likely worse than mere unconsciousness.

Painfully rolling over onto his side, Blaise reached for the Stone that lay next to him. The simple movement sent his stomach roiling, but he managed to close his hand around it and grab a few cards before he had to close his eyes to combat the nauseating dizziness. After a few moments, he forced his lids open again to study what he was holding.

There was only one card that was even remotely related to a healing spell. Cursing, Blaise spied his pencil lying on the floor and reached for it, his hand shaking from the effort it took to grab the object. Then, ignoring the churning sickness in his stomach, he began to slowly write the appropriate spell.

Knowing that he was not in his best mental shape, Blaise took extra time to accomplish his task, making sure the spell would be safe. If he accidentally killed himself, he would never see Gala again. Anger surged through him again at the thought, and as soon as the spell healed him, he jumped to his feet, every cell in his body clamoring for vengeance.

Walking over to Augusta, he stared at her prone figure, a vengeful plan forming in his mind. His former lover had tried to make him an unwilling instrument of Gala's destruction, and Blaise would make certain she regretted it.

Going down to his storage room, he carefully selected a few droplets. The first was a Life Capture of what Blaise had felt during the vote on the day Louie had been sentenced. *Let her experience what it's like to learn that your brother is condemned to death.* The next one was of Blaise's conversation with

Augusta about the vote, when he learned that she had voted in favor of his brother's punishment. *Let her experience the betrayal of the woman you love.*

Then, reaching for the bottle that had the skull-and-bones label, Blaise paused, wondering if this one would be too cruel of a punishment. Then Gala's words flashed across his mind again, and his resolve solidified. *Let Augusta experience Louie's death through his own eyes. Let her see the consequences of her actions.*

Grimly decided, Blaise walked back to his study to write the appropriate spell. When it was done, he loaded the cards into his Stone and went downstairs to see if it had worked.

The spell was simple, yet beautifully complex. The fact that the droplets could be reused was what made it possible. It was a loop—a loop of the Life Captures he'd chosen, playing over and over in Augusta's mind.

Standing over her, he watched it happen.

A needle flew up to Augusta's finger first. The Life Capture Sphere then floated next to the little bit of blood, beginning the recording process. After that, the first Life Capture droplet Blaise had chosen flew into Augusta's mouth.

He didn't watch the rest—he knew that after a time, a new droplet would be formed in the Stone and join the queue that was waiting its turn to be consumed by Augusta. This would go on and on, until either the paralysis spell or the looping spell lost its potency. Which would be a very long time, if

Blaise had done his job properly. With each subsequent recording, Augusta would experience a bit of her own reaction as well. It would be an endless loop of despair and regret—or so Blaise hoped, at least.

"Maybe you will learn something from this," he told her, even though he knew Augusta couldn't hear him right now. Steeling his heart against any hint of weakness or remorse, Blaise walked back to his study.

He couldn't afford to think about Augusta anymore. He needed to figure out how he could reunite with Gala.

* * *

Blaise spent the next few hours reviewing everything related to the Spell Realm.

He wished he could simply bring Gala back, but he couldn't think of a way to do it. During her creation, the spells to make her mind and to have her manifest in the Physical Realm had been intertwined. As far as he knew, there was no way to simply reach into the Spell Realm and bring her back here. It would require a thorough understanding of the Spell Realm, and the only person who might even attempt something of that complexity would be Gala herself.

However, he had once succeeded in sending an object to the Spell Realm, Blaise realized, thinking of the needle that had come back as that strange sword. It was a crazy idea, but it was the only way he could think of to reach Gala. The thought of her alone out there was unbearable to him.

Reworking and scaling up the needle spell, Blaise made himself the target, trying to perfect the spell along the way to the best of his ability. When he was done, he still wasn't certain of the result. It would take months of careful testing and experimentation to ensure the spell's safety, but he didn't have the luxury of time.

Mentally bracing himself, Blaise loaded the cards into the Interpreter Stone and waited to see the results.

CHAPTER FORTY-EIGHT

❊ BARSON ❊

His clothes soaked through with blood, Barson quietly opened the door to the room where two of his next targets were sleeping. Dara slipped in behind him, her steps whisper-silent. She was pale with fatigue, but the look on her face was that of grim determination.

Two sorcerer apprentices were sharing this room. The one whose bed was closest to the door was Jundi—a name that was on Barson's list. Though the room was quite dark, Barson could make out her shape in the dim moonlight streaming in from the window. Gripping his dagger, Barson stepped closer to the sleeping woman, and in one smooth motion slit her throat. There was a quiet gurgle, followed by the sharp, metallic scent of blood and death.

Jundi's roommate continued sleeping, blissfully unaware. It was Hanta—a young sorceress whose name was not on his list.

Dara approached Hanta's bed and touched the woman's shoulder. "Wake up," she said gently, loading a spell into her Stone. A second later, the room was illuminated by a pale yellow light.

The girl opened her eyes, a look of shock forming on her face. Gasping, she jackknifed to a sitting position, holding up the blanket protectively in front of herself. As her eyes fell on her dead roommate, the look of shock turned to horror.

"You will not make any noise or try to do anything stupid," Barson said evenly, keeping his bloody dagger visible.

The sorceress stared at him, her body starting to tremble under the blanket. "Captain? W-what's going on? W-why are you doing this? I thought you were dead—"

"Yes, yes, I've heard that a lot today," Barson said impatiently. "Now listen to me carefully, Hanta. I'm not here to answer your questions. You have two options: you can join Jundi today—or you can join me."

"Join you?" The woman looked like she was going into shock, her face utterly bloodless. "What do you mean? You're our Guard—"

Dara smiled, sitting down on the bed next to Hanta. "Not anymore, dear," she said softly. "He's about to be your king. And you can join him, or try to fight against him. Either way, the outcome will be the same—but with the first option, you will be richly rewarded for your loyalty, whereas with the second..." His sister let her voice trail off and glanced meaningfully at the dagger in Barson's hand. Hanta's eyes followed her gaze, and she visibly flinched.

"Now," Barson said calmly, stepping toward the sorceress. "What do you choose?"

"I choose you," Hanta said hurriedly, scooting backward on the bed.

"I knew you would be reasonable," Dara said reassuringly. "That's why I kept your name off the list. Now let's discuss the Life Capture surveillance program I came up with, a program that will make sure there is never a misunderstanding between us..."

For the next few minutes, Barson's sister explained all about how sorcerers' thoughts would be carefully watched and monitored via Life Captures, to prevent any treachery. Hanta kept nodding to show her understanding, tears running down her face, and Barson knew that this sorceress would be just like the others they'd dealt with on this bloody night—that she would fall in line with the new regime.

As Dara was finishing her explanation, the door to Hanta's room opened, and Zanil walked in. "Larn sent me to tell you that we couldn't find at least forty people on our list—some of them quite dangerous."

Barson frowned. That was not good. He'd been hoping for a swift and controlled operation, and it looked like things were about to get messy.

His thoughts were interrupted by an ear-splitting

noise that vibrated through the tower.

"The gong," Dara said, jumping to her feet. "Someone has gotten into the Council Hall and is warning the rest of danger. They could be gathering there as we speak."

Leaving Hanta crying over her roommate's body, they ran down the twisted corridors of the Tower to the Hall, gathering soldiers and their sorcerer allies on the way. When they got there, they saw Larn and a group of soldiers standing in front of the giant doors.

"They're locked," Larn reported, coming up to Barson. "How do you want us to approach it?"

Barson turned to Dara. "Can you and our allies prevent anyone from teleporting, or otherwise leaving that hall?"

"Hmm." She looked thoughtful. "It's the biggest room in the Tower, so it will be tricky, but I've picked up a thing or two from Jandison. We can create this field of force—"

"No offense, sis, but I am not interested in details," Barson said, waving in greeting at another group of soldiers that was coming down the hallway.

"Then the answer is yes, we can keep them there," she responded, looking mildly annoyed.

"Good, then I will leave some soldiers outside with you, so if anyone runs out, you can deal with them."

There were now at least fifty soldiers in front of the Council Hall doors. Thinking about the best course of action, Barson decided that he first needed some information about what awaited them in that chamber. "Dara, which one of our allies do you trust the most?" he asked, glancing at his sister.

She considered that for a moment. "Kira and I had been friends for a few years before I told her about our plans," she said slowly. "I think I can trust her the most."

"Do you think you can get her in and out of that room safely?" Barson asked.

Dara contemplated his request. "Does she need to move around, or can she be stationary?"

"It's best if she moves around freely."

"In that case, we could combine a locator spell with a cleverly written teleportation spell—" Dara began when Barson caught her eye, giving her a sardonic look. His sister had never been in a battle before and obviously didn't understand the value of brevity in critical situations.

"Oh yes, sorry, master commander," she said mockingly. "You don't care about these details. The answer to your query is yes. We can get her in and out."

* * *

"I have never done something like this before," Kira said nervously, staring at Barson. "I don't know a single thing about reconnaissance . . ."

"You don't need to know," Barson explained calmly. "You will be using Life Capture. When you get back, I will be able to look through your eyes at that room. And I know about recon. Just look around casually and appear to be scared. They won't know that you're with us."

"I don't think appearing scared will be hard to do," she said wryly.

They had Kira start a Life Capture session, and Dara implemented the teleportation and locator spells, to get Kira in the room. Vashel, Mittel, Pavel, and Noriella had joined them too, and were frantically writing spells to strengthen the already-enhanced armor of the soldiers. Dara also insisted all members of the Guard get protected against psychological attacks. This involved temporary spells, unfortunately, but Barson made a mental note to work on something more permanent with his sister. Perhaps enhanced headgear of some kind, to protect his mind from sorcery when he was king.

Kira's return distracted him from his musings. As soon as she appeared in front of them, she pricked her finger and put a tiny drop of blood on his Life Capture Sphere.

Picking up the droplet that had formed as a result, Barson immediately placed it under his tongue.

* * *

Kira wanted to be brave. She wanted to impress Dara's powerful brother.

No. She stopped herself from thinking about Barson, realizing that the Life Capture would make her thoughts known. Trying to focus, she looked around the room where she'd just appeared. There were at least thirty sorcerers gathered inside the Council Hall. They were clustered on the far side of the room, away from the giant doors.

"Come join us, quickly," said a voice she vaguely recognized as belonging to Pierre, one of the more senior apprentices. "We need the center of the room clear, so people can teleport in safely. And send a Contact message to anyone you trust. We need everyone to gather here as quickly as they can. It looks like the Guard faked their deaths and turned on us. They're slaughtering people left and right, and I don't know how long the doors will keep them out."

Kira nodded, pretending to go along with the instructions. Clearly Pierre and the rest didn't realize that Barson had help from sorcerers. They assumed anyone who was able to get into the locked room was on their side.

As she walked across the large hall, she saw more people teleporting in. Approaching one of the sorcerers, she started to ask him a question when she felt that strange sensation that precedes teleportation. She was being brought out, she realized, and in the next moment she was facing Barson again, her heart beating faster in her chest. Her finger was still bleeding from before, and she pressed the wound against the Sphere . . .

* * *

"You did well, Kira," Barson said, trying to

suppress a smile. He apparently had an admirer among his allies. "I have all the information I need. Dara, prepare to get us in and block the room from teleportation. Keep in mind, we need to appear as close to the middle as possible, since there is an empty space there."

While Dara worked on the spell, he walked over to his soldiers. Given the number of sorcerers inside, he decided to split up his men. The majority of them would go into the Hall, while the rest would guard the doors to the chamber, in case any sorcerers tried to escape on foot.

Now that he had a moment to think, Barson realized how desperate the people in that room were. In their panic, they acted like chickens with their heads cut off, instead of thinking strategically. Ringing the gong might've alerted others of the danger, but it also pinpointed their location to Barson—and their choice of a gathering spot was even worse. They should've run—or teleported themselves—outside, instead of barricading themselves indoors, where they couldn't utilize their most destructive spells without also killing themselves. Their inability to think like warriors was to his advantage.

When Dara's spells were ready, Barson addressed his troops.

"Soldiers, you know I don't give fancy speeches," he said calmly, "but on this occasion, some words need to be said. We are at a crossroads now. If we succeed—and I have no doubt that we will—this day will forever be remembered as the start of a new era. Each and every single one of you will be written about in history books. Today we are about to change the world." He paused, looking at them. "Are you ready?"

An approving roar was his response. Studying their faces, Barson could see that his soldiers were just as hungry for this as he was. They all longed for victory, and each could already see it, taste it.

"Remember your training and utilize their weaknesses," he said when the roar died down. "Every sorcerer in that room must die."

CHAPTER FORTY-NINE

✻ GALA ✻

So this was the Spell Realm, Gala thought. This time, unlike right after her birth, she would get more than a brief glimmer of it with her conscious mind.

Everything was achingly familiar and extremely strange at the same time. Gala realized with surprise that the dreams she couldn't remember before were of this place. Only even her dreams did not prepare her for what it was really like. If anything prepared her for this, it had to be those moments when she was born—moments she had not remembered until now.

Just as when she had woken up to self-awareness here for the first time, she was not in possession of her familiar body—the body that she'd grown used to, the body that Blaise found attractive. No, here she was something she could best understand as a pure mind. The feeling, if it could be called that, was that of flying or floating in water. Only this was infinitely more serene and peaceful.

She knew she should be petrified at having no body, but she took it in stride. Having a body was meaningless in a place where none of her human senses worked. Existence was of a different sort here. Of a kind she was just beginning to understand.

Though Gala didn't have the now-familiar human senses, she still *felt*. It was as though her mind was connected with the fabric of the Spell Realm itself— as though the Spell Realm was permeated with sensory organs, and she was somehow able to access them.

She still felt some of the emotions she'd experienced before. Anger at Augusta. Sadness at her own loss of control in the battle with the Council. And, overwhelmingly, she felt love and longing for Blaise.

She tried to not let the emotions confuse her. It would be easy to get confused in this place. Instead, Gala focused on her surroundings.

When she analyzed them, she understood more. There were colors and chaotic patterns that appeared here from time to time. These colorful displays were spells from the Physical Realm, she decided, not knowing where the certainty came from. Perhaps like knows its like, she reflected. Now that she thought about it, Gala realized that she herself was a pattern of lights and connections. Her pattern was much more complex than any she saw—and much more structured—but she could still see the kinship. *I am a spell that learned how to think,* Gala thought with amazement.

She also comprehended that if she concentrated on the different shapes and colors, she could discern the effects these spells would have in the Physical Realm.

Someone was casting a fireball spell, which looked like a blue fractal pattern here—a pattern that didn't resemble a ball of any kind. And yet Gala knew that it would produce a ball of fire. This pattern was more than just the shape; it was also the temperature, trajectory, and location in space and time in the Physical Realm. A lot of information was encoded in that blue pattern.

Then there was another grand display. Instinctively Gala knew that a magical object would be formed when this spell affected the Physical Realm. There was information about the permanence of this object in the Physical Realm, and details about what it would look like, with all of its various attributes. There were myriad stipulations on how and when it would break the laws of nature in the Physical Realm—how it would be lighter than air under most conditions—and Gala knew that this would be a flying chaise, like the one she and Blaise had ridden.

Another fantastic shape looked like a giant fountain, spewing colors and sounds; that was someone's Interpreter Stone doing what it was made to do.

Gala imagined that when she was in the Physical

Realm, she must have been creating displays not very different from this.

* * *

She wasn't sure how much time passed while she admired these displays. After a while, some of her overwhelmed awe faded, and Gala began trying to figure out where she was. As soon as she focused on that, it became clear to her that the concept of 'where'—the concept of location—had a different meaning here in the Spell Realm from what she was used to on Koldun.

She was wherever her attention was. Her thought was what seemed to determine her location in the Spell Realm. How this process worked, Gala didn't know, but that didn't seem to matter.

She knew she wanted to go back to Blaise. She *needed* to go back. However, focusing on getting back to the Physical Realm didn't work the same way as simply moving about in the Spell Realm. Gala tried to demand it from her surroundings, but she had no idea how to achieve what she wanted. A disturbing thought crept in, a thought she had been trying to push away this whole time . . . What if she never saw Blaise again?

No. Gala refused to give in to it, to admit defeat. She would find a way to get back to Blaise.

Suddenly, her attention shifted. She sensed something out there. There were things here, Gala realized, things that were not spells from the Physical

Realm, but something else entirely. Something completely foreign to her mind.

There was thought here. Some kind of alien reasoning.

Fascinated, Gala tried to discern what these intelligent entities were. Their thought patterns were constantly moving and shifting, and she could occasionally glimpse something in their minds. These brief glimpses revealed intelligences that were beautiful, yet frightening in their otherness.

Intelligences . . . Something nibbled at the back of her mind, some memory that had long been suppressed. Gala had a feeling that she was forgetting something important, and then it suddenly came to her.

The dreams. She'd dreamed of the Spell Realm before—and in her dreams, she'd interacted with an intelligence here.

An intelligence that she knew as Dranel.

As soon as Gala recalled Dranel, she sensed a thinking pattern. It was recognizable as the one from her dream, but at the same time, there were differences. It wasn't just the fact that the Spell Realm of her dreams had been different from the way she was experiencing it now. No, it was a change in the nature of the being she now sought. There was something like a flaw in the otherwise beautiful pattern.

"Dranel," she called out in her mind, trying to talk to the pattern as she had done in her dream.

There was no response coming her way, but Gala

was suddenly immersed in a vision.

* * *

Dranel became lucid. The being he had found so interesting, Gala, was casting spells again. He had observed her do this many times, and the algorithms she produced evoked serenity in Dranel, the kind of serenity he otherwise only felt when he was not lucid.

Somehow he knew the effects these spells would have in the Physical Realm. The concepts were distant and foreign: floating, healing, thunder . . . Dranel had only a vague understanding of what those were.

He observed it all with a faint sense of curiosity, his mind sifting through the different patterns of the spells. It was only when he felt something powerful gathering out there that he realized it was not going to be a pattern that reached into the Spell Realm next— it was going to be the destructive energy of that spell itself.

He felt the jolt as the energy entered the space surrounding him, and he instantly knew that, if left alone, this force could wreak havoc on his world. Without hesitation, Dranel made a decision, taking the energy into himself.

His mind exploded in agony, and lucidity faded.

* * *

Horrified, Gala emerged from the vision, separating her mind from the shreds of the pattern that had once been Dranel.

She had done this, she realized in despair. She had sent the energy of the spell the Council directed at her into the Spell Realm, seeking to protect herself from its destructive force. And in the process, she'd managed to hurt this intelligent being.

Desperate to fix her mistake, Gala closely examined Dranel's pattern, trying to determine what went wrong with it. She could feel the breaks and misalignments, the damage from the explosive force she'd inadvertently introduced into this entity's habitat. She found the errors and tried to mend them, letting her mind focus on what the pattern should be. What it used to be in her dream. As she fixed the errors, she could sense Dranel changing, his mind healing in a way that felt almost physical.

After what seemed like a long time, but could easily have been a moment, Gala knew that Dranel's pattern was as it had been before. He was not conscious yet, but that would come eventually.

She was waiting for that moment when she became distracted by something far, far more important.

She sensed Blaise casting a spell.

As she focused her thoughts on the pattern he was generating, Gala again 'traveled' somewhere. Wherever she now was, she saw a complex shape with sounds and tastes that she found mesmerizing. She soon knew what the spell in front of her was meant to do.

It was meant to bring Blaise to her, to the Spell

Realm.

Except it was doomed to fail in its goal.

Blaise had made a number of subtle, but fatal mistakes in his calculations. It was clear to her that the spell would not work as intended. If allowed to run its course, it would end up killing Blaise's mind, but even if it didn't, the next part of the spell—the part that was supposed to take Blaise back to the Physical Realm afterwards—was flawed. Still, it did give Gala an idea of what a return spell might look like, and she tucked away the knowledge for later, focusing on the more immediate task in front of her.

Reaching out toward the spell, Gala tried to change it, to fix the errors that she could see as she had fixed Dranel's pattern. She had no idea if it would work, but she had to try. Everything inside her trembled at the possibility that Blaise's spell might go through in its current form, that he would perish in his attempt to reach her. She only had time to implement a few tweaks in his spell. Her priority was to ensure that he survived the trip in.

She focused on the problems in the fabric of the spell. Fixing the spell came naturally to her. The mistakes dulled the bright colors and the subtle patterns. All Gala had to do was make it beautiful again, like all complete spells were. Following her intuition, she broke the spell structure down into smaller parts. If she succeeded, Blaise would arrive in the Spell Realm, and no other parts of the spell would take effect. Once Blaise arrived, she would work out the other details.

Having set the fix in motion, Gala anxiously watched the pattern unweave, desperately hoping that she herself had not made any errors.

CHAPTER FIFTY

※ BARSON ※

As Dara and her colleagues completed the spell to teleport them into the Council Hall, Barson braced himself. He knew enough about sorcery to realize that this was a dangerous maneuver. In a flash, he was standing inside the room. His soldiers were here as well—all except two. He could see a bloody mess on the floor, and a cold shudder ran down his spine as he understood what happened.

Two of his men had materialized in the same spot, dying gruesomely in the process.

It was an honorable death, and one Barson couldn't dwell on now. Seeing the shocked looks on the sorcerers' faces, he yelled, "Charge!" and started running across the giant hall toward the frightened group of sorcerers. His men followed, letting out a fierce battle cry.

As they ran, a barrage of powerful spells began

assaulting them. Terrible heat, bone-chilling cold . . . Pierre and his comrades were trying every elemental spell in their arsenal. The spells slowed Barson and his men, but the enchanted armor protected them from the worst of it, absorbing the energies of the spells. Barson knew there was a threshold, a limit to this protection, but he also knew that this was one advantage of this battleground. In an enclosed space like this room, the sorcerers' hands were tied when it came to some of their more powerful spells.

Then the attacks on the mind began. The Guard had protection for this as well, but Dara had warned Barson that some mild effects would still be felt. The fear that gripped his whole being, however, was anything but mild. Still, Barson didn't let it stop him; he had been trained to face fear and utilize it to his advantage. Running faster, he yelled, "Now!" and lifted his bow into the air.

His men joined him, and a moment later, a small cloud of arrows flew toward the sorcerers. Instead of reaching the target, however, the arrows fell harmlessly to the ground, bouncing off the shimmering protective shield that the sorcerers managed to put up. Barson was not deterred, however. "One arrow," he roared, signaling a different strategy—one that had been developed specifically to deal with this magical defense.

His men focused all their arrows on one particular spot, magnifying the impact of the strike. It was his sister who had come up with this strategy, and it worked. The combined force of the arrows hitting the same spot caused the sorcerers' protective shield to weaken, and the next batch of arrows dissipated it completely, leaving Barson's opponents without their primary defense. Now the soldiers' arrows pierced flesh, and screams filled the air as sorcerers tried to scatter, running in every direction.

"Contain the perimeter," Barson ordered, unsheathing his sword. And as the screaming intensified, he and his men swiftly dispatched the remaining opponents.

When it was all over, the floor was red with blood and corpses lay in piles at his feet. Surveying the room, Barson saw that all of his men had survived this portion of the fight.

The takeover of the Tower was complete.

It was a victory as grand as any Barson could've imagined.

CHAPTER FIFTY-ONE

※ BLAISE ※

Blaise slowly became aware of being conscious.

He could still think—which he reasoned meant he was still alive. However, when he tried to open his eyes, he discovered that he could not. As far as he could tell, he had no eyes . . . and no body that he could feel.

Panic came at him in waves. The sensory deprivation was so terrifying that his mind retreated into the darkness again, conscious thought fading again.

Upon the second awakening, Blaise felt a bit calmer. The realization of where he was—in the Spell Realm—was something for his mind to latch on to. And as Blaise slowly processed that fact, he realized that he did *feel,* though not in the same way as he had experienced things in the Physical Realm. It was as if the structure of his own mind was changing, acclimating to his new surroundings.

After a while, he became cognizant of shapes with colors, tastes, and smells mixed together into strange mathematical patterns. These patterns were mesmerizing in their complexity. As Blaise studied them with awe, he felt a peculiar sense of belonging, as though he was becoming a part of something bigger than himself. The sensation was soothing and frightening at the same time, because Blaise realized he could easily lose himself in this bigger whole and forget that he ever existed.

No. Focus, Blaise, Focus.

That wasn't why he was here. Gala. He needed to think about Gala. Concentrating on her, Blaise tried to imagine what she would look like here, and to his shock, as soon as the thought came to him, so did an avalanche of sensations.

He saw, tasted, and smelled something wonderful.

It looked like an intricate web, only it was three-dimensional, a bit like branches of a tree in the winter, and it was covering all of the nearby space. The web was buzzing with activity, small flashes of lightning traveling up and down the tiny strands within the pattern. At the same time, Blaise smelled the color red and tasted the number seven. He knew these concepts didn't have scent or taste in his world, but they did here. In a strange twist, red smelled peaceful, like chamomile flowers, and the number seven tasted sweet, like raisins.

And somehow Blaise knew what was in front of him.

"Gala," he thought with joy, addressing the intricate design.

"Yes, this is me," her thought came at him in response.

The feeling of relief was so strong, Blaise would've shook with it if he had a body. His mind pulsated with joy. He found her. He had succeeded.

There were a million things he needed to ask her, but all he could say was, "How could you do this? How could you disappear like that?" The words came across as angry, yet anger was the last emotion he was experiencing right now.

There was no response for a moment. Instead, Blaise could see the colors in the Gala pattern changing. Lightning flashed, and the chamomile color red became violet—which smelled like rosemary for some reason—and Blaise tasted thirteen, which reminded him of a peach. Overwhelmed, he experienced the wonder that was his creation. "You are beautiful even here," he thought at her, unable to help himself.

Instead of a thought, he felt a response of a different sort. Suddenly, he was overcome by a deep sense of belonging, an intense feeling of happiness that somehow was not his own.

He was feeling Gala's emotions, Blaise realized, and he tried to project his own feelings at her. All the love and worry had now transformed into an almost incandescent joy, and he let her feel it, opening his mind as he had never done before. She responded with a plethora of her own sensations. It was intense, but he did not want it to stop.

And then he felt the pattern that was Gala begin to join his. Slowly and methodically, they became a bigger, joint pattern. It was strange and wonderful, reminding him of the night before, when they made love for the first time.

As the merging was coming to an end, Blaise received visions of Gala. He saw her whole life, as short as it was. He saw himself through her eyes, that first time in his study. Then he became her, reading all those books in his library. He was seeing her time in the village, the trial and the fair, the wonder and horror of the coliseum. He suffered with her in the battle with the Sorcerer Guard, and felt regret at the lives she destroyed. He saw himself teach her magic, felt her battle the storm, and in one violent flash he saw their night together and the battle afterwards. He even saw the Spell Realm through Gala's eyes and realized that she was experiencing it in a different manner. The spells, the strange being she'd encountered, even himself—Blaise saw it all. The culmination of the vision was an ecstasy unlike any other, an exquisite pleasure that was born of the mind, not the body. It seemed to last forever.

When it did end, he felt her explore his own mind the way he just did hers, and the ecstasy began again.

CHAPTER FIFTY-TWO

✳ BARSON ✳

The day after the takeover, after all the corpses had been removed from the Council Hall and the room had been thoroughly scrubbed, Barson gathered his men and the sorcerers who had been spared.

Looking at the faces in front of him, he felt jubilant. This was the moment he had dreamed of all of his life, ever since he had learned that he was a descendant of the rightful kings.

Dara and Larn stood to the right of him, holding hands. On his left were his sorcerer allies and his closest lieutenants. All present were dressed in their best clothes, and Barson himself wore decorative armor that had been passed down from times of old.

The only thing missing was the woman he had planned to have by his side at this ceremony—Augusta. Where was she? Where was the Council? The questions tormented Barson, interfering with his joy at this victory, and he knew his first order of business would be to find answers.

But first, he had to get through the ceremony.

Stepping forward, he surveyed his new subjects, watching as a pair of young women walked toward the throne, carrying a golden crown on a velvet-wrapped tray. As they got closer, Dara took the crown from them, raising it high over her head. Then she reverently placed it on Barson's head.

"Long live the king!" she shouted, turning toward the crowd.

"Long live the king!" Their answering cry echoed through the hallways, filling the Tower with the sound of a new beginning.

CHAPTER FIFTY-THREE

❋ BLAISE ❋

When the merging of their minds was long over, Blaise thought back to what he'd learned through the experience. He was particularly fascinated with whatever intelligences seemed to exist in this realm. "What do you think Dranel is?" he asked Gala silently, remembering the brief image he got from her mind.

"I don't know," Gala responded, a bit dreamily. She appeared to be still under the influence of their joining. "He seems to be more like you than me, though his pattern is still quite different."

Blaise thought about it, remembering seeing his own pattern through her eyes and comparing them in his mind. He could not see any resemblance, but then he didn't have Gala's ability to process complex information quickly. Being in her mind here had been a very different experience. She was less like a human being here; instead, she was something different, something greater.

Dwelling on it, Blaise slowly felt his thoughts fade as his newfound senses took over. It was so beautiful, so peaceful, that the nothingness lured him in.

* * *

"Blaise?" Gala's thought brought him into consciousness.

"Yes?" he responded, confused.

"You have not thought for a while," she explained, and he could detect a hint of worry in her pattern.

What had happened? Did he pass out? Was it possible to do that in this place? Mildly disturbed, Blaise tried to refocus on something he almost forgot, though it was on his mind earlier.

"How do we go back?" he thought, finally remembering his original intent. He had come here to retrieve Gala. To save her. To take her back to his world.

"Do you want to go back?" she thought back, her pattern seeming to pulsate with a feeling Blaise could only describe as hesitation.

He was not sure he did. This existence was very direct and pure. Blaise could feel what Gala felt, and she knew his innermost thoughts. But somehow, he still felt like an intruder here, though the feeling lessened with every moment. Yet as the feeling lessened, so did his sense of identity, of knowing what and who he was. It was only Gala's presence that seemed to ground him somewhat, and Blaise had a bad feeling about the episode he'd just experienced. It was possible that he would have more periods of time without thought, his mind getting absorbed into the serene, mathematical beauty of the patterns around him. Could he slowly lose himself here? The idea was frightening.

"Then I will go back with you," she said simply. Blaise hadn't voiced his thoughts, but she was answering them anyway. Blaise could also sense Gala's feelings on this matter. She was much more ambivalent about returning. He understood her hesitation; she was a product of both realms and was nearly as at home here as she was in his world. In many ways, she preferred this serene, startlingly different place. There was no ugliness here, no injustice that she could not abide.

"Maybe we could do something about that," Blaise thought, remembering his original intentions. He still wanted to help people, to eliminate the suffering that made Gala so uncomfortable.

For a short time, she appeared to muse about something that he could not discern. Then a pattern appeared in front of him. A strange, complex shape that didn't contain the intelligent components he could see in Gala.

"This is part of the spell you wove before," she explained, projecting her thoughts at him.

Blaise studied the shape curiously. All he saw, tasted, and smelled were unusual textures and things that had nothing in common with the arcane words he'd written on cards.

Gala, however, seemed to know what to do with it. He could see that she was altering the structure, changing it as she went along. Looking closer, Blaise could tell that there were flaws in the spell's intricate mathematics—errors that he had inadvertently made—and he could see that Gala was fixing them. The changes started small, but with time they almost recreated the structure, giving it new life. With each tweak that Gala made, new tastes, smells, and associations occurred to Blaise, overwhelming his new senses.

Finally, after what seemed like hours, the activity stopped.

"Are you ready?" her thought came.

"Yes. Take us home," he thought back, and watched the colors in the spell structure flare brighter as they departed for the Physical Realm.

EPILOGUE

※ DRANEL ※

This time, when lucidity came, Dranel knew himself instantly. The last thing he remembered was observing Gala. She had done something, and he had reacted. Whatever it was, it had brought him the deep calm he longed for. But now the lucidity he often cursed was back.

Dranel's thoughts were clearer than he could ever recall, and he arrived at a decision. He strongly preferred the serenity of not thinking to this state of lucidity. Yes, lucidity had its moments, like when he was observing Gala, but as fascinating as those small moments were, on the whole they did not seem worth leaving the blissful state he so often found himself in.

Thinking of Gala distracted Dranel again. He felt something related to her. A sense of urgency. A sense of awe. She was here. And not in the ephemeral presence he had witnessed before, when he'd learned her name. No, she was here in the same way Dranel was here.

Quickly he brought his attention to her and saw that he was too late. She had just become interwoven in a spell. He examined the algorithm of the spell. What the mathematics implied was genius.

It was a way out of this realm—something Dranel had thought impossible to initiate from within the Spell Realm itself.

He reacted instantly. He didn't want Gala to leave. He wanted to interact with her once more.

He tried to change the pattern responsible for her departure, to stop its unfolding, but it didn't work. Still, Dranel knew he should be able to do something to that pattern, so he tried again. This time, he attempted to slow the spell down, and that seemed to have a small effect. Even so, he only had mere moments to observe her before she left. Fleetingly, he wondered if this slowdown would harm Gala somehow, but decided that it would not. In the worst case, as a side effect, it could tamper with the timeline of when she would appear in the Physical Realm.

With no time to lose, Dranel began examining Gala and her handiwork. As he marveled at her beauty, he became aware of something else. She was not the only strange pattern interwoven into this departure spell. There was another. Curious, Dranel took a closer look at this other being—and recoiled.

Something about this other pattern filled Dranel

with dread—and it was only when he felt it that he realized what dread meant. It was an emotion, and emotions were the reason he preferred never to be lucid.

This pattern evoked a barrage of emotions in Dranel, each one worse than the one preceding it. It wasn't the pattern itself—Dranel was certain he had never seen it before—but rather the way the pattern made Dranel feel. There was anger and a sense of loss, desperate longing and regret. He felt overwhelmed with feelings. And in the midst of all this turmoil, Dranel wished for one thing above all: for the silence of the Spell Realm to take all of these emotions away.

Before he could even start to contemplate how to regain his serenity, the spell he tried to slow down finished its execution, taking Gala and whatever accompanied her to the Physical Realm.

Dranel stayed behind, his thoughts in turmoil. He wanted to return to his former peaceful existence, but he didn't know how. Something about what had just happened disturbed him deeply, and he didn't understand what it was.

As he drifted, lucid, in the pattern-filled world surrounding him, he found himself resenting every bit of noise, every spell that felt like an intrusion. He tried to be someplace where there were no disruptions, no echoes from the Physical Realm, but such a place could not be found.

And as time went on, Dranel slowly came to the realization that nothing would ever be the same again—unless he did something to restore the peace and quiet he longed for.

Unless he silenced the source of his distress.

SNEAK PEEKS

Thank you for reading! We would love to hear what you thought of the book, so if you would consider writing a review, it would be greatly appreciated. Anna and I use reader reviews to objectively determine which of our many book series to work on next, and to see what works and what doesn't, so any and all honest feedback is invaluable to us.

Additional works in progress include *The Thought Readers* and *Mind Awakening*, as well as book 3 in The Sorcery Code series. Please sign up for my newsletter at www.dimazales.com to learn when the next book comes out.

I love to hear from readers, so be sure to:
-Friend me on Facebook
https://www.facebook.com/DimaZales
-Like my Facebook page
https://www.facebook.com/AuthorDimaZales

-Follow me on Twitter
 https://twitter.com/AuthorDimaZales
-Follow me on Google+
 https://www.google.com/+DimaZales
-Friend or follow me on Goodreads
 https://www.goodreads.com/DimaZales

Thank you for your support! I truly appreciate it.

And now, please turn the page for sneak peeks into my upcoming works . . .

EXCERPT FROM
THE THOUGHT READERS

Note: *The Thought Readers* is the first book in a new urban fantasy series, *Mind Dimensions*. The excerpt below is unedited and subject to change.

* * *

Sometimes I think I'm crazy. Right now I am sitting at a casino table, and everyone around me is motionless, as though frozen. I call this the Quiet, as though giving it a name makes it seem more real—as though giving it a name changes the fact that all the players around me are sitting there like statues, and I am walking among them looking at the cards they have been dealt. Doesn't that sound crazy?

The problem with the theory of my being crazy is that when I 'unfreeze' the world, as I just did, the cards the players turn over are the same ones I just saw in the Quiet. If I were crazy, wouldn't these cards just be random? Unless I am so far gone that I am imagining the cards on the table.

But then I win also. If that's a delusion—if the pile of chips on my side of the table is a delusion—then I might as well question everything. Maybe my name isn't even Darren.

No. I can't think that way. If I am truly that confused, then I don't want to snap out of it—because if I do, I will probably wake up in a mental hospital.

Besides, I love my life, crazy and all.

My shrink thinks the Quiet is an inventive way I describe 'the inner workings of my genius.' Now that sounds crazy to me. She also might want me, but that's beside the point. Suffice it to say, she is as far as it gets from my datable age range. In any case, her explanation would not work, as it doesn't account for the way I know things even a genius wouldn't know—like the exact value and suit of the other players' cards.

I watch as the dealer begins a new round. Besides me, there are three players at the table. The Cowboy, the Grandma, and the Professional, as I mentally call them. I feel that now-almost-imperceptible fear that accompanies the phasing—that's what I call the process: phasing into the Quiet. Worrying about my sanity has always facilitated phasing; fear seems to be helpful in this process.

I phase in, and everything gets quiet. Hence the name for this state.

It is eerie to me even now. This casino is usually

very loud. Drunk people talking, slot machines, ringing of wins, music—the only place louder is a club or a concert. And yet, right at this moment, I could probably hear a pin drop. It's as though I've gone deaf to the chaos that surrounds me.

Having so many frozen people around adds to the strangeness of it. Here is a waitress stopped mid-step, carrying a tray with drinks. There is a woman about to pull a slot machine lever. At my own table, the dealer's hand is raised, and the last card he dealt is hanging unnaturally in the air. I walk up to it from the side of the table and reach for it. It's a king, meant for The Professional. Once I let the card go, it falls on the table rather than continuing to float as before—but I know full well that it will be back in the air, in the exact position it was when I grabbed it, when I phase out.

The Professional has the look I always pictured for people who make money by playing poker. Scruffy, shades on, and a bit odd-looking. He has been doing an excellent job with the 'poker face'— basically not twitching a single muscle throughout the game. His face is so expressionless that I wonder if he might've gotten some Botox to aid in maintaining such a stony countenance. His hand is on the table, protectively covering the cards dealt to him.

I move his limp hand away. It feels normal. Well, in a manner of speaking. The hand is sweaty and hairy, so moving it aside is unpleasant and is an abnormal thing to do. The normal part is that the hand is warm, rather than cold. When I was a kid, I expected people to feel cold in the Quiet, like stone statues.

With the Professional's hand moved away, I pick up his cards. Combined with the king that was hanging in the air, he has a nice high pair. Good to know.

I walk over to the Grandma. She's already holding her cards, and she has fanned them nicely for me. I am able to avoid touching her wrinkled, spotted hands. This is a relief, as I have recently become conflicted about touching people—or, more specifically, women—in the Quiet. If I had to, I would rationalize touching the Grandma's hand as harmless—or at least, not creepy—but it's better to avoid it if possible.

In any case, she has a low pair. I feel bad for her. She's been losing quite a bit tonight. Her chips are dwindling. Perhaps her losses are due, at least partially, to the fact that she's not good at keeping a poker face. Even before looking at her cards, I knew they wouldn't be good because I could tell she was disappointed with her hand as soon as it was dealt. I also caught a gleeful gleam in her eyes a few rounds ago when she had a winning three of a kind.

This whole game of poker is, to a large degree, an exercise in reading people—something I really want to get better at. I have been told I am great at reading people at my job. But I am not. I am just good at using the Quiet to make it seem like I am. I do want to learn how to do it for real, though.

What I don't care that much about in this poker game is money. I do well enough financially to not have to depend on hitting it big gambling. I don't care if I win or lose, though quintupling my money back at the blackjack table had been fun. This whole trip has been more about going gambling because I finally can, being twenty-one and all. I was never into fake IDs, so this is an actual milestone for me.

Leaving the Grandma alone, I move on to the next player—the Cowboy. I can't resist taking off his straw hat and trying it on. I wonder if it's possible for me to get lice this way. Since I have never been able to bring back any inanimate objects from the Quiet, nor otherwise affect the world in any lasting way, I figure I wouldn't be able to get any living critters to come back with me either. Dropping the hat, I look at his cards. He has a pair of aces—a better hand than the Professional. The Cowboy may be a professional as well. He has a good poker face, as far as I can tell. It will be interesting to watch those two in this round.

Next, I walk up to the deck and look at the top cards, memorizing them. I'm not leaving anything to chance.

With my task in the Quiet complete, I walk back to myself. Oh, yes, did I mention that I see myself sitting there, frozen like the rest of them? That's the weirdest part. It's like having an out-of-body experience.

Approaching my frozen self, I look at him. I usually avoid doing this, as it's too unsettling. No amount of looking in the mirror or seeing videos of yourself on YouTube can prepare you for viewing your own body in 3D. It's not something anyone is meant to experience. Aside from identical twins, I guess.

It's hard to believe that this person is me. He looks more like just some guy. Well, maybe a bit more than that. I do find this guy very interesting. Usually, I don't consider other guys capable of looking interesting, but I am curious about how my frozen self looks. Or, more accurately, I like the way my frozen self looks. He looks cool. He looks smart.

I think women would probably consider him good-looking, though it's not a modest thing to admit.

I am not good at rating the attractiveness of guys—never have been—but some things are common sense. I can tell when a dude is ugly, and this frozen me is not. I also know that generally, being good-looking requires a symmetrical face—and the statue of me has that. A strong jaw doesn't hurt either. Check. Having broad shoulders is a positive, and being tall really helps. All covered. I have blue eyes—that seems to be a plus. Girls have told me that they like my eyes, though right now, on the frozen me, they look creepy—glassy and shiny. They look like the eyes of a wax figure. Lifeless.

Realizing that I'm dwelling on this subject too long, I shake my head. I can just picture my shrink analyzing this moment. Who would imagine admiring themselves like this as part of their mental illness? I can just picture her scribbling down words like 'narcissistic.'

Enough. I need to leave the Quiet. Raising my hand, I touch my frozen self on the forehead, and I hear noise again as I phase out.

Everything is back to normal.

The king that I looked at a moment before—the king that I left on the table—is in the air again, and from there it follows the trajectory it was always meant to, landing near the Professional's hands. The Grandma is still eyeing her fanned cards in disappointment, and the Cowboy has his hat on again, though I took it off in the Quiet. Everything is exactly as it was the moment I phased into the Quiet.

On some level, my brain never ceases to be surprised at the discontinuity of the experience in the Quiet and outside it. It's almost hardwired into us to question reality when such things happen. When I was trying to outwit my shrink, early on in the therapy, I once read a whole psychology textbook during our session. She, of course, didn't notice it, as I did it in the Quiet. The book talked about how babies, even as young as two months old, get surprised if they see something out of the ordinary, like gravity appearing to work backwards. It's no wonder my brain has trouble adapting. Until I was ten, the world behaved normally, but since then, everything has been weird, to put it mildly.

Glancing down, I realize I am holding a three of a kind. Next time I will look at my cards before phasing. If I have something this strong, I might take my chances and play fair.

The game unfolds predictably because I know everybody's cards. At the end, the Grandma gets up. She's clearly lost enough money.

And that's when I see her for the first time.

She's hot. My friend Bert at work claims that I have a 'type.' He even described to me what my type is, after he saw a few of the girls I dated. I reject the overall idea of a 'type.' I don't like to think of myself as shallow or predictable. But I might actually be a bit of both because this girl fits Bert's description of my type to a T. And my reaction is extreme interest, to say the least.

Large blue eyes. Well-defined cheekbones on a slender face, with a hint of something exotic. Long, extremely shapely legs, like those of a dancer. Dark wavy hair in a ponytail, which I like. And without bangs—even better. I hate bangs—not sure why girls do that to themselves. Though lack of bangs was not, strictly speaking, in Bert's description of my type, it probably should have been.

I continue staring at her. With her high heels and tight skirt, she's a bit overdressed for this place. Or maybe I'm a bit underdressed in my jeans and t-shirt. Either way, I don't care. I have to try to talk to her.

I debate phasing into the Quiet and approaching her, so I can do something creepy, like staring at her up close or maybe even snooping in her pockets. Anything to help me when I talk to her.

I decide against it, which is probably the first time

that has ever happened.

My reasoning for breaking my usual habit, if you can even call it that, is very strange. Talk about jumping the gun. I picture the following chain of events: she agrees to date me, we date for a time, we get serious, and because of the deep connection we have, I come clean about the Quiet. She learns I did something creepy and has a fit, then dumps me. It's ridiculous to think this, of course, considering that we haven't even spoken yet. She might have an IQ below 70 or have the personality of a piece of wood. There can be twenty different reasons I wouldn't want to date her. And besides, it's not all up to me. She might tell me to go fuck myself as soon as I try to talk to her.

Still, working at a hedge fund has taught me to hedge. As crazy as that reasoning is, because I know it would be the gentlemanly thing to do, I stick with my decision not to phase. In keeping with this unusual chivalry for me, I also decide not to cheat at this round of poker.

As the cards are dealt again, I reflect on how good it feels to have done the honorable thing—even without anyone knowing. Maybe I should try to respect people's privacy more often. Yeah, right. I have to be realistic. I wouldn't be where I am today if I had followed that advice. In fact, if I made a habit of respecting people's privacy, I would lose my job within days—and with it, a lot of the comforts I have grown used to.

Copying the Professional's move, I cover my

cards with my hand as soon as I receive them. I am about to sneak a peek at what I was dealt when something unusual happens.

The world goes quiet, just like it does when I phase in . . . but I did nothing this time.

And at that moment, I see her—the girl sitting across the table from me, the girl I was just thinking about. She's standing next to me, pulling her hand away from mine. Or, strictly speaking, from my frozen self's hand—as I'm standing a little to the side looking at her.

She's also still sitting in front of me at the table, a frozen statue like all the others.

I don't even consider the possibility of that second girl being a twin sister or something like that. I know it's her. She's doing what I did just a few minutes ago. She's walking in the Quiet. The world around us is frozen, but we are not.

A horrified look crosses her face as she realizes the same thing. She lunges across the table and touches her own forehead.

The world becomes normal again.

She's staring at me, shocked, her eyes huge and her face pale. I see her hands trembling as she rises to her feet. Without so much as a word, she turns and begins walking away, then breaks into a run.

I don't hesitate. I get up and run after her. It's not exactly smooth. If she notices a guy she doesn't know running after her, dating would be the last thing on her mind. But I am beyond that now. She is the only person I've met who can do what I do. She's proof that I am not insane. She might have what I want most in the world.

She might have answers.

* * *

If you'd like to know when *The Thought Readers (Mind Dimensions: Book 1)* comes out, please visit Dima Zales's website at www.dimazales.com and sign up for his new release email list. You can also connect with him on Facebook, Google Plus, Twitter, and Goodreads.

EXCERPT FROM
CLOSE LIAISONS BY ANNA ZAIRES

Note: *Close Liaisons* is Dima Zales' collaboration with Anna Zaires and is the first book in the critically acclaimed erotic sci-fi romance series, the Krinar Chronicles. It contains explicit sexual content and is not intended for readers under 18.

* * *

A dark and edgy romance that will appeal to fans of erotic and turbulent relationships . . .

In the near future, the Krinar rule the Earth. An advanced race from another galaxy, they are still a mystery to us—and we are completely at their mercy.

Shy and innocent, Mia Stalis is a college student in New York City who has led a very normal life. Like most people, she's never had any interactions with the invaders—until one fateful day in the park changes everything. Having caught Korum's eye, she must now contend with a powerful, dangerously seductive Krinar who wants to possess her and will stop at nothing to make her his own.

How far would you go to regain your freedom? How much would you sacrifice to help your people? What choice will you make when you begin to fall for your enemy?

* * *

The air was crisp and clear as Mia walked briskly down a winding path in Central Park. Signs of spring were everywhere, from tiny buds on still-bare trees to the proliferation of nannies out to enjoy the first warm day with their rambunctious charges.

It was strange how much everything had changed in the last few years, and yet how much remained the same. If anyone had asked Mia ten years ago how she thought life might be after an alien invasion, this would have been nowhere near her imaginings. *Independence Day*, *The War of the Worlds*—none of these were even close to the reality of encountering a more advanced civilization. There had been no fight, no resistance of any kind on government level—because *they* had not allowed it. In hindsight, it was clear how silly those movies had been. Nuclear weapons, satellites, fighter jets—these were little more than rocks and sticks to an ancient civilization that could cross the universe faster than the speed of light.

Spotting an empty bench near the lake, Mia gratefully headed for it, her shoulders feeling the strain of the backpack filled with her chunky twelve-year-old laptop and old-fashioned paper books. At twenty-one, she sometimes felt old, out of step with the fast-paced new world of razor-slim tablets and cell phones embedded in wristwatches. The pace of technological progress had not slowed since K-Day; if anything, many of the new gadgets had been influenced by what the Krinar had. Not that the Ks had shared any of their precious technology; as far as they were concerned, their little experiment had to continue uninterrupted.

Unzipping her bag, Mia took out her old Mac. The thing was heavy and slow, but it worked—and as a starving college student, Mia could not afford anything better. Logging on, she opened a blank Word document and prepared to start the torturous process of writing her Sociology paper.

Ten minutes and exactly zero words later, she stopped. Who was she kidding? If she really wanted to write the damn thing, she would've never come to the park. As tempting as it was to pretend that she could enjoy the fresh air and be productive at the same time, those two had never been compatible in her experience. A musty old library was a much better setting for anything requiring that kind of brainpower exertion.

Mentally kicking herself for her own laziness, Mia let out a sigh and started looking around instead. People-watching in New York never failed to amuse her.

The tableau was a familiar one, with the requisite homeless person occupying a nearby bench—thank God it wasn't the closest one to her, since he looked like he might smell very ripe—and two nannies chatting with each other in Spanish as they pushed their Bugaboos at a leisurely pace. A girl jogged on a path a little further ahead, her bright pink Reeboks contrasting nicely with her blue leggings. Mia's gaze followed the jogger as she rounded the corner, envying her athleticism. Her own hectic schedule allowed her little time to exercise, and she doubted she could keep up with the girl for even a mile at this point.

To the right, she could see the Bow Bridge over the lake. A man was leaning on the railing, looking out over the water. His face was turned away from Mia, so she could only see part of his profile. Nevertheless, something about him caught her attention.

She wasn't sure what it was. He was definitely tall and seemed well-built under the expensive-looking trench coat he was wearing, but that was only part of the story. Tall, good-looking men were common in model-infested New York City. No, it was something else. Perhaps it was the way he stood—very still, with no extra movements. His hair was dark and glossy under the bright afternoon sun, just long enough in the front to move slightly in the warm spring breeze.

He also stood alone.

That's it, Mia realized. The normally popular and picturesque bridge was completely deserted, except for the man who was standing on it. Everyone appeared to be giving it a wide berth for some unknown reason. In fact, with the exception of herself and her potentially aromatic homeless neighbor, the entire row of benches in the highly desirable waterfront location was empty.

As though sensing her gaze on him, the object of her attention slowly turned his head and looked directly at Mia. Before her conscious brain could even make the connection, she felt her blood turn to ice, leaving her paralyzed in place and helpless to do anything but stare at the predator who now seemed to be examining her with interest.

* * *

Breathe, Mia, breathe. Somewhere in the back of her mind, a small rational voice kept repeating those words. That same oddly objective part of her noted his symmetric face structure, with golden skin stretched tightly over high cheekbones and a firm jaw. Pictures and videos of Ks that she'd seen had hardly done them justice. Standing no more than thirty feet away, the creature was simply stunning.

As she continued staring at him, still frozen in place, he straightened and began walking toward her. Or rather stalking toward her, she thought stupidly, as his every movement reminded her of a jungle cat sinuously approaching a gazelle. All the while, his eyes never left hers. As he approached, she could make out individual yellow flecks in his light golden eyes and the thick long lashes surrounding them.

She watched in horrified disbelief as he sat down on her bench, less than two feet away from her, and smiled, showing white even teeth. No fangs, she noted with some functioning part of her brain. Not even a hint of them. That used to be another myth about them, like their supposed abhorrence of the sun.

"What's your name?" The creature practically purred the question at her. His voice was low and smooth, completely unaccented. His nostrils flared slightly, as though inhaling her scent.

"Um . . ." Mia swallowed nervously. "M-Mia."

"Mia," he repeated slowly, seemingly savoring her name. "Mia what?"

"Mia Stalis." Oh crap, why did he want to know her name? Why was he here, talking to her? In general, what was he doing in Central Park, so far away from any of the K Centers? *Breathe, Mia, breathe.*

"Relax, Mia Stalis." His smile got wider, exposing a dimple in his left cheek. A dimple? Ks had dimples? "Have you never encountered one of us before?"

"No, I haven't," Mia exhaled sharply, realizing that she was holding her breath. She was proud that her voice didn't sound as shaky as she felt. Should she ask? Did she want to know?

She gathered her courage. "What, um—" Another swallow. "What do you want from me?"

"For now, conversation." He looked like he was about to laugh at her, those gold eyes crinkling slightly at the corners.

Strangely, that pissed her off enough to take the edge off her fear. If there was anything Mia hated, it was being laughed at. With her short, skinny stature and a general lack of social skills that came from an awkward teenage phase involving every girl's nightmare of braces, frizzy hair, and glasses, Mia had more than enough experience being the butt of someone's joke.

She lifted her chin belligerently. "Okay, then, what is *your* name?"

"It's Korum."

"Just Korum?"

"We don't really have last names, not the way you do. My full name is much longer, but you wouldn't be able to pronounce it if I told you."

Okay, that was interesting. She now remembered reading something like that in *The New York Times.* So far, so good. Her legs had nearly stopped shaking, and her breathing was returning to normal. Maybe, just maybe, she would get out of this alive. This conversation business seemed safe enough, although the way he kept staring at her with those unblinking yellowish eyes was unnerving. She decided to keep him talking.

"What are you doing here, Korum?"

"I just told you, making conversation with you,

Mia." His voice again held a hint of laughter.

Frustrated, Mia blew out her breath. "I meant, what are you doing here in Central Park? In New York City in general?"

He smiled again, cocking his head slightly to the side. "Maybe I'm hoping to meet a pretty curly-haired girl."

Okay, enough was enough. He was clearly toying with her. Now that she could think a little again, she realized that they were in the middle of Central Park, in full view of about a gazillion spectators. She surreptitiously glanced around to confirm that. Yep, sure enough, although people were obviously steering clear of her bench and its otherworldly occupant, there were a number of brave souls staring their way from further up the path. A couple were even cautiously filming them with their wristwatch cameras. If the K tried anything with her, it would be on YouTube in the blink of an eye, and he had to know it. Of course, he may or may not care about that.

Still, going on the assumption that since she'd never come across any videos of K assaults on college students in the middle of Central Park, she was relatively safe, Mia cautiously reached for her laptop and lifted it to stuff it back into her backpack.

"Let me help you with that, Mia—"

And before she could blink, she felt him take her heavy laptop from her suddenly boneless fingers, gently brushing against her knuckles in the process. A sensation similar to a mild electric shock shot through Mia at his touch, leaving her nerve endings tingling in its wake.

Reaching for her backpack, he carefully put away the laptop in a smooth, sinuous motion. "There you go, all better now."

Oh God, he had touched her. Maybe her theory about the safety of public locations was bogus. She felt her breathing speeding up again, and her heart rate was probably well into the anaerobic zone at this point.

"I have to go now . . . Bye!"

How she managed to squeeze out those words without hyperventilating, she would never know. Grabbing the strap of the backpack he'd just put down, she jumped to her feet, noting somewhere in the back of her mind that her earlier paralysis seemed to be gone.

"Bye, Mia. I will see you later." His softly mocking voice carried in the clear spring air as she took off, nearly running in her haste to get away.

* * *

If you'd like to find out more, please visit Anna's website at www.annazaires.com. The ebook of *Close Liaisons* is currently available for free at most retailers.

ABOUT THE AUTHOR

Dima Zales is a science fiction and fantasy author residing in Palm Coast, Florida. Prior to becoming a writer, he worked in the software development industry in New York as both a programmer and an executive. From high-frequency trading software for big banks to mobile apps for popular magazines, Dima has done it all. In 2013, he left the software industry in order to concentrate on his writing career.

Dima holds a Master's degree in Computer Science from NYU and a dual undergraduate degree in Computer Science / Psychology from Brooklyn College. He also has a number of hobbies and interests, the most unusual of which might be professional-level mentalism. He simulates mind-reading on stage and close-up, and has done shows for corporations, wealthy individuals, and friends.

He is also into healthy eating and fitness, so he should live long enough to finish all the book projects he starts. In fact, he very much hopes to catch the technological advancements that might let him live forever (biologically or otherwise). Aside from that, he also enjoys learning about current and future technologies that might enhance our lives, including artificial intelligence, biofeedback, brain-to-computer interfaces, and brain-enhancing implants.

In addition to *The Sorcery Code (The Sorcery Code: Volume 1)*, which was nominated for a 2014 Roné award, and *The Spell Realm (The Sorcery Code: Volume 2)*, Dima has collaborated on a number of romance novels with his wife, Anna Zaires. The Krinar Chronicles, an erotic science fiction series, has been a bestseller in its categories and has been recognized by the likes of *Marie Claire* and *Woman's Day*. If you like erotic romance with a unique plot, please feel free to check it out, especially since the first book in the series *(Close Liaisons)* is available for free everywhere. Keep in mind, though, Anna Zaires's books are going to be much more explicit.

Anna Zaires is the love of his life and a huge inspiration in every aspect of his writing. She definitely adds her magic touch to anything Dima creates, and the books would not be the same without her. Dima's fans are strongly encouraged to learn more about Anna and her work at http://www.annazaires.com.

CPSIA information can be obtained
at www.ICGtesting.com
Printed in the USA
LVOW04s1601210416
484700LV00019B/1107/P